LITTLE PIECES

ISSA MARIE

This book is dedicated to the people who thought they didn't deserve love, who thought they were too much, too loud, or too broken. I love you, and fuck all the people who made you feel that way.

"For You, YES."

H.L. Swan

"Just because he can't love you the way you want him to doesn't mean he doesn't love you with everything he has."

-Landon to Tessa by Anna Todd

Thank you for inspiring me, without you I would have never read nor written those first words, reviewed those first books, and started following my dreams. Here's to my female Hardin.

Preface

There may be some triggering topics in this book, we all have different triggers and this one includes off-page, suggestive behaviors that may be triggering for some. Some include trauma, PTSD, mental health, toxic behavior and/or relationships. Some aspects of the story don't match reality, for instance how some features of cell phones work, etc. While I know this story may not be for everybody and I am not the best writer/author in the world, thank you for taking a chance on Alex, Kohen, and me. The journey for this book has been a rough one, the first half was written before my brother passed and the second half two years after. My growth and the character's growth are linear. So I left it as it was. I hope you like it.

Playlist

Top 10:

You broke me first- Tate Mcrae

Last Night- Morgan Wallen

Flowers- Lauren Spencer Smith

Under the Influence -Chris Brown

Escapism- RAYE

Nonsense- Sabrina Carpenter

Only Love Can hurt Like This- Paloma Faith

Tell Me You love Me- Demi Lovato

Midnight Rain- Taylor Swift

Rescue- Lauren Daigle

Prologue

Alex

When is love enough? When will I ever be enough?

I stare at the vase of flowers he left on the table and the note beside them. My eyes tear up as, ironically, "Flowers" by Lauren Spencer Smith blasts through the speakers in my bedroom. I don't want to read it. I don't want the apologies. If he loved me, he would be here with his arms wrapped around me as my tears fall. He would catch them and whisper, "*Beautiful girls don't cry, Angel.*"

Why isn't he here to remind me?

What the fuck is wrong with me? Everywhere I go, darkness follows. I try and try to be my best self and with Kohen, I was, wasn't I? *Who the fuck are you kidding, Alex? You are a broken doll, no one wants to play with a broken doll.* I feel like I deserve this after the constant flow of mistakes I've made in my life. Why couldn't I just let someone love me? Instead, I sabotage anything that looks like happiness and sunshine, yet that's all I want; all I've ever wanted.

Every time I fight the waves and try to catch my breath, the deeper down I'm plunged into dark waters, the vicious cycle never ends.

I'm like Alice in Wonderland, wandering around in a fairytale land that's only twisted and corrupt. Every time I think I'm figuring my way out of this labyrinth, I'm right back at the beginning, suffering more loss and heartache.

I scream at the top of my lungs for help, but of course, no one hears me. All I have is this emptiness... no one, and nothing, and it's all my fault. Will it always be this way? I bet we could have been happy; if anyone could've succeeded in making me truly happy, it would've been him.

I squeeze my eyes shut, feeling my wet lashes touch the tops of my cheeks, I beg the tears to stop falling. But, like me, they're stubborn and they don't listen. All I can do is open them again, look out the window, and stare up at the moon praying someone or something up there hears my broken heart's plea.

The sound of a fist meeting the wood of my front door startles me; probably my Tinder match. What's the saying? The best way to get over a guy is to get under another. I shout, "Just a minute," at the door, run into the restroom to check my appearance, and put my bad bitch face on. I smile, almost sadistically in the mirror at myself. "Let's do this shit, Alex. You have played this role several times." One more heartache won't break us.

Like the Mad Hatter told Alice, I tell myself, "We're all mad here." I turn the light off and make my way to the door to meet my next victim. *Damn, I'm toxic.*

Chapter 1

Alex

I sit here waiting for class to start, and all my brain is focusing on is how much I hate my first name. It's a boy's name and it isn't even short for anything. What the hell was my mother thinking? It's a random thought but, I have tons of those, thank you ADHD. My phone chimes in my purse and right on time, it's Cora for her afternoon check-in. I roll my eyes as if I don't love the check-ins. I'm lucky she loves my crazy ass, she is too good of a friend to me. Sometimes I feel like I don't deserve her.

She loves every piece of the angry, fucked up mess that I am, and I don't show her how much I love her enough! Cora is the calm to my storm. She knows what to say to defuse the bomb that is Alex Monroe.

I open up the text thread and see a GIF of two girls partying, which can only mean one thing: she got us into a frat party. We are freshmen in college, and she is determined to get in with the upperclassmen. We haven't been to a party since our Junior year of high school, but we made a pact recently to live our lives to the fullest. It proves to be a little hard because we used to have another best friend that should be doing all these things with us. The three of us were inseparable, but she passed away tragically that year.

Cora: Alex guess what?

Me: what?

Cora: I said guess :(

Me: You bought a pony?

Cora: Alex :/

Me: okay sorry what?

Cora: We got invited to Edward's friends party!!!!!!

Me: oh em gee! girl for serious?!!!

Cora: Alex Monroe, I'm gonna kick you in the pants.

My timer goes off on my phone to alert me that I have five minutes to get to class so I shoot her a quick text while I walk there.

Me: I'm just teasing Cinderella, don't lose your glass slipper, I gtg, class.

She already knows not to message me when I'm in class. The way my crazy brain is set up, if she texts me I'll be anxious about responding the whole time. Yay, trauma!

I walk into my class and some dude bumps into me in a rush out the door, causing me to knock into the door frame. I rush to grab the elbow I hit, as if that could aid the shooting pain to my funny bone, and spill the entire contents of my purse in the process. He doesn't so much as look back to see if I'm okay as he rushes down the hallway and out the double doors to the courtyard. I'm instantly pissed and more so embarrassed that everyone is just staring at my dumb ass and whispering about how pathetic I must be.

I feel my cheeks flushing with embarrassment. My elbow is aching, which only causes my anger to rise. Anxious and hyper-aware of these people whispering around me, I look up at the stupid sorority sluts watching me stuff all the shit back into my purse. One of them smirks as she looks straight into my eyes, and I lose it.

"Do you have a fucking problem?" I shout.

Her eyes widen in shock as if she didn't expect me to confront her blue-eyed, blonde-haired ass.

"Umm no. I'm sorry, I was saying we should offer to help you." Rolling my eyes, pure heat radiates through my veins, and I envision myself yanking her out of the chair by her perfect hair.

There goes your anger issues, my subconscious reminds me.

Ah yes, my anger issues. They consume me no matter how hard I try to control them. A small part of me wishes that it didn't take over so easily, but hey, I am passionate about the things I love and the things I hate. My mind and body just react accordingly. It's the aftermath, though, it will hit me and I'll feel guilty about getting so angry. I fuck up time and time again, reacting to the little devil on my shoulder. That's why Cora is my best friend; she loves me regardless.

Cora!? What would Cora tell me to do?

I grab the rest of my shit and tell the professor I have to go. He nods and continues teaching, not caring either way.

Chapter 2

Alex

Fresh air hits my face as I exit the building my class is in. I make my way to the courtyard, as I pull my phone out of my purse to text Cora.

Me: Hey bitch. I left class because I was about to choke a hoe, where r u?

While I'm waiting for her to respond, I take a seat on a bench near the fountain to try and calm down a little bit. I stare at the sky and take some deep breaths. My brain feels like it's vibrating inside my skull, I'm so overstimulated by that whole situation. It's usually hot as fuck in Texas, but I'm lucky because there is a cool breeze in the air. I close my eyes and imagine I'm at the beach. It's my happy place. My phone pings but instead of rushing to it, I wait a few seconds as I center myself.

Finally able to release some of the tension in my chest, I pull my phone to my face to check the notification.

Cora: At the mall, picking out something new for tonight!

Cora: It's our first party!

Cora: Come meet me, you need an outfit too, Alex.

Me: k

I will never understand why we need new outfits for every fucking thing, but here I go. Anything to make my bestie happy.

Walking into the mall, I see tons of smiling faces and loud laughter. People are just enjoying their lives and I'm immediately annoyed with all the noise. There is a torture that comes with being in public places: I hear everything. The sensory overload drives me crazy.

I know she is going to be inside of Steve Madden. I head there first because, ironically, all the stores Cora prefers to shop in are lined up perfectly one after another, as if just for her.

I would never admit it to Cora, but I am a little bit excited about tonight. I won't allow myself to feel too excited, though. If one thing is certain in my life, it's that if something bad is going to happen, it's going to happen to me.

As soon as I walk in, I can see my best friend's head towering over the racks of clothes. She is at least 6 ft tall, has a long athletic frame, and just the right amount of goods in all the right places. She has subtle curves that I would kill for, my own personal Kendall Jenner. She has long straight strawberry blonde hair. She is stunning. I always try to force her into modeling, but despite being drop-dead gorgeous, my friend doesn't see her beauty.

I walk up behind her and shout her name, she jumps and I burst out laughing.

"Alex! What the heck? You scared the crap out of me!"

"Well, that's kind of the point, Cora. It's not my fault you're taller than the damn racks. You should have seen me coming." She smacks her lips in annoyance.

"You know I hyperfocus when I'm shopping, Alex. I'm in the zone. Besides, it's not my fault you're so short that the racks hide you like a toddler." Ooh, burn.

"Ouch, Cora." I place my hand over my heart. "That really hurt my feelings."

She stares at me with a flat expression on her face and rolls her bright blue eyes.

"Spare me the dramatics, Alex Monroe. You have no feelings. In fact, how are you even breathing? Do you even have a pulse?" That's fair, I think to myself.

"Ha-ha. Very funny. Keep looking for your damn outfit and leave me alone. As a matter of fact, I'm gonna go to the side of the store for people with no soul and you stay here in bubblegum pink fairytale land, k? K."

She sighs in defeat because she knows I never stop talking shit back and she loves me enough to let me win. I walk over to the dresses, short black and skintight. That's what I'm looking for. I can't wear anything that doesn't cling to every curve of my body. I get stared at hard and not just by men. It's mostly women looking at me like I'm trying to steal their man. That would never happen, girl code and all.

I am 5'1" and not as blessed as my gorgeous best friend. Listen, I know I'm a bad bitch who is also madly confident, but I am snack-size. I am extra curvy, and I have a handful of tits and ass. I may be short, but my legs are long for my height, and my dark hair falls past my waist in loose curls. I am thick everywhere it counts, and I'm reminded every time some asshole tries to hit on me. It's so hard to know who is really trying to get to know me, and who just wants in my pants. I can't remember a time when my body didn't place me at the center of attention, even as a kid. Guys always thought I was older, and that put me in several uncomfortable situations. I guess it doesn't help that I never dressed my age either, but that shouldn't mean I'm up for grabs.

My mom never cared and always told me I was asking for attention. Maybe I was but, not from any man. She was fine as long as she had her quiet time. That meant me being gone, and her in a dark room feeling like she was floating on cloud nine. I hate her. I look nothing like her, thank God. She always made fun of my figure. In her opinion, my thighs and butt were too thick and my breasts too big. I needed to lose weight so I could be thin like her. No, thank you. As perfect as she looked, she was damaged and broken inside, never capable of loving anyone as much as she pretended to love herself. Wait, I'm wrong. Let me correct myself. She never loved anyone or anything as much as her drugs.

Aside from the differences in body type, Cora and I typically end up on opposite sides of the store because our styles are so different. Black is my signature color. Cora always jokes about how it matches my soul, and she isn't wrong. Her signature color is pink and she loves every shade, although now that we are in college, I have noticed her trying to tame it down with more nude tones. Her soul will always be bubblegum pink, though.

Cora is the sunshine to my dark cloud. If you placed us next to each other, no one would believe we are best friends. Different esthetics, styles, and personalities. The only similarity we seem to have is an unconditional love for each other. A love that has been a light in the darkness that was our childhood. We grew up on different sides of the tracks but were equally neglected and lonely.

Our moms were best friends. Also from different worlds, the same small town, doing all the same shit that every generation did before them. They never outgrew it, so because of them, we vowed to leave and make something of ourselves. We promised that we would be the only family we ever needed. My mom gave up her inheritance for my father, a lowlife good-for-nothing drug dealer. I thought she had sealed my fate, but my grandparents saved me. I was given her inheritance and mine. I don't live like I have it, though. I grew up with nothing, so it's hard to allow myself to feel safe with it. I feel like the rug can be pulled out from under me at any time. I only use it to pay for school and necessities.

My grandparents passed away a while back. I didn't even get to meet the people who saved me. Their lawyer contacted me when I enrolled in college. It was the shock of a lifetime. I was already accepted because, despite my reckless behavior, my grades were on point. I had a partial scholarship and used financial aid for the rest. I am so thankful to my dance teacher. She paid my application fee because she believed in my dreams. "Your talent will take you places, Alex," she always said.

I'm so deep in my thoughts, I don't see that Cora is waiting next to me. We have this tradition of not going into the dressing room unless we are together and we can't check out unless both of us find outfits. She is studying me with sad eyes and I roll mine at her.

"What, Cora?" The tone of my voice matches my annoyance.

"What were you thinking about?" Concern laces her tone.

"Nothing," I say, trying to send her vibes that I don't want to talk about it.

"Your mom, then. Figures." She places her hands on her lap, waiting for my response.

How does she even know? "Are you a psychic?"

She giggles. "Because I know *you,* best friend, and I know that look. Your mom was on your brain."

"Ugh, fine. She was, but not just my mom. I was thinking about us and where we came from." I look away from her so she doesn't see the tears welling in my eyes as I force them away.

"Enough of that," I say before she can respond. She doesn't push. She knows I don't like talking about it.

"Okay, but hurry up. I want to try this on. It's getting late." I'm glad for the quick subject change she makes.

I grab two black dresses I was checking out from the rack to try on. They are exactly the same, but depending on how short it is, I may need an extra large instead of a large. Cora is much more modest than me and will definitely have a heart attack if my ass pops out of the bottom. I want tonight to be perfect for both of us and don't want to cause any unnecessary waves, so I'll try to cover up.

"See, I'm getting one that won't show my ass. I'm not that much of a selfish bitch," I say, smiling at her as I walk into the fitting room she's in.

"Oh, you're so kind, Alex. Thank you for not showing your vagina to the world." Her teasing tone makes me happy. I love when we roast each other.

I laugh at the fact she whispers *vagina* like it's illegal to say when we are adults.

"I thought you would appreciate that. Also, I will wear underwear this time." I wink at her and she smiles.

"You should always wear underwear, Alex," she says, rolling her eyes.

I hate underwear. The only time I regretted not wearing any was when I wore a mini skirt to class the first day and fell flat on my face in front of everyone. I'm sure the hot professor got a nice show, though. Hopefully, I get an A plus because math isn't my strong suit.

I try on the large dress first and I love it. It's a mini dress, skintight with a sweetheart neckline. Thank God it doesn't run small and is the perfect length. Cora won't kill me. We all win. I can picture the heels I'm going to wear with it.

My ex bought them for my birthday last year. They are shiny black square-toe pumps that wrap up around my ankle and up to my calf and tie in the back. Sooo sexy.

As I check myself out in the mirror, I notice Cora staring too.

"Damn, Alex. That dress looks amazing on you and it's the perfect length."

“I know, right?" I respond, looking myself up and down in the mirror.

“A ‘thank you’ would be nice before your head gets too big." We laugh in unison, she knows me well.

"Yes, thank you, best friend. So is this okay with no underwear, then?" She smacks my arm.

"It isn't like you would wear any if I told you to anyway, Alex."

I turn around to see what she has tried on, and I'm in awe. She stayed modest but looks so good. She is wearing a light pink pleated skirt that looks shorter than it is with her long legs, a nude tube top that covers her breasts and torso completely, and she finished the look with nude peep toe pumps. She looks hot.

Very...Cora.

“Cora, you look hot as fuck!”

“Thanks, I definitely thought you were gonna make fun of me,” she admits, smoothing out the skirt.

“Me? Make fun of you? Never!”

We break out of the dressing room in a fit of laughter as we head to the checkout line. Tonight is going to be a good night. I can feel it.

Chapter 3

Alex

"It's so loud in here!" Cora shouts. I laugh at her. Does she honestly think it would be quiet at a frat party? "What were you expecting? Tea and crackers?" We continue our trek through the house and it's huge!

The doors are at least 12 feet tall, and when you step inside and look up, the ceiling seems miles high. This place is kind of amazing. It's very James Bond. The door locks are touch pads and there are what looks like Google Home hubs in every room we have passed through so far. I am loving the modern décor, all sleek, with black and gold accents throughout the entire home.

I'm feeling anxious as we travel deeper into the party. The possibility of things happening that are out of my control puts my senses into overdrive. No doubt, PTSD from the way we lost Cecille. This is part of why we haven't been to a party in so long. I want Cora to have a good time, so I need to relax. I take some deep breaths, hoping I'm discreet.

She must sense my unease because I feel her hand grab mine as we make our way into the kitchen. It's quiet here and there aren't as many people hanging around as there were in the living room. There aren't many people, period, but everyone that's here is in there.

It's 10:30 pm and I tried to tell Cora no one worth it would be here this early, but she insisted. She is a very punctual person, and I'm lucky if I even remember to be somewhere important. You would think she would have learned from our high school party days that being early is for losers because we were always teased about it. We didn't mind it, though, because, by the time everyone showed up, we were the life of the party. Secretly, I think that's why she liked to be early: to be able to talk to everyone who walked through that door first. As if that somehow made us easier to remember. I guess it worked because we always ended up being the center of attention.

Thoughts of those days bring Cecille to the front of my brain, and I have to push it to the back of my mind quickly. Especially since I already have anxiety. I don't want to go there right now or the night will definitely end up ruined. I faintly hear Cora's voice saying my name and that brings me back to the present. I must have been in my own head for a while because I look around and notice a lot more people have filed into the house now.

"Earth to Alex. Is anyone in there?" She taps a finger to my temple to get my attention.

"Yes, you asshole. I was thinking about what I wanted to drink while checking out the meat market," I lie.

She smirks. "Gross," she laughs. "Meat market? You're such a guy."

"Always thought that I should have a dick, but..." I pause, holding a finger up, "...only if I could fuck myself with it," I laugh out loud, but Cora doesn't.

Her eyes widen as she looks to her left with a slight nod that only I could notice. There are a group of guys surrounding us.

Oops.

"Alex, this is Edward." She introduces her dickwad boyfriend and I don't approve.

I look him up and down. *Edward, huh?* "Nice to finally meet you." The fake smile that adorns my lips must not hold up well because she widens her eyes at me.

He looks like a preppy jock asshole, but hey, who am I to judge? Oh, that's right. I'm Cora's best friend, so, hell yeah, I'm gonna judge.

He holds his hand out to give me a handshake like a stiff. "Hello, Alexandrea."

I roll my eyes, and I see Cora's eyes almost pop out of her pretty little head.

She knows, bitch mode activated.

I ignore his hand. "It's *just* Alex. Not short for anything." I don't even bother trying to be nice.

He swallows and I see his jaw tighten. I'm not sure why because he is the one who assumed my name was short for something else, which I hate. I have a feeling it's because he thinks I'm out of line for a woman. I caught the vibes and I don't like him one fucking bit.

"Oh, I apologize, Alex," he says sarcastically, turning away as he speaks to me like I'm not important.

Asshole.

He excuses himself as some of his douchebag friends call him over to where they're standing.

I make it a point to look around once more, paying close attention this time. This house is full of snobs, dressed as if they belong at a country club instead of a party. I get that I'm the one judging right now, but I must stick out like a sore thumb. Not only because of my outfit of choice but, also because I don't look like these people. The darker complexion of my skin against all the lighter ones in this room is duly noted. This house is probably owned by some spoiled rich kids. Daddy bought them a house, how nice. Life must be really nice when you have daddy's money and daddy's love. Something I will never have.

Cora and I can barely afford the apartment we share. There is a third bedroom, but we haven't had the heart to rent it out. Cecille would have stayed in there. I mean, technically I can afford it, I just don't want to depend on that money, so I pretend I don't have it and live my life like any other college kid.

I want to smack one of the Google things off the wall and make these rich pricks pay. I hope they make some genius mad, and he hacks all their high-tech smart house bullshit. I'm always assuming the worst of people, so I make sure to protect myself. Fight or flight, another stupid fucking trauma response. It takes me a minute to realize Cora is talking to me again. I didn't hear one word she said.

"What did you say? Sorry, I was inside my head again."

"What did you think of Edward?" Curiosity fills her eyes.

I give her *the look.*

"I hate him, Cora." Well, that came out a little harsher than I intended, but whatever.

"Alex, you don't even know him." I feel bad that I've upset her, but I'm not going to sugarcoat it, she knows me better than that.

I scoff, "I don't need to know him. His vibe is off and that tells me everything I need to know."

"You and your fucking vibes. I knew you weren't going to like him once he called you Alexandrea. I told him not to."

"Even more of a reason not to like the idiot. He doesn't listen to my best friend. Besides, you know my vibes are always right. Mark my words."

We see him making his way back over, bringing different douchebag friends with him this time. What fun.

Two of them are staring at us with such anticipation, that I'm glaring right the fuck back, not breaking eye contact at all. Both of their eyes rake my body up and down, moving to Cora's body and back to mine. The dark-haired one licks his lips and I smile a bit, still not breaking eye contact. I have zeroed in on him. He caught my attention first. Probably because he looks like an asshole and I'm a sucker for a bad boy. He is at least 6 feet tall and well-dressed, but not in the way the rest of the guys are. His style is more relaxed. He's wearing dark wash Levi jeans and a black button-up with a crisp white t-shirt underneath. He has his sleeves rolled up, displaying all his tattoos. They are colorful and traditional, which is *so* sexy because it isn't the norm anymore. The icing on the cake is his classic black and white Vans. Yup, he has my complete undivided attention.

I'm suddenly so grateful Cora made me meet her at the mall because I know I look like a badass bitch in this dress.

Cora whispers in my ear, "The guy in the black button-up looks like he is undressing you with his eyes."

"Great, maybe he can actually undress me later."

She nearly spits out the sip she just took of her drink, and we giggle.

The guys finally reach us after being stopped several times by girls in the crowd and Edward begins to introduce them. Here we go.

"Ladies, this is Aaron, Eli, and X. Fellas, this is Cora and her best friend Alex."

He looks over at me and smirks. I want to actually slap him for acting like a little bit of a dick, but I let him slide because I want to bang his friend. God, I'm such a slut. Oh well. No shame in my game.

Edward speaks loudly, interrupting my thoughts. Clearly, he is already buzzing. "Has anyone seen Kohen?" he asks.

The guys all look at each other and then back at Edward.

X speaks up first. "He said he was on his way an hour ago." He's making serious eye contact with me. He runs his tongue across his bottom lip and I bite mine in response. Damn, he's sexy.

"He told me he wasn't going to head here until he heard the house was packed," I hear another guy say, but all I can focus on is X. His smile, his vibe.

I'm brought back to reality when I hear my best friend's voice.

"He probably won't be here at all then because it's already midnight, babe."

"Who are you talking about Cora?" I ask, still staring at X.

I'm curious because I love his name. I'm a sucker for a sexy name. Since his name was mentioned, everyone seems excited. You can feel the rise in the energy around the room. It's at this moment that I realize, everyone is looking at me like I grew another head.

"What?" I whisper to Cora, and even though no one asked him, Edward answers me.

"He is our best friend, and he owns this house. We aren't a frat, but he lets us live here. We are all brothers."

Of course.

"So, this is his house, and he isn't here?"

I don't know if it's the alcohol running through my veins or if it's just the trauma of my past, but it really pisses me the fuck off that he isn't here at his party, at his house. How irresponsible.

My unanswered question repeats in my head.

It's *his* house and he isn't here.

"Alex, it's fine. The guys take care of everything. He is never here."

She knows me well, and she knows why it upsets me that he isn't here. If this is his house, then he should be here. Anything could happen and the person who owns the home should be here. What if something bad happened? No matter how much I try to push the thoughts down and have fun, my mind goes straight to Cecille. I need some air.

"I'll be back, I need to pee."

"Wait, I'm coming with you. I have to go potty, too."

I love her, she knows me like the back of her hand and why I'm really making my escape. Cora leads me up some stairs and into a guest bathroom that is the size of my bedroom.

I wait for her to start her whisper-yell as I gawk at the unnecessary shit they have in here.

"What is wrong with you?" she asks me.

I scoff. "Me? What's wrong with me?"

"Go on, Alex. Let it all out because when we leave this restroom we will not address it again. I like Edward, Alex. I just want things to go well."

"OKAY, MOM." I don't like that this Kohen guy isn't here. It is his party, his house, and what if something bad happens? I really don't like any of these guys. They all seem like assholes, but I don't tell her that.

She stares at me with sadness in her eyes. "Well, it's pretty obvious you already hate Edward."

"It's not that I hate him, Cora. You know how I am. I just don't like the energy he gives off. If he truly is a good guy, then there's nothing to worry about and I'll admit I was wrong."

"That's highly unlikely," she says, rolling her eyes.

"That's because I'm almost never wrong and you know it."

Her eyes tear up and it tugs at my heartstrings. Heartstrings I only have for her. I pull her into a hug. I'm not trying to be a bitch. I know I come off harsh when I am just trying to protect the last person on the earth I love.

"I'm sorry C, I'll try."

"I want so badly for you to be wrong, Alex. I really like him."

"Trust me, best friend, I hope I'm wrong too. I want nothing more than your happiness, but you deserve the love you give."

"I know, Alex."

"Well, then you also know I won't let you settle. I'm going to protect your heart."

"I'm going to protect your heart, too."

I release her from our hug, take a few steps back, and smile. She returns the gesture, and my heart settles.

"Besides..." she says, as I look back up at her in the mirror and she looks nervous as hell. "...We thought you might like Kohen."

I begin to turn, slowly taking a moment, so my head doesn't pop off my shoulders.

"Cora, tell me you didn't bring me here as a blind date setup. Tell me you know me well enough to know I would hate that. Tell me you didn't, Cora. Wait, better yet, don't tell me because I'm going to lose my shit."

She shushes me because the acoustics in this restroom make it sound like I'm in an amphitheater as it is.

"Alex, before you pop off, listen."

"No, Cora!," I interrupt. "And don't shush me. This could have been avoided by telling me this was a setup."

"It wasn't a setup," she whisper-yells.

Cora isn't one to cause a scene and she is constantly defusing the bomb that is me.

"Please fucking explain to me how bringing me here, thinking I would like meeting Edward's stupid asshole friend Kohen, wasn't a setup?"

"Well, when you say it like that..."

"Yes, Cora, because that's what it is. And to top it off, the asshole isn't even here. He isn't here, Cora, at his own party!"

"Stop yelling!"

"No! Stop trying to defuse me. I have a right to feel everything I'm feeling."

"Don't be a bitch, Alex."

"You know it's easy for me to be a bitch when my friend is a goodie two shoes."

"That is not fair!"

"Life isn't fair."

Cora's eyes narrow "Oh, I know. I know as well as you do, so can we drop this? I'm sorry. I'm not trying to defuse you, I promise I just don't want to fight. You're right, but I did it out of love. I just wanted us to have a great start to this year and Kohen is a good guy. I'm sure he has an excellent reason for not being here."

"I'm sure he does, Cora. I'm sure he is saving babies in third-world countries. I guess it bothers me because he is responsible for all the people here. Me and you know better than anyone that anything can happen. If something does, he isn't here!"

She stays quiet. I know she finally pieced it together.

"Cecille," she says in a whisper with sadness in her eyes.

We stare at each other. Without words, we both decide to let it go. I count to ten in my head and realign my thoughts.

"Okay, I don't want to fight either. It isn't worth it. He isn't here anyway. I'm overreacting. I'm sorry. Just don't try and set me up anymore, please."

"Deal," she says.

I wonder if anyone heard us outside. Not that I care, I just don't want to embarrass my best friend any more than I already have. I know how she gets. We can't have one of her pretty and perfect blonde hairs out of place.

"Okay, enough bullshit. I'll give Edward a real chance. Let's go out there, forget this even happened, and have a badass night!"

Her smile is huge. It's all the confirmation I need to know that all is well.

"Also, have you looked around this restroom?" She takes a look around and giggles. There are bowls of ChapSticks, condoms, wet wipes, and gum. There are at least a dozen different perfumes, colognes, and lotions for people to use at their discretion.

I smirk sarcastically. "Ridiculous, right?"

"Absolutely ridiculous." She rolls her eyes, feigning annoyance.

We look at each other and laugh.

"Okay, best friend, let's go let loose and have fun. No more fighting."

"Okay, pinky promise?"

"Pinky promise," I state.

We wrap our pinkies around each other and seal it with a kiss before making our way out of the restroom and back downstairs into the raging party.

Chapter 4

Kohen

The party is raging when I walk in the door and the buzz of energy is palpable. The vibrations of the music hum through my body. Erica has been on my ass all night trying to get back with me. I guess the NFL player she tried to level up with didn't like spending all his money on her gold-digging ass. Ditto, bro.

We've been over for too long. I thought she was the love of my life, and I've tried to remain friends, but I just can't do it. She's a cold-hearted user and a cheater. I want no part of it. She says we need closure and I'm sure it's in the form of sex.

This entire house believes I have a reputation of being a playboy and I let them. I give no fucks about what anybody thinks or says. I am the king of this fucking campus, so do girls line up on their knees? Yes. Do I fuck every tight little hole they throw my way? Hell nah. I was with Erica for a long time, and I never cheated. My mom taught me better than that. One thing that stayed with me after she passed is how to treat my woman. Erica isn't my woman anymore and I'll be honest, I'm a little buzzed, so I'm gonna go upstairs to get this so-called closure and call it a night.

I have three weeks of intense training and I need to get focused. Being an Olympic athlete is a full-time job in and of itself, and I have no time for bullshit. I must continue the family legacy as my father would say. He's a dick and the reason I need to be buzzed tonight. He thinks he can pressure me to marry Erica because her family comes from wealth and status. Fuck him and fuck her. Well, I will fuck her. She pulls me through the party by my hand, loving the way people stare at her while she's with me. I hate it.

I see Xzavien and Edward with a group of our friends. X looks up at me and laughs as I ascend the staircase with Erica. I shake my head and he shakes his back. X is like a brother to me, my best friend if I could say I had one, but our friendship hasn't been the same for about a year now. We have been competitive with each other our whole lives, but it's gotten pretty fucked up lately. It seems like he wants to step into my shoes or my life. I care about the dude, even love him, but I don't tolerate the disrespect and he knows better.

We are almost at the top of the stairs when I see a few girls coming down from the restroom. To avoid one of Erica's classic meltdowns due to jealousy, I keep my eyes to the ground. Last thing I need is one of these women trying to get my attention and then Erica causing a scene. I'm tired of all that shit.

The girls finally pass us and suddenly I'm hit with the most intoxicating scent. Floral yet sweet, like lavender and pear. I must be more buzzed than I thought because it's as if everything around me slows down.

I turn my head to look at where the sweet scent is coming from, and I see the most beautiful woman I have ever laid my eyes on. She's flipping her long raven-colored locks over her shoulder. Her thick eyelashes flutter open and closed as she continues to make her way past us. Her caramel-colored skin is flushed, and I find myself wanting to reach over and run my thumb across her cheek. I want to feel the heat there. My eyes roam the rest of her face as I follow the perfect line of her nose down to her luscious wine-red lips. I want to fucking bite them. Gravity is pulling me to this girl and I don't even know who the fuck she is. I continue my trek down her body. It's heavenly fucking perfection. Her breasts bounce with every single step she takes in those high heel shoes, her curvy body beckoning me like a moth to a flame. I bite the knuckle of my free hand, but I really want to take a bite out of her.

I'm captivated.

I notice Erica trying to lead me to the private set of stairs that go to my room, but I quickly stop her.

"You know we don't go in there," I remind her as I guide her to the empty guest room.

"I know but I thought since we are going to get back together, we could finally go up there." Pleading eyes meet mine, but I don't care. All I can think about is going to find the girl I passed on the stairs. Her scent is banked away permanently in every corner of my mind. I wonder how her pussy tastes. How it feels or what her sexy body will look like writhing under me as I please her.

The door slams shut, bringing me out of the naughty thoughts I'm having about that girl. I turn to look at Erica and excuse myself from the room when I see her standing there completely naked. How long was I suspended in thought? "What are you doing?"

"I'm going to make you feel good, babe."

I cringe. I have a picture-perfect girl standing in front of me, ready to make me feel good by letting me do anything I want to any hole in her body.

Yet all I want to do is get the fuck away from her. Don't get me wrong, her tits are large and perky perfection, and her small waist and long legs may be every man's dream, but not mine.

"This was a mistake." I shake my head in disappointment. I said I'm tired of these same old habits and yet here I am, back on track to repeat the same pattern.

"No, babe. We aren't a mistake." She walks up to me in nothing but her spiky Louboutin heels. My dick doesn't care. "We are meant for each other." She reaches for the place that would usually be a bulge in my pants and her eyebrows raise. Nothing. She leans in to kiss my neck and her scent repulses me. I have to be batshit fucking crazy to have every emotion and attachment to Erica I have ever felt just completely shut off for a random fucking stranger.

It can't be that. I'm just realizing I'm finally done with her.

"Put your clothes on, Erica. Get your shit and get the fuck out. We're done." I walk around her to open the door. I don't care if she's naked. It's not like she doesn't already post her body on Only Fans and Twitter.

She scoffs. "Are you kidding me?" she asks incredulously.

"No, I'm not. Like I said, I'm done." I slam the door closed behind me and make my way down to the party to find out who this girl is that possessed my mind.

It doesn't take me long to find her in the crowd. Of course, she is with Xzavien and Edward's crew. I should have known she would be. She has that plump ass on display in that tight little dress. Fuck. I don't go to where they are right away. Nah. Instead, I bide my time. I'm sober now, so I'm observing, watching, and I like everything I'm seeing. She sways to the music randomly when no one's paying attention, her body moving to the rhythm like second nature. Every curve on her body deserves to be admired, but only by me.

She flirts with Xzavien, but I have yet to determine if it's innocent or if she actually likes him. I don't want to step on anyone's toes, but I know I need to be near her and it's getting harder to watch her interact with him. He says something to her and she laughs, her hand grazing his arm, and my heart starts to pump. I want her hands on me. They are small and feminine and they look so soft. Images of them wrapped around my cock as she sucks my dick with those luscious lips fill my head and my dick twitches.

The music changes and I see her get excited. Her eyes light up like it's Christmas and I laugh. She shakes her friend to get her attention and they start to dance, all eyes on them. They bump and grind into each other and X has his eyes all over the girl, my girl. Suddenly, she climbs up on the table, her friend following suit as another shorter girl they were with joins them. A crowd gathers and I remain watching, moving in the shadows because once my boys see me, the entire party will know too and I want to stay under the radar as long as possible.

I guess it helps that everyone is piss drunk and it's two in the morning. I just need to see her for now, her energy is a force to be reckoned with, I can tell. When Taylor Swift said, *'I knew you were trouble when I walked in,'* this must be what she meant. I have to know her name. She is the most gorgeous woman I have ever seen, and her curvy little body is sexy as fuck. She is the perfect size all the way around, and I want to grab all the soft parts of her body. Thick curly, jet-black hair ends right at the curve of her back, and there sits the perfect peach. Her thick thighs and muscular calves are on display as she moves her body, calling me to her. God damn, she's intoxicating.

The song ends and X helps her off the bar. I almost intercede as they begin to dance, but I wait. He places his hand on the small of her back and she moves it. Good girl. He excuses himself to go to the restroom and that's when I come in.

I waste no time telling everyone hi, and I learn the name of the blonde she's with, and that she's Edward's girl. So this is who they were trying to set me up with. Call it fate.

"Hi, I'm Kohen." I move in for a hug but she moves back. Feisty.

"So you're the asshole who didn't show up to his own party, where someone could get hurt." She is drunk for sure, and such a little spitfire. I fucking love it and only fuels my obsession more.

"Yeah, that's me. Just a big dick."

She snorts out in laughter and her hand lands on my chest. "Oh, asshole has jokes. Okay, I like it. But next time you have a party, Kohen..." My name on her lips sounds so fucking good. "...make sure you're at it. I mean, imagine, you may have met me much sooner." She winks, and that's it. I'm a dead man walking and I would die happy for her.

"I'm sorry, I didn't catch your name," I smile, laying on the Kohen Ventura charm. Her eyes meet my dimple and she smiles.

"I'm Alex, and no it isn't short for anything."

"Got it, nice to meet you, Alex. If I may say so..." I pause and she waits for the next words to come out of my mouth intently, biting her own lip. "You are the most gorgeous woman I have ever laid my eyes on."

Her honey-brown eyes meet mine and it's like an electric current flowing through my veins at the connection. I place my hand on her hip as I catch her swaying to the beat and she leans into the touch. Fuck yes. She's into me, too. Before I know it, her lips are on mine and it's like everything and everyone in the room disappears. She breaks the kiss and brings her fingers to her lips in wonder, lust filling her eyes.

"I'm sorry, I'm a little buzzed. I wouldn't normally do that."

I lean in to whisper in her ear, making sure to graze my chin along her neck and her breath hitches. "It's okay, Angel. I wanted you to." I place a soft kiss there and back up a bit, as I appreciate every single bit of the glory that God himself had to have created just for me.

Chapter 5

Alex

I wake up with a massive headache. My eyes feel like they are pounding behind my eyelids. Forcing them closed causing swirls of light behind them. I don't even want to think about what's going to happen if I try to open them again. A symptom of some type of alcohol brain damage.

Last night is a blur, but from the bits I can remember, I *think* I had fun. I hear Cora's feet shuffling down the hall, and then I hear puking. Yup, we had fun. I don't want Cora to know I'm awake yet. She'll make me do things and it's too early to do things. I also don't want to think about what the hell we did if we woke up like this. I know that if I let myself get drunk enough to feel this hungover I must have been acting crazy.

"Alex?"

I don't respond. I feel like a little girl, giggling under the sheets pretending I'm still asleep so I don't have to go to school.

"Alex, are you awake?"

I take some deep, nauseating breaths, still not ready to respond. I want more sleep, but my brain doesn't allow me to take naps. So, it's not like I could go back to sleep anyway. Once I wake up, that's it. I'm up all day. It sucks. I hear her walk away and turn on the shower. Getting up slowly, I make my way to the restroom.

"Cora?"

"Come in, Alex."

The bathroom is already filled with steam as I make my way inside our vintage restroom.

She peeks at me from behind the powder blue shower curtain, wasting no time. “Remember anything from last night?” she asks, wiggling her eyebrows. She has a grin that spreads from ear to ear. Now I’m scared.

“No, I don't remember a single thing from last night after we left the restroom. Everything is fuzzy.”

She giggles.

Fuck.

“You don't remember anything at all?”

“Just tell me, what did I do?”

She giggles some more and now I know I’m fucked.

“The bits and pieces I do have don't make sense, so I’m not sure if it was just like a hangover dream. I think I remember grabbing drinks and going to dance?” I ask more of a question than a statement. “Do you remember? Because you sure are smiling fucking huge.”

“I do.” A mischievous smirk graces her face.

“That's it? You do? Elaborate, please. Now!” I demand.

“We had the time of our lives. I haven’t seen you let go like that in a long time!” excitement radiating from her body.

She is behind the curtain again, but I can picture her smiling from the sound of her voice as she continues to recap me. My palm slaps my forehead and I have a feeling my alter ego made an appearance.

"It was crazy!" she starts.

It’s at this exact moment that I feel like I’m watching *The Hangover*- The Alex and Cora version.

"I don't think we have had that much fun ever," she continues. "Alex, you got on the bar, and everyone was yelling and cheering while you danced."

"What? OMG! What else? Tell me," I laugh.

“You were hyping everybody up, rallying everybody onto the dance floor. It was so much fun. You were always a natural at being the life of a party. You danced with Xzavien and- oh!- Kohen was watching you dance all night!”

I pause, my smile fading. I must look like a confused puppy with my head tilted to one side. "Kohen?" I question.

She peeks out of the curtain and looks at me like I should know what she is talking about. "Alex, you were all over him." She laughs, and I forget to breathe.

I gag like I'm gonna vomit. "Lies," I deadpan.

"Alex, don't start. He came up to you, and you thought he was *so hot* when he introduced himself."

"And," I interrupt her, "What? I don't remember that at all. You better be kidding, Cora."

She has to be kidding. I would remember that. To be fair, I hadn't drunk alcohol in a very long time, so I was probably acting like an idiot.

"I can't believe I danced on the bar," I groan with my head in my hands. I had been the most outgoing version of myself in a long time and I don't even remember. I was introduced to the most popular and handsome guy at our school and don't even remember what he looks like. How the fuck is that fair? This is unbelievable and, in his house, no less.

"Cora! Ugh, this is just my luck." I pull my hair out of frustration.

She just laughs in response. She turns off the water and opens the curtain, still smiling.

"Don't your cheeks hurt? Have you been smiling this whole time?" Her smile fades as she walks to where I sit.

"What's wrong?"

"I'm just pissed because I wish I remembered. I hate having questions and not knowing for myself."

"I know, Alex, but trust I had your back and you were safe. I'm sorry, but you were having so much fun and I decided to just let you be."

"I'm not mad at you, Cora. Well, I am, but not too bad." We laugh. "And I know you kept me safe. Thank you. I love you mucho."

"I love you dos." I roll my eyes at her poor attempt at Spanish, even though I've taught her the right word, it's become our little thing.

We make our way down the short hallway to her bedroom, and I climb up on her tall ass *Princess and the Pea* pink bed. I need a damn stool to get on it.

"Wait, so what time did that Kohen guy even get there? I thought he had flaked." Well, that's one of the last things I remember anyway.

"He got there around two in the morning. You were already buzzed and flirty. I thought you really liked Xzavien, but once Kohen arrived, the poor guy didn't exist anymore."

I'm sure my face is as red as a tomato. I am so embarrassed. I would never want to lead someone on and treat them like that.

"I need to apologize to him. I feel so bad. How long were we there?" I can't take anything back, the damage is done, but my toxic ass can take some damn responsibility. I may be a bitch, but I don't treat people like shit for nothing.

"We were there until around four. It was a long night, or should I say *morning.*" She moves her eyebrows playfully and I throw a shirt at her. It hits her smack dab in the face. Cora's reflexes are shit. "You have to remember something, Alex."

Is she not listening? I stare at her, clearly annoyed because I said from the get-go that I don't remember a damn thing. How many times will I have to say it?

"Cora, I don't remember anything. I wish I did but I don't. But maybe it's better that way."

"I call bullshit, Alex. You have to remember getting his number. I feel like you're saying you don't remember so you don't have to call him. He was an alpha for sure. It's okay if you're scared," she smirks. "But yeah, he grabbed you, asked for your phone, and put his number in it. Everyone was talking about it, Xzavien got jealous and that's why he took off."

Okay, now I *am* scared. My stomach feels like it falls onto the floor. I think I'm going to be sick. I have to know more.

"Tell me everything now," I say seriously. I have to know what else I missed. I know if anything really bad or embarrassing happened she would tell me that first, so it must have all just been good fun, but still. I hate not knowing. I'm too much of a control freak for this.

Chapter 6

Alex

I feel a little lost inside when I can't remember everything I did. I hate that feeling. I'm glad I allowed myself to let loose at the same time, though. I'm proud of myself in that regard. I'm young and I deserve to have fun, but the loss of control is what makes me seem like a stuck-up bitch. I have to feel like I'm in control of everything. It's the aftereffects of the trauma we went through, and the way Cecille died. If I had only paid attention, been less drunk, wasn't such a fucking party whore... The feelings of anxiousness remain.

My thoughts are interrupted as Cora claps her hands together and speaks.

'"Okay. I'm going to tell you everything, Alex. But you have to promise you won't freak out any more than I can tell you already are."

"Fine," I huff in response. I hate that she knows me so well sometimes. I shut my mouth so she can continue.

"We left the restroom and grabbed a couple of drinks."

"Well, I know that, Cora. You already mentioned that part and clearly, since I blacked out, I had more than a couple."

"Hush! If you want me to tell you everything, I'm going to have to go through it in my own mind step by step, from beginning to end. So have some damn patience or I won't tell you."

I giggle because she thinks she is speaking with authority, but she only sounds soft and sweet, like a damn bubblegum princess. She also knows it annoys the living fuck out of me when she takes forever to tell a story, especially if it's stuff that is irrelevant.

"So, anyway. We grabbed our drinks and went to talk to the boys. The DJ had taken a break and his assistant was playing some badass remixes. We were taking shots and having a good time, and friendly conversation. Then BAM!" she exclaims. "It hit us like a ton of bricks. We were drunk off our asses." She laughs, her eyes wide with excitement. We look at each other and I join in on the laughter, shoving her with my shoulder playfully. I don't respond yet because she looks so happy recalling all the events of last night. So, I just have fun watching it replay in my mind as she continues.

"Right when we were about to head to the restroom for the hundredth time, your song came on."

I immediately know what song she means by the sparkle in her eyes. My alter ego song!

"No!" I gasp playfully.

"Yes, Alex! Yes! Ester Dean!"

I'm a whole other woman when that song comes on.

"Then what?" I ask, genuinely curious because that must have been when I blacked out indefinitely.

"Then a bunch of girls joined us and cheered you on as you shook your big ass. They were spanking you and giving you compliments on how nice your ass is."

I'm sure that got us even more attention. Somehow my ass always becomes the top topic of conversation. I even got in a fight once because a girl was arguing about how a guy would choose her huge tits over my big ass any day and we went around a party taking surveys. When I won, she got pissed!

I facepalm myself, remembering all the stupid shit I have done and all the equal amount of times I promised myself I wouldn't do it again. And yet, here I am years later doing the same shit. Peter Pan- take me now because I'll never grow up.

"Yes, Alex," Cora continues. "But we lived it up and we loved all the attention! We were the life of the party, just like old times. The guys joined in and you danced with Xzavien as I danced with Edward. It was like we made our own little club right there on the dance floor."

"How long were we dancing?" *No wonder my legs are so damn sore.*

"I'm not sure, but it seemed like forever, though. The music, the vibes, it just kept us going... But then we took off our shoes and got on the table."

"Of course, we did," I mutter, facepalming again. Wouldn't be us if we didn't. I'm just annoyed that I can't remember any of it.

"Oh, and you ran into an old friend. Do you remember that? Danielle or something like that. She said your moms were best friends growing up."

"Danielle? Wow, I haven't seen her in years. How was she?"

"Good, apparently. She was on the table, too. You got extra crazy when she started to hang out with us. But no worries, you got her number!"

That's right. Cora said I got Kohen's number. I want to check my phone and see if I actually have it. I'll wait, though. I don't want Cora to think too far into it as I know she will. Besides, I want to hear the rest of the story.

"Okay, so we danced on the table. Then what?"

"Well, that Danielle girl is just as nuts as you are, and y'all decided to do a damn strip tease while you were on the table."

"Oh my god, Cora. Please tell me you stopped me?"

"Is there such a thing as stopping Alex Larae Monroe? No! There isn't. I told you to stop, and that just lit more of a fire under your ass. It's you!"

I thought that version of me died a long time ago. "I can't believe I did that. I'm so embarrassed."

Cora lets out a loud laugh. "Alex, are you serious? Of course, you did, and you two loved every second of it. Listen, I'm glad you were able to let go like that. You deserve to be crazy. You aren't 40 years old. You're not even 21. It's okay."

I take a little pause from the conversation as Cora cleans up and think to myself. Damn, I really did let loose last night. I'm a little shocked about it but I also feel a little free. I'm still kind of ashamed and that's new for me. I never feel guilt or shame because I have always been so unapologetic about who I am and why I'm like this. I guess it feels different because I promised a change on Cecille's behalf. After she passed, I promised to take my life more seriously and to give myself a chance at life. Set goals and have some ambition. I owe it to her. Just when I think I'm doing shit right for once, life reminds me I don't deserve anything good. I suck in all these negative thoughts before Cora notices and I ask more questions about last night.

"So did Xzavien or Kohen have anything to say? How did they react to my craziness?"

"Oh my gosh, Alex. Yesss. Kohen was infatuated with you. He told Edward he had never met a girl that was as confident as you. You told him he was sexy, but you also called his butt out for not being at his own party on time. You went on and on about how rude it is and how unsafe it could be if something happened, and he wasn't there."

"I didn't! Why didn't you stop me, Cora? Omg, how embarrassing."

"No, Alex, it was the cutest thing! He kissed your hand and apologized. He had joked around about it making him seem mysterious so you would be more interested, and you told him he failed because you met X."

I gasp. What the fuck was I thinking? I'm a hot fucking mess. No, I'm a damn dumpster fire. I am so embarrassed. I laugh, because if I don't, I might just throw up. My head is spinning from all the information I just got. I have so many more questions but I don't know if Cora will know the answers. Did he like me? What about X? God, if I hurt his feelings I'm going to feel like a bitch. Then again, when have I ever cared about another man's feelings? They never spared mine. That's why I'm such a bitch. Every heartbreak, every broken piece, reminds me that men ain't shit. I laugh.

Cora looks at me puzzled as I continue to chuckle quietly at myself.

"He did not back down at all and I think that's why X ended up leaving. Originally, X was trying to make you seem less interesting to Kohen once he got there. Edward says Kohen doesn't date much and he loves a challenge. So when X tried to make it seem like you were hard to get, it only made him more interested and X got upset."

I wish I felt bad, and I almost did, but then I remembered men don't give a shit when they hurt us. So, too bad for him. If I was worth it, he wouldn't have left.

"All I know, Alex, is you're on Kohen Ventura's radar, and he always gets what he wants."

Me? A challenge? I guess that's fitting. But if Kohen thinks he is going to get what he wants out of me, he has another thing coming. He is on my radar now, too, and I'm not afraid to play with sharks.

Chapter 7

Alex

It's been a week since the party. We have been so busy with our second week of classes and time really flew by. We have barely seen each other at home between school and trying to find jobs. I went back through my texts and pictures from the night of the party at Kohen's house, but I don't remember what he looks like so I wouldn't even be able to tell who he is in any of the pictures I have. Aside from that, most of them are blurry as fuck because my dumb ass was drunk. There are pictures in there that someone else took because I'm in them, but so is Cora. There are pictures of me dancing and taking shots with Cora and Danielle.

I'm happy that everything went down the way it did. I wouldn't change a thing. I was able to take a step forward, even though it felt like a step back. It reminded me that it's okay to live a little. Maybe not to blackout state, though.

I just can't seem to get Kohen out of my head. If he liked me, he would have texted me by now, right? I don't know why, but I find my mind wandering to thoughts of what he looks like, what I liked about him, what his voice sounded like. I know I liked X. I know I liked so many things about him. What was so special about Kohen that I would ditch X for him? He must be fine as fuck! God, I'm so fucked up. Why do I keep thinking so much about a guy I don't even remember meeting? There are two texts in a thread between us, but no way am I making the first move.

K: hey it's Kohen

K: save my number, you know you want it.

Me: yeah, yeah, I know YOU want THIS.

That's it. Those are the texts. What the hell is wrong with me? I ask myself this question all the time. What in the ever-loving fuck is wrong with me? Clearly, I lost my mind that night. A small part of me wants to text him and figure out if he remembers me. If he can tell me anything else that happened and, better yet, find out what the hell he looks like! I can't bring myself to do it, though. Part of me is still super annoyed by him and the fact that he assumed I wanted his number. I lock my phone and roll my eyes. My phone vibrates. My heart races with excitement, I look at it so fast, hoping it's Kohen, but it's just X.

Xzavien: hey gorgeous.

Me: hey X, whats up?

Xzavien: haven't heard from you since the party, just seeing what you were up to. We should get lunch soon.

Me: sure! I'd love to. don't h8 me?

Xzavien: of course, not gorgeous. Why would I h8 you??

I breathe a sigh of relief as I respond.

Me: oh, idk because i blacked out and ruined the fun at that party.

Xzavien: nah babe. you just made it a lot more interesting.

Babe? Why did he have to call me *babe?* It gives me the ick. It's like a staked claim. And I belong to no one.

Danielle pops into my mind right at that moment and I open our text thread. It's been good catching up with her, but I can only take her in small doses. She has big energy, and it can be a lot sometimes.

Me: hey hoe, what you up to?

DD: nothing much. just headed to the beach wanna come?

ME: you don't have class?

DD: yeah, but fuck class YOLO

ME: my YOLO days are over, we did enough of that in middle school, lol how are we even alive?

DD: no idea lol, suit yourself BORING. always gotta be a scared little bitch

DD: Jk don't get your panties in a wad.

I don't respond. This is part of why I stopped hanging out with her. The party never stops and I find myself lost as fuck, just drunk all day, every day with her. I don't want to miss my classes. I'm looking forward to them and the goals I laid out for myself. Where Danielle is...trouble follows, and that's just something I'm not trying to be mixed up in anymore.

I block her number because that's a black hole the white rabbit will definitely pull me into. Might as well remove the temptation altogether. She always has the ability to rile me up, even when we were kids. Not anymore. I'm on a road to recovery and I don't want to give anyone this kind of power over me anymore. I got into a lot of shit when we were young from that type of manipulation. I won't be opening that can of worms.

I text Cora to let her know and start to make my way to my next class. While I walk, I change Kohen's contact info in my phone from Hot Guy with a K, to Kohen.

I silence my phone right as Professor Watkins begins to speak. I can't help but notice this really good-looking guy staring at me. Maybe I recognize him from another class.

He looks really familiar, but I know I've never met him. I look right at him as he looks right at me and I'm not looking away first, so we kind of just stare each other down. He smirks as if he already knows I'm difficult. I see a hint of a dimple on his left cheek. He looks so cute.

He looks away first and I feel like I won some sort of trophy, as if we were playing the staring game. I'm such a dork, but I want to make sure that he knows I'm not some shy girl and I wasn't going to back down.

I look at my professor and then open my laptop. Just then, my phone vibrates and I'm sure it's Cora, so I just hit the volume button to ignore it. I look up to see the guy staring at me intensely. He has the most amazing hazel eyes. Eyes I could melt in.

I can't focus on what this damn teacher is saying because all I can feel are his eyes on me. I want to look but...fuck it. I'm looking. Wow, he is so fucking hot. He is the sexiest man I ever laid eyes on.

Professor Watkins calls my name, only I can't for the life of me peel my eyes off this man. Why does he look so familiar? My phone buzzes again, but I ignore it despite the fact that I wish I could text Cora what's happening right now.

I hear Professor Watkins again. "Miss Monroe?"

I finally snap out of it. "Yes, sir, Professor. I apologize. What was the question?"

"There was no question, Miss Monroe. I was just checking if you are all right. You seem to be in a bit of a daydream."

Oh my God! How embarrassing.

"I'm sorry, Professor. I didn't get much sleep the last few days. Tomorrow is my day off, so I'll make sure to rest up."

I look over at the stupid guy who caused all this to happen, and he is smiling the biggest smile I have ever seen. And he's laughing! Wow! He is *laughing* at me. I feel the heat rush to my cheeks and my heart is beating so fast. This must be what hummingbirds feel 24/7. I have no idea what I'm supposed to be learning in class today and I don't know where the time went. This guy hypnotized me. I need to find out who he is.

Before I know it, the timer goes off to signal the end of class. I get my shit together and stand up. I take a quick glance at Mr. Right and see that he is also tall. Ding ding ding, winner, winner chicken dinner. Damn, this man is a God. He is at least 6'2 and has a lean muscular body, but not the gross kind that looks big and scary.

His body is perfect. I glance down at his shoes because that matters. If his shoes are dirty, he doesn't really take care of himself.

I don't know if that's true or just something girls came up with because we care too much about looks, but he has some nice clean white Nike's on, so he must care. His hair is dark brown and pushed back. It is styled perfectly, and long enough that, if given the chance, I could run my fingers through it. Kind of reminds me of Johnny Bravo hair but my God does he pull that shit off.

I begin to walk out of the door, and I notice him out of the corner of my eye. He's walking over to the side I'm on and heading for the same exit. I feel butterflies in my stomach and weak in the knees. What the hell is wrong with me? He hasn't even said a word yet and I'm falling apart. I'm the girl guys are after. I play with them and then toss them away like toys because that's all men do to us and I'll be damned if I'm ever hurt again.

"Hey, you're Alex, right?"

How does he know who I am? Up close, he looks even better. His facial features are pure perfection. He has a jawline chiseled by God himself. *Breathe, Alex. Stop gawking at him.*

"Yes, I'm Alex. Do I know you?"

I can see confusion on his face, but I have no idea why. I also notice him checking me out, but I don't want the excitement of knowing he finds me attractive to show on my face.

Make him work for it, Alex.

"Well, damn. I usually leave an impression and by the way you were staring, I thought you remembered."

My heart is racing. What don't I remember? Who the hell is this guy? My butterflies turn into hornets and my anxiety takes over.

"We met at a party a couple of weeks ago. We took some pictures and I gave you my number. My party, actually. Ring any bells?"

I stare at him, half in awe of his amazing lips, and half in annoyance because he is talking to me with some attitude like I should know who *he* is. Like *everyone* knows who he is.

I see a couple of girls looking at him and gossiping on the way out the door. Who the fuck is he? I want to ask but I also want him to just tell me. Why am I such a bitch like that? I should just ask.

“Hey wait," he shouts as I try to exit the classroom. "I texted you a few times while you were drooling at the sight of me. But you didn't respond and left me on read. What's up with that?"

The nerve of this guy...

"Well, first of all, my phone is on vibrate, and second, I must have opened it by accident while looking through my purse. Besides, what makes you so special that you think I would respond anyway?” I let out a giggle I didn't expect to, mostly because I don't know who this guy thinks he is. I mean he is sexy and all...but no sir. I don't like that he has a big head.

"I'm sorry, but I don't remember you. Also, I was not drooling over you. *You* were staring at me, so I was just staring back. You do look familiar but that's common since all of you cocky assholes look alike."

He laughs the sexiest laugh I have ever heard. On top of that, his voice is so fucking smooth and sexy. Just hearing him speak while I stare at him and knowing he knows who I am makes me tingle. I'm such a perv.

"Well, damn, Miss Alex. I didn't think you were going to be that hard on me. Don't you remember this face? You know you do. I love this stubborn, and confident attitude you have. I love the fact that you don't back down. Like I told you that night, you're one of a kind and I collect one-of-a-kind things."

I smile, even though I don't want to smile. I'm not something anyone can collect. That pisses me off. I have a gut feeling about who this is, but I don't know for sure. I want to make him work. If it is him, he deserves to work for it. I can't remember what Kohen looks like for sure but I just have a gut feeling. I feel like a giddy schoolgirl inside. Please sir, just take me here and now over these desks, on the floor, wherever. Man, I guess it's been a little bit. I'm not even sure who he is, yet I want him to take me.

"Sorry, but I just don't remember. I felt my phone vibrate, though, so I got your text. I'll try to find time to respond later. Bye."

Trying to keep it short, I turn to walk away, but he grabs my arm and gets really close to me from behind. I want to jerk my arm away- that's just my natural instinct- but his hand feels so good touching me. Damn, he smells good too. Everything feels like it's in slow motion, even though it's just been a few seconds. I can feel his body close to mine. and then I hear him, he whispers in my ear. His breath smells so good- like sweet mint. His touch is cool on my warm skin- like a fresh breeze on a sweltering day. It feels good.

"Don't play with me, Alex. I know you know who I am. I couldn't forget you, so I know you didn't forget me. Like you could ever forget my name. You are the only girl to ever stand toe to toe with me and not back down. You're so intriguing to me. Text me back," he says in the most demanding way.

Just like that, he lets me go and walks out. I can't even move. I think I'm in shock. I feel glued to the floor here. I'm not even sure if I am breathing. My phone vibrates and I begin to take it out of my purse. His scent is fading, and I just want him close to me again...whoever he is. I look at my phone screen. The sight makes me melt inside. I feel like throwing up. I knew it. On my screen the name *Kohen* flashing. I stay standing there, staring at my phone, stunned. It's him. Holy fucking shit. He's gorgeous but a lot of guys are. There's something about him, though. Something special. Different. I can't place my finger on it. I finally get the courage to actually read the texts. The first one makes me smile.

Kohen: Hey Alex, you look so fucking sexy. I need you to stop making eye contact with me or I'll make you pay.

Kohen: Okay, I'm sorry. I know you said you don't like compliments. Smile though.

Kohen: Wow, just ignoring me huh. Shaddddy

Kohen: I thought we liked each other. don't be shy now.

I'm at a loss for words and that doesn't happen often. I screenshot the texts and send them to Cora. She is going to flip! I scroll down to the last text he sent when he left the room.

Kohen: I want you. You will be mine.

Damn, do I text back or not? I feel like he probably tells every girl stuff like this. I don't want to fall into his trap. I don't want to be like every other girl on his lineup, but I want him, too. What should I do? I have to talk to Cora. She hasn't seen my texts yet, so I'm just going to walk to her building and wait outside her class.

I'm waiting for half an hour. I missed a lecture, but I need to ask her how I should respond to the text. She is going to think I'm so dumb for this. I laugh out loud. Finally, I hear people rustling around, so I know her class is over. Finally, I see my best friend's beautiful face right in front of me.

"Cora, did you get my text?"

"Hey, girl. No, class went over. You know I turn my phone off. What's up?"

"Kohen," is all I respond.

"Oh my gosh, Alex! What happened?"

"Read the texts, bitch. Hurry. I sent screenshots."

Her jaw drops and her little gasps are everything. I get butterflies again thinking about the screenshots I sent. She looks up at me as she puts her phone away. I see the excitement in those pretty brown eyes.

"Alex, I can't believe it. Have you responded?"

"No. I was waiting for you. Tell me what to say, you know I'm mean. I want a mix of you and me in my response."

She looks confused. So am I. I haven't felt this way since....my ex, my first love. My stomach turns at that thought and I feel nauseated. He was the worst thing that ever happened to me. The reason I trust no one, the reason I didn't ever want to be in a relationship again. Suddenly, I don't want to text Kohen back. Cora stares at me knowing what I'm thinking.

"Alex, not all guys are like him. Let the past go. We're moving forward. It's what Cecille would want."

She's right. I'm going to text Kohen. I'll be damned if I let my ex take another thing away from me.

Chapter 8

Alex

My hands are shaky from being nervous. I unlock my phone, hit the message icon, and tap on the text messages. I look at Cora to make sure she is locked and loaded to help me respond to him. She's staring at me, waiting for me to make the first move.

My mind blanks and I can't think of anything to say to Kohen. Negative thoughts enter my mind already, yelling at me to not text him first. *You will look weak,* the voice says. I pull down on the messages and that causes the thread to refresh. I see ones that weren't there before. At the bottom of the thread, it says hidden messages are turned off. What? I immediately begin to read the messages I didn't see there before. They're from the night of the party.

Kohen: it's me Kohen. save my number

Kohen: I know how badly you want it.

Me: I dnt want it. YOU. want mi

I slap my palm to my forehead because I'm not even spelling correctly from how wasted I was.

Kohen: Alex, Alex, Alex don't make me spank you. Be a good girl and listen for once.

Me: oh, hell no i listn ti no ione

Me: who do you think u r?///??

Kohen: I'm the guy you just secretly made out with.

We couldn't have kissed, could we? I think I would remember if I kissed someone. Ugh, this is what I get for getting drunk off my ass. I close the message thread, deciding not to say anything right now until I process the fact that I kissed this guy and don't remember.

Cora looks at me with confusion clear on her face. *don't worry, bestie- I am just as confused as you.*

"Cora, did you see me kiss Kohen?" I don't know if I actually want her to answer.

Just as she starts to respond, I feel a soft tap on my shoulder. I turn around to see Xzavien with his million-dollar smile.

"Hello gorgeous, how are you on this fine day?"

I shoot a stare at Cora, hoping she gets the telepathic message I'm sending that this conversation needs to be tabled for now. She does. I look at Xzavien and smile.

"Hey, X. I'm good. I'm just so tired. What are you up to? You remember my best friend, Cora, right?"

"Hey, Cora. Yeah." He walks over and gives her a side hug.

"Nice to see you again. Do you ladies have class in this hall?"

Cora answers him, knowing I'm processing, and I'm so thankful because all I can think of is Kohen. I'm so shocked that I just found out I kissed him. I really shouldn't be surprised that my alter ego tends to be a slut, but that's on top of what just happened less than an hour ago with Kohen. He has my senses on overload and he isn't even here.

"Alex?" I hear Xzavien say as Cora giggles.

"Yeah, no I don't have class here. I just came to walk Cora to her class so we could see what we are going to do for dinner." Lies.

Cora rolls her eyes and X seems to take the bait. We continue to talk for about five minutes before Cora excuses herself for class, and it feels awkward being alone with X. I hear him talking but I can't think clearly enough to focus on what he's saying. I think back to the attraction I had to him at the party. I was interested in him when I met everyone and I'm curious what happened. How did I end up kissing Kohen? I want to ask but also, I don't want to throw myself under the bus if he doesn't know. I decide against it, and I think it's for the best.

I zone back into what he is saying, and his voice is so nice, deep, velvety, and confident. Listening to his ramblings about the campus and where his favorite places are to eat, I remember why I found him so attractive. He dresses so nicely, commands a room, is friendly, and on top of everything else, his smile is to die for.

"So have you explored at all, or are y'all more of the homebody types?" X asks with that radiant smile stretched across his face.

"We haven't explored much at all. And the party we met you at is the first one we have been to in ages. I'd say we are more homebodies, although Cora is hell-bent on trying to change that."

He smiles. "So y'all don't party at all?"

"Well, we used to, but we had a friend of ours pass away at a party our junior year. So we kind of laid off the partying."

"Oh, I'm sorry, doll. How did she pass- if you don't mind me asking?"

I gulp, this was not a topic I expected to discuss but I know I need to get past it.

"She had an aneurysm. We thought she was just drunk from the party we were at since she hadn't ever drank before. She was the responsible one, I was the crazy party girl, and Cora was the social butterfly."

"Oh shit, I'm sorry Alex."

"It's okay. There was nothing we could have done, the doctors said it could have ruptured at any time in her life. I just..."

My eyes well up with tears. I decide I'm not ready to admit that I feel guilty, that she died alone because of me. I blink away the tears and X brings me in for a very unwelcome hug. I tense up. I'm not good with this type of emotional shit. So, I pull back.

"Thanks, but I don't want to talk about it anymore. This just isn't something I'm prepared to talk about. That's typically why we don't party anymore."

"I'm sorry to hear that, but hey. At least you were able to let loose and have fun once Kohen showed up. I actually felt left out once he stole you from me. We even argued about it that night."

I don't know how to respond. They argued? About me? Why? Who the hell would argue about a girl they just met?

He must read my expression and take my silence for unease because he follows with his version of an explanation. "We are best friends and we butt heads a lot. I guess you could say we are pretty competitive".

He must be nervous because I catch him running his hand through his hair multiple times.

"Wow, well I'm sorry you felt left out but I'm not some prize to win. So if you two think this is some sort of competition, I'm definitely not the one."

I start to grab my things off the table to leave and he looks a bit taken aback by my response.

It was unexpected.

He instantly starts to apologize, as he should because I am not just some piece of meat. If he wants to be my friend, he better learn really quick just how hard to get Alex Monroe really is.

"No, Alex. Hey, I'm sorry. I didn't mean it like that. I don't want you to think I'm an asshole, but I wasn't sure if you were into me or not because it seemed like you and Kohen were really getting along." He starts to backtrack.

"What's that supposed to mean?" I ask.

"Nothing. I just...never mind. I don't want to put my foot in my mouth. Look, there's Kohen now."

My brain freezes and my body melts. How those two things can happen at the same time, I have no clue and it makes zero sense, but it's happening.

I turn to face the direction that X is staring in, and sure enough, there he is. He isn't alone. He walks our way with a short redhead woman by his side, and my stomach drops. Of course, everything he said was bullshit. Especially when he has some other girl at his side just two hours later.

I feel like an idiot, and I sure feel it as I watch him walk closer to us. I'm confident, but I can recognize beauty when I see it. This girl is gorgeous. She's smiling and saying hi to people as she passes them, making everyone feel welcome in her presence. I wish that I could say she is ugly, but she isn't. I am *not* the type of person to hate on someone else just because I'm jealous, and let's be real- I am jealous. I look away and gather my thoughts as Kohen brings X in for a bro hug and handshake.

I look away quickly so I can gather my thoughts and decide how I want to react. I hear Cora's voice in my head saying, *kill them with kindness, Alex.* I can't text her since she is already in class, and I know her notifications are off. Fuck! If there is a god up there, please help me keep fucking calm!

I turn back, rubbing my eye, pretending like I had something in it, but I see Kohen's eyes locked on me. The audacity of this man to be staring at me so intensely in front of the girl he is with. I smile at them both and act like I don't give a fuck. I see him still looking at me and I keep my eyes on X. I'm not about to let him see me bothered. He hasn't said anything, and I won't be the first one to speak to him either. Instead, I introduce myself to the redhead.

"Hi, I'm Alex. I just wanted to say you are so damn gorgeous," I say, holding my hand out to shake hers. We shake hands. Hers are small, soft, and suddenly I find myself wondering if mine are soft. Nothing about me is soft. "I'm Xzavien's friend. It's nice to meet you."

I pull my hand from hers. Smiling, I look over at X, and even though he and Kohen are having their own conversation, I can tell he was paying attention to mine. She responds to me in the mousiest voice I have ever heard, reminding me of Ariana Grande in *Victorious.*

"Thank you, doll. I'm Sarah. It's nice to meet you. I just want to say you have a gorgeous body. I wish I had curves and an ass like that." She giggles, and I can't help but join her in laughter.

Blushing I look up through my lashes and make eye contact with Kohen, who is biting his bottom lip and staring straight at me. I hope neither Sarah nor X notices.

"Thank you. Sometimes I wish I was less curvy, though. It would be easier to find jeans or wear skirts."

"Oh, baby, I hear you but can't say I understand it. You are perfect. I, on the other hand, look like a little boy. So, wear the skirt, dammit." We break out in laughter again. She's a breath of fresh air, and clearly, he is an asshole for gawking at me right in front of her.

I rub X on the arm to catch his attention since a couple of his other friends came up to chat. Right when I'm about to speak, Kohen clears his throat to try and grab my attention, demanding the attention of the circle. I start to talk to X because I refuse to allow him to think he can demand that type of attention from me. He can do that with his little circle of friends but not me. He can sweat it out. He can talk to me first if he wants to.

"Hey, X. I have to go. Sarah- we will have to chat again soon. I'll find you on Instagram."

We say our goodbyes and I hug X and start to walk away. I take a couple of steps and turn back. "Oh, I almost forgot about that date. I'd love to, so text me with the details, okay?"

"Sure thing, babe," he says with a wink, and my heart skips a beat.

Mission accomplished. I continue to walk, taking slow steps as I dig through my purse for my phone. I feel bad that I'm using X to make Kohen jealous, but no harm no foul. Besides, I was interested in him first and Kohen is with Sarah. I stop a few steps away from them. I start texting Cora to let her know we need to meet at the campus Cafe.

And then I hear him. Kohen.

"So, you weren't going to say hello, Alex?"

The entire hall goes quiet. That's the power his voice has, it gives me goosebumps all over my body. I didn't think he was even going to acknowledge me, the little playboy he is. I don't say anything, I just turn to stare at him.

"That's a little rude, Angel. You and X man on a date? That's interesting." He smirks and my panties fucking melt. Why the fuck does he have to be so damn sexy? X looks uncomfortable and now I feel awful. I was not expecting Kohen to actually say something in front of everyone. What the fuck is wrong with him? He was with me in class just hours ago, pressing up against me, and now he's here with Sarah. If he wants to play games, I'll show him how fun it is to play with me.

"I'm sorry. Kevin, right? I didn't realize you knew my name."

He puts his arm around Sarah's shoulder, and my blood starts to boil. She giggles as if she is in on his game. Hell, maybe she is and knows when he is trying to make someone jealous.

"Well, hi, and bye. I'm late for a work thing. Nice meeting you, Kevin."

I don't have the patience for this. I *will* lose it.

"Bye, honey," Sarah says sweetly. For her sake, I hope she means it.

"Have a good day, Alex. I will text you when class is over," X smiles. It looks a little forced and I give him a small smile back. He really is so sweet.

I make a right down the next hall and call Cora instead of texting her.

Like I'm being haunted, I hear a voice saying my name again. His voice. I think it's in my head until I hear it again.

"Alex, wait," he calls, jogging up to me.

My heart is pounding so hard that he might be able to see it. I freeze as he gets to me. What could he have to say to me?

"You forgot your book."

I look in my purse and sure enough, it's not in there. When did I put it down? I must have dropped it when I was searching for my phone. I politely grab it, thank him, and turn to walk away without saying bye.

"What- no goodbye kiss?"

Heat floods my body. The fucking nerve of this guy. I like it- this little game we are playing- but I know I shouldn't. I look over my shoulder at him and he's staring at my ass, so I pause and turn to face him.

"Why would I do a silly thing like that when I'm about to go on a date with your best friend? Don't flatter yourself, Kevin."

He laughs. "Now, Angel, you know what my name is. If you keep pretending like you don't, I'm going to have to remind you. I'll make you shout it *loud* in bed and make it so you never forget it again."

I only have seconds to think before my body naturally reacts and I don't know if I want to kiss him or slap him.

"Save that for Sarah. You know- the girl you just had your arm around?"

I start to walk away again because I don't want to say or do anything else that makes him think I care. I stare down at my phone, remembering I was calling Cora, and see that she is still on the call. I pick it up to my ear and turn to look at where me and Kohen were standing. He's gone. Good.

"Oh my god, Cora. Did you hear all that?"

"Yes, bitch I did. He is a cocky one. Where are you?"

"I'm at Camden Hall. I'll meet you at the Cafe."

"Okay, bye."

"Love you, bye."

I make it out of the building and my notifications are going off. I see a text from X and one from Kohen. Of course, perfect.

Kohen: you ran away so quick.

Me: maybe it's the fact that you have a girlfriend. I don't come in second to anyone.

Kohen: Sarah is my cousin.

Me: sure, she is.

Me: convenient you failed to mention that in person.

Kohen: maybe I just like the way you squirmed when you saw me with her.

I don't respond. I don't know how to.

Kohen: don't be mad at me, sexy. that's why you should make me YOURS

The audacity of this dude. He's getting to me already. I can tell he's going to drive me crazy.

Kohen: oh, and by the way....

Kohen: don't even think about going on that date with X. wouldn't be a good idea for either of you. I don't want to have to break any hearts or any arms.

Kohen: you are mine.

I want to respond but I won't. I'm too angry and I need my best friend to give me some advice. I'm his? Pfft. Yeah, right. What would make him think I would ever be his?

Chapter 9

Alex

My head is spinning as I sit here waiting for Cora to show up. I order a lavender tea and a vanilla sweet cream cold brew for her. Would Kohen even make me his? Do I want to be his? This feels a little crazy. My mind is conflicted. I feel like I just met him but I know I met him before. Either way, it isn't enough time for either of us to be so infatuated with each other. Cora needs to hurry because I really need to know how I should respond to these text messages.

He seems to be falling a little fast for such a notorious playboy.

Do I want to be his? No, that's insane. I don't want to belong to anybody ever again.

I feel like I screwed myself up because I don't know what to do here. I told X I would go on a date with him, but I do want to get to know Kohen, or at least test him out. I don't want to be anything more than friends with X, and if Kohen says he wants me, I need to make things clear with X.

Cora is walking up to the table and relief washes over me. She's the calm to my crazy. She smiles at me and I respond with a smile back.

"Hey, lovie, are you okay?" she asks, concern clear on her face as she rubs my shoulder.

"I'm okay, but I have so much to tell you. I don't even know where to begin."

"Start with what happened with X after I went to class."

I recap her on everything that happened and she looks at me like I've grown three heads. Her mouth opens wide as she listens.

"He said you're *his?*"

"Yes, Cora. Now close your mouth before a fly goes in there."

It feels like I'm out of breath, recapping her on everything in one go.

"Look at the text messages between us. Some of them I didn't see and were in some private mode thing. How I managed that...I don't know," I laugh, explaining.

She grabs my phone from my hand and scrolls, gasping as she reads.

"Oh em gee, Alex Larae," she teases. "He is hot for you!"

"So, what should I respond?" The anticipation is killing me. I have to say something. I need.... Well, I don't even know what I need.

I don't like how he makes me feel. Like I'm a little girl falling head over heels for a boy and I don't want to. I don't want to hurt ever again. That's all men do: hurt you. I should know.

"I honestly don't know, Alex. Let me think. First off, I can't even believe you kissed him. This all feels like it's happening so fast. It's a whirlwind."

"I know and now he is calling me *his.* What the fuck is that? We met twice now and it's only been two weeks. That's not normal."

"It's kind of romantic though, don't you think? Like love at first sight?"

I laugh. "That shit doesn't exist, Cora."

"You never know, it could exist. Just because you don't believe in it, doesn't mean it doesn't exist."

"I'm sorry, I didn't mean it that way. Of course, it can exist for you, best friend. Only for you."

I pull her in for a hug. I never want to hurt her feelings, and I know she believes in true love. Her parents set a good example of it. I wasn't as fortunate.

"It's okay, Alex. Back to you and your love life."

"Right, okay. I'm just shocked. Like who the fuck does he think he is?"

We say that part at the same time and burst out laughing. The negative thoughts enter my mind and I immediately start to question his motives. If he was or is so interested and captivated by me, why hasn't he texted me since the party?

"Okay!" she says, breaking me out of my thoughts. "Let's come up with a plan. You like him, and he clearly likes your crazy ass. Edward said he usually gets bored easily. I'm sure all your personalities can keep him entertained, but I don't want you to get hurt."

"Hilarious, Cora. Are you a comedian now? So funny," I deadpan.

"So what? What do you suggest?"

"Let's text him."

My hands are shaking uncontrollably as I open the text messages and get ready to respond. Flashes of Kohen and his demanding presence fill my head. The party, my class, the meeting in the hallway... I feel Jumanji-sized butterflies in my stomach, and I don't want them there, so I snuff them out. I hate that I'm so excited to text him.

What is this guy doing to me? His hazel eyes, and the dimple in his cheek when he smiles is one of the most captivating things I have ever seen. The smirk he made when he knew exactly who I was and was secretly texting me... How could I not remember meeting this irritating boy? More visions of his muscular frame dance around my head like they do in cartoons. I can't deny how fucking hot he is.

I want him, I must have him. To claim him before he can claim me. Every fiber in my body feels like it's on fire when I'm around him. I have never felt anything like it before.

"Alex? Did you hear me? Are you going to text him back?"

"What? Yes. I was waiting for you to tell me. Any ideas on what I should say?"

She slaps her palm to her forehead. "Do you listen at all? Of course, you don't. When have you ever listened? Why do I even bother?"

"Text him and let him know you aren't going to play his games, which it was shitty of him to pretend Sarah was his girl."

She continues on about all the things I should say to him to let him know I'm not playing his games, but she doesn't need to know that I have every intention of playing the game. I want to because I'm going to show the heartbreaker of

Texas state that he has met his match. I will break his little heart before he even has the chance to break mine. I wanted her help but now I remember I'm a badass bitch and I got this. So, I start to respond.

Me: to your first set of messages in class, I had no idea who you were lol, I didn't remember anything from that night including what you looked like. does that happen often?

Me: I also don't remember a kiss so how do I know you're not making that up?

Doesn't show he has read anything yet, so I send one last message.

Me: the only heart that will be breaking is yours. Not mine and not Xzavien's. I know you want me, Kohen, so come and claim me. Until then, I am going on that date with X. may the odds be ever in your favor.

I know I said I would friendzone X and I will, but Kohen doesn't need to know that.

I see the bubbles. He is typing his response, so I turn my phone off. I don't want to be tempted to respond.

I look over at Cora, who is probably on the phone with Edward I'm sure. So I wait for her to hang up and tell her the truth about what I responded with. She rolls her eyes and gets up, shaking her head at me.

"This isn't going to end well. Come on, let's go home," Cora says.

I don't plan on it ending at all but let the chips fall where they may.

"Okay, best friend. We can order in. I'm tired."

Chapter 10

Kohen

My text messages to Alex aren't going through. She doesn't know me well enough yet to know I can find out where she lives easily. I have connections as the king of this campus.

The fact that she was brave enough to respond to me like that, to test me that way. This is what makes me want to possess her, make her mine in every fucking way. She challenges me. She stares straight at me and does not back down. Fuck, she's sexy.

I stare at the texts she sent going over them again. She's so feisty.

Alex: to your first set of messages in class, I had no idea who you were lol. I didn't remember anything from that night including what you looked like. does that happen often? LOL

Alex: I also don't remember a kiss, so how do I know you're not making that up? If you need me to pretend, then just say that.

Alex: the only heart that will be breaking is yours. Not mine and not Xzavien's. IF you want me, Kohen, come and claim me. Until then, I am going on that date with X. may the odds be ever in your favor.

She clearly doesn't know who she is messing with. It drives me crazy that I don't have the effect on her that I do with most girls. My charm goes unmatched. She doesn't seem to be falling for it, though. Alex isn't like the other girls in this god-forsaken city. That's what draws me to her. She drives me crazy already, and we aren't even official. Well, in my head we are but that doesn't count for much if she isn't in agreement. I wouldn't know. I have never dealt with this before. She is strong, confident, beautiful, and- *damn-* that fucking body. Curves in every fucking right place. Exquisite.

When I saw her at my party, I was intoxicated. Not in the way that everyone else was because, in that way, I was sober. Her body glistened in sweat under the strobe lights, and the way she moved her hips seductively and sexually to the rhythm of the music, it was like she was speaking to me in another language as her body moved. I wanted to snatch her up at that moment and fuck her on that dance floor. I don't know exactly what it is but the primal need to make her mine overtakes all common sense.

I try to text her a few more times and I am still receiving the same automated message:

Alex: You're BLOCKED- lose my number.

So, I call her and it goes straight to voicemail.

"This is Alex, leave a message and maybe I'll get back to you."

She blocked me! What the actual fuck? She sent those messages and blocked me so I couldn't respond. She is crazy, but I like that.

This is making me feel uneasy. The fact that I could see the guys all interested in her and just as captivated by her as I am. Xzavien especially. I need to let him know to back off. No one will have her if I can't have her. The way that angry kiss felt after she called me out on my shit at the party turned me the fuck on. Never have I ever been called out like that before, and definitely not in my domain. I *need* to see her.

Dialing Xzavien's number, I climb into my car to see if he knows what's up with her. Do I even want to know if he knows where she lives or has spoken to her when she won't even give me the damn time of day? I don't want this to cause more competition shit between him and me, but that's what it's looking like since he asked her out.

To be honest, I don't give a fuck if he likes her. She will be mine. I hang up the phone and decide not to turn to him. He won't want me to have a leg up on him. Alex will give in to me if it's the last thing I fucking do. Xzavien will ruin this just like he has ruined everything else in my life since we were kids.

Just when I pull into campus headquarters, he calls me back. Shit.

"Hey bro, I missed a call from you. What's up?"

"Oh, nothing man. I was just at the gym. I thought I forgot the key to the top floor of the house, but I had it."

"Oh, okay. That's a coincidence, I'm walking into the gym right now."

"Oh, alright. Well, have a good workout, my dude. Oh, and you might want to leave your phone in the car. There was some guy going through the lockers earlier. I almost knocked his ass out."

"Ah shit, thanks, man. I'll do that."

"I GTG, bro, I'm driving."

"Alright, brother. Talk to you later."

I walk up to the administration building and scan my badge. I look up at the brick walls lined with vines and greenery until I see the security camera and salute. Being the son of the mayor in this town means something to some people and I know the guys watching from the security room will delete this footage. My aunt is also the dean. She has spoiled me rotten since my mom passed, so I tend to get away with a lot, which only adds to my reputation around here.

The air smells fresh here, probably because it rained this morning. The dew still sits on the rose bushes lining the sidewalk. The door finally beeps to let me know it's unlocked. I run up to the secretary's computer. They're closed today, so other than a few janitors, I should be alone. I power it on, type in the master passcode, and I'm in.

Alex Monroe is the name I type in the database. That I know for sure because I asked our professor what her full name was that first day of class. Her file pops up. I hit print and impatiently wait for the pages. Everything finishes printing and while the pages are still warm, I enter her address into my GPS and drive.

She is going to find out really quickly how resourceful I am and exactly who Kohen Ventura is.

My phone rings but the name flashing on my screen reminds me that I do not want to answer it. I'm done with that bullshit. I have new goals for my life, and it doesn't include any toxic people from my past. I roll my windows down and the cool breeze whips my skin as I wave my arm through the air.

I feel nervous as I turn down the street and look for her house. This was impulsive. The adrenaline that was pumping through my body is dying down. My impulsivity didn't allow me to think this through. Imagine if people saw me looking up and down the streets for this girl. Everyone knows everyone around here and I don't want this to make me look like a pussy whipped little bitch. I'll kill any rumors of that by making my little Angel scream my name loud enough that her neighbors know it's the other way around. I finally find her house, shut off my lights, and pull up to the curb. My heart is beating a hundred miles a second, and it feels like I could pass out. Damn, I'm acting like a little bitch.

I run my hands through my sweat-drenched hair and take some deep breaths. This isn't me. I don't do this type of shit for a girl. I start to second guess my actions for the millionth time, arguing with myself about why I'm doing something so stupid and desperate.

I didn't realize my body had ever left my car as I find myself at the bottom of her steps. I turn around to leave and begin the walk back to my Corvette. I take one last glance back at her house and everything stops when I see a silhouette in the window upstairs.

I hope it's her. The crickets are chirping, and the leaves are rustling on the ground around me as the wind blows. Goose bumps erupt on my skin and move like a wave from my arms, to my shoulders, and up to my neck, causing a shiver to ricochet down my spine. The timing of it all is not coincidental, because right when I glanced back and saw the silhouette of her body through the curtains, it gave me all the courage I needed to walk up to her door and knock.

Chapter 11

Alex

Today has been eventful. Who knew so much could happen in a day? We came home and just as we were about to order food, Edward shows up and whisks Cora away on a surprise date. I want my best friend to be happy, I really do, but I hate that douche. He gets on my damn nerves. He smells like cheap cologne and peppermint and the combination is nauseating. I'll play nice, though. My version of it, anyway. I hope for his sake he does right by my best friend because I will go off on him. For her, I'd burn the world down. He isn't prepared for hurricane Alex.

I plug my phone into the charger and curiosity is killing me. I want to know if Kohen has texted. I go to my filtered messages and see that he has sent several. I giggle internally as butterflies flutter through my stomach. He tried to message me, yet I'm still not going to respond even if I want to. I refuse to give him the satisfaction of a response. Deciding to be a little petty, I text Xzavien instead.

Of course, X responds quickly. I start to reply when I have an unfamiliar feeling gnawing at my insides. It might be guilt. Guilt that I'm using him to make his best friend jealous. He handed me the ammo and everything I needed when he told me they were competitive, and I plan to use all of it against them. So why should I feel guilty?

Men don't think twice when they use women. They don't even bat an eye. They use, abuse, break, and replace. I shake my head as if that will make the ping of guilt vanish, but it doesn't work. I don't want to hurt anyone. I decide to be honest and friend-zone him, so he knows where he stands. I look back at our texts to make sure I didn't lead him on. It's flirty but I'm like that with everyone, so I hope he doesn't take that as a sign of anything between us.

Me: hey X, what are you up to?

Me: just thought I'd say hi.

X: hey pretty girl! Glad to hear from you.

X: I'm a bit surprised but I'll welcome it.

Me: surprised, why?

Me: We're friends, right?

X: friends? Yeah, I just didn't expect a text or anything since I saw you and Kohen talking, but like I said I want to take you out. Is that still, okay?

Me: yes of course, I really don't know Kohen like that he just handed me a book I left behind.

X: a book he seemed adamant on talking to you himself. He snatched it out of my hand.

Me: weird.

Me: well lmk when you wanna hang out I gtg need to shower. Ttyl

X: okay gorgeous ttyl

I hope my responses are enough for him to know we aren't going to be anything more than friends. My mind floats to Cora. She looked so happy when Edward showed up to get her. Her radiant smile was ear to ear. She sprayed on her Daisy perfume and rushed around the room changing into something cute for her date, leaving little notes of her scent all around the room. She really does deserve all the happiness in the world.

I hope she is having fun on her date. Edward spares no expense when he spoils her because he lacks in every other area, but if he truly makes her happy, I need to try and get along with him. It became a habit of mine to push away her boyfriends since she is all I have left in this world.

I turn the water on and undress while I wait for it to warm up. The clothes fall to the floor with a plop and take the weight of the day with them. I tie my hair up into a messy bun and run my hand under the water to test the heat. It's hot enough that it leaves my hand red- just how I like it. My ex used to joke that it must be a comfort to the little demon inside me.

I don't even know why my mind went there. *Gross*. That's the last person I want on my mind.

Steam fills the restroom, rising to the ceiling and covering everything in dew, which is my cue to step into the tub. I sit in the tub and the hot water engulfs me and relaxes all the tense muscles in my body.

I hear my phone go off, interrupting the music I have playing, and I roll my eyes at whoever it is. I ignore it and close my eyes. Whoever it is can wait until I'm done. I begin to relax and then somewhere in my half-melted brain it hits me, and my eyes shoot open. That particular notification is for filtered messages. It's Kohen. He is still trying to reach me.

A little giggle slips from my lips. I look around as if anyone else could be in here to ask me why I'm laughing. It goes off a couple of more times and the anticipation builds inside me like a volcano, wanting to check what he's sending, but I don't. I can't. He must know I won't bow down at his feet like all these other little gym bunnies that follow him.

I'm not surprised when it doesn't go off anymore, because hey, I didn't even expect him to go this far. I can't be that interesting to this guy. It's not that I'm not worthy, it's just that I'm more than sure I'm not his type. He seems like he likes them easy, and that's one thing I will never be. I'm intelligent, strong, confident, and blessed to be beautiful inside and out.

There's always that little voice, though. It has to remind me that I'm broken. A damaged girl with a broken heart that never fully healed, and just like that I doubt my worth.

I soak for a while, but I can feel my hands start to wrinkle. I hate when that happens. I drain the tub and when the water runs out, I stand up. The bathroom smells of fresh lavender and eucalyptus. Cora loves to have natural plants in the restroom, so the steam releases the scent into the atmosphere. Lavender is my kryptonite. I love it, the scent of it immediately calms me down. I wrap the fluffy white towels Cora says I'm not supposed to use around my body and look for the face mask mix we made last week.

I just spread some of the mint julcp mask on my cheek when I hear a loud knock on the front door. I walk to the top step and another loud knock reverberates through the hall. I freeze, like a deer in headlights, startled by the loudness of it. I run to the restroom and grab my phone, readying 911 on the keypad.

I don't know who the hell this is, I wasn't expecting anyone, and Cora would have called if she forgot her key or something. She knows unexpected guests freak me out. There were several times when I was a kid that we had men break into our house in the middle of the night to try and reach my mom when she wouldn't respond to their calls or texts. Those were some of the scariest nights of my life. I had nightmares for years. One night in particular sticks out to me and that is why I get so panicked when someone shows up unannounced. I don't like to think of that night so I whisk the thought away to the far reaches of my mind.

I tiptoe down the stairs, trying not to make a sound. I pad my way into the kitchen and head for the junk drawer where I know the pepper spray sits. I grab it, pull the pin, and press down on the button in preparation to use it on whoever stands outside the door. Another knock startles me and I jump like a mouse ran over my foot. I yank the door open, ready to spray, but when I see who it is, I feel frozen to the ground. It's Kohen. Butterflies erupt. He looks so fucking good. He can break in anytime. I wouldn't do a damn thing.

"Kohen? What are you doing here?"

I blink a few times to make sure he is actually here and it's not some hallucination from me hitting my head and I'm actually passed out in the tub. I still feel like I'm imagining this so I don't even realize what I'm doing until it's too late. I feel the scruff on his chin underneath my soft fingertips. The feeling sends chills down my spine. I move my hand away as quickly as my brain and body allow.

With a smirk on his face, he responds, "Hey, I'm sorry to just drop by but I remembered you mentioned the street you lived on at my party and I had to come find you."

I have no words. It's as if my mind is black and I no longer know how to form sentences. Shocking, since I never shut the fuck up any other time, but this is the last thing I ever expected to happen.

"I'm sorry, I just don't know what to say."

Thank you brain for forming a sentence for me.

"Are you mad? I only came because you blocked me and I had to know why."

"No, I'm not mad. I was just..." I pause, inhaling his scent. It smells like strawberry and leather and it's so intoxicating as it fills my nostrils, making me dizzy. "I just got scared. I wasn't expecting anyone. I'm a little shocked to see it's you, if I'm being honest."

He half smiles and a dimple appears in his cheek. I love dimples.

"Well, I'm so sorry to have scared you, ma'am," he says in a poor attempt at a southern drawl, and I laugh.

"Ew, Kohen! Do not call me *ma'am.*" He joins me in laughter and my heart feels like it does a little flip. The sound of his laughter sends a warm comforting feeling throughout my body, grounding me here on the earth like my own personal gravitational pull. He looks so fucking good. His outfit is simple- gray sweatpants and a crisp white t-shirt that fits him like a second skin, complete with pristine air forces. Jesus Christ.

"You look good, Kohen."

I slap my hand over my mouth, not meaning to say that out loud. I am so embarrassed. What the fuck is wrong with me? It's a question I feel like I'm asking myself a lot lately. I look up at him and see a huge smile adorning his handsome face, and it is everything.

"Oh my god, are you blushing?"

I turn on the porch light for a better look at him, causing him to squint at the unexpected brightness of the bulb.

"Oh, shit. Sorry!" I'm rushing to turn it off when he grabs me by the wrist, stopping me from reaching the switch.

"Thank you, Angel. You don't look so bad yourself. Sexy as hell. You make that bath towel look good."

Holy fuck, I'm in a towel! I opened the door to Kohen Ventura in a towel! To be fair- I didn't know it was going to be him, but I think that actually makes it worse. The knocking scared me so much that I forgot I wasn't dressed.

"Oh, my GOD! Close your eyes!"

He laughs again, causing me to break out in more laughter.

"I am so fucking embarrassed. I'm so sorry, Kohen."

First, I touch his face, then I tell him how good he looks without meaning to, and the cherry on top is doing all of that in a damn towel that doesn't even cover the right side of my legs and hip. Your girl is thick.

"It's okay, Angel. I would have seen it sooner or later."

I'm blushing. I just know I'm blushing. His words make me all giddy. We make eye contact, and he licks his lips.

"Well, do you want to come in and sit down? I'll just go get dressed really quick. I'm home alone. Edward came over and surprised Cora with a date, so girls' night was ruined."

I don't know why I just said that, but I hope he comes in. Not only do I want him to come in because I like him, but I also want him to because now I am too scared to be alone again. PTSD is a bitch.

"I'd love to. Are you sure? I wouldn't want to impose. I just came over because my calls and texts don't seem to be going through. So now that I know you're okay, I can go if you want me to. It's cool."

I respond a little quicker than I would have liked, "No, please come in. I don't want you to leave." He looks pleased to hear me say those words and starts to walk toward me. I move aside so he can come in, breathing in as much of him as I can.

I'm thankful I just took a shower. It's crazy where a day can take you.

He steps past the threshold of my little house and my heart flutters wildly in my chest. He is inside *my* house. I keep repeating it in my head like the warnings at the bottom of the news when a storm is brewing. He walks into the living room and sits on the couch like he owns the place.

He watches me intently as I sit next to him. I feel like I'm forgetting something, but I can't remember what. Too many jumbled thoughts running around in my brain. It's like a cuckoo clock. I sit on the couch but I'm careful not to sit too close. Nervousness takes over my body and I feel myself blushing. He smiles at me, right on cue, as if there's a prompt somewhere giving him all the right moves to make.

He pats the seat next to him. "Come here. Why are you so far away?"

This is so unlike me. I'm not shy and timid. I'm a force to be reckoned with. I never get nervous around guys, and I don't really even like this one. Sure, he is fucking hot, and his smile, and oh that dimple. But that's it. He is all looks and no depth. It must be the hormones. I'm just horny. It's been a long time. That's it. He's just a guy with money, and he's probably an asshole. This is just a facade to get in my pants.

When Cora and I left the cafe, I did do a little intel. Kohen is an only child from what I can tell, so probably spoiled. His family has several businesses they own as well as hitting big in oil. It looks like they did a ton of volunteer work and had several scholarships for underprivileged teens to get to college, but I bet that's to cover up something shady. I did see he had a girlfriend for a while, a gorgeous Victoria's Secret model-worthy one who he looked serious about. He tagged her in everything until a few months ago. He probably broke her fucking heart. He hasn't been with any other girl publicly since her.

Kohen's voice brings me out of my spiraling thoughts. "Did you hear me, Angel?"

Angel. He has called me that a few times now. I wonder why, and does he call every girl he's trying to get in bed that?

"Yes, my bad. I was just thinking."

"Thinking about what exactly?" he asks, smirk in tow.

He is so cocky. Ugh. There's a really fine line between hating it and loving it.

"Nothing important, and wipe that smirk off your face because it had nothing to do with you." I look down at my feet and it hits me, I forgot to change. I'm still in a fucking towel.

"Don't be shy, Alex. I'm not that intimidating." He emphasizes that as if he really thinks he's intimidating me. That's all it takes to light the fire back under my ass. Whatever shyness I have is long gone now.

"Okay asshole, calm down. You do not intimidate me."

"There's my spicy girl." He lets out a little laugh, smiling as if his goal is achieved.

There's a little throb at my core with that comment. I bite my lip, trying to mask my smile.

A notification pings from my phone before I can speak, and I remember for the second time now that I need to change. I grab my phone off the coffee table and I see it's Xzavien texting me.

"I'll be right back. I forgot to change."

"You don't have to change. I don't mind the view."

I roll my eyes and he follows the line of sight to the ceiling. "Is there something up there you're looking at?"

The smirk! I want to smack it off his stupidly handsome face. "You are an asshole, Kohen."

"Ooh, say my name again. It sounds so good coming from those gorgeous lips."

I walk away, not engaging with him anymore.

X: hey gorgeous, wyd??

Me: hey, headed to bed.

Me: night.

I return to the couch in sleep shorts and an oversized T-shirt. I don't miss the way he eyes my thick thighs. Sitting closer to Kohen this time, my thigh rubs against his muscular one. It feels like little sparks travel up my leg where our bodies meet. Our skin didn't touch but it didn't have to. I can't deny that there is...something between us. It's magnetic and strange. I want him here, but I don't want to want him at all. It makes me angry with myself.

"Who was that?" he asks nonchalantly while popping a Jolly Rancher in his mouth from the candy dish on the coffee table. I'm a little taken aback by the bravery of his question. I like that he wants to know who is texting me. I bet he isn't used to that type of curiosity. Waiting a few seconds to respond, he clears his throat. "My bad, you don't have to tell me. It's none of my business."

Half of me wants to say *you're right, it isn't your business,* but the other half of my stupid brain wants to reassure him it's no one and they mean nothing. A thought pops into my head and it's from the little red devil on my shoulder. She whispers for me to push his buttons a little. *Make him sweat,* she says. So, I do.

"No, it's cool. It was X." My eyes move to his face faster than lightning strikes to catch his reaction. Right at that second, my phone pings again. I don't really care what it says. The only thing on my mind is how bothered Kohen looks right now and it's turning me the fuck on. I see the hints of jealousy and I wonder how possessive he is of his women, how possessive he would be with me. I rub my thighs together, the friction teasing the parts of me I wish Kohen was touching right now.

"You gonna answer that?" he asks, the annoyance clear in his tone. It didn't sound like a question but more like a dare.

"And if I do?" I say, challenging him.

"Do it and find out," he challenges back.

So, I do.

> X: I'm going to tell Kohen I want to ask you out. I know he likes you and I want to make sure he knows that I want to date you.

I panic. I don't want X to tell Kohen anything. There are no plans to date him. He is going to ruin this. But also, why does he have to be so damn nice?

I take my time to answer, even though I'm not actually typing anything. Kohen's stare has been fixed on me since I unlocked my phone, and I can feel it burning into me. I have a feeling he is not going to like X trying to stake this claim. This infamous rivalry I have heard so much about is going to come into play sooner than I thought. This is what I wanted, right?

I look back up at him wondering if he already knows it's X. What if they are playing me? If I'm being honest with myself at this moment, I am intimidated. It's the way he is looking at me, leaning back on my mediocre sofa, like he's a king on his throne and I'm just a peasant- the woman at the well unworthy of his admiration. I shake the negative thoughts away and realign my body to face him.

"It was Xzavien."

I sit here, nervous in anticipation of what he has to say. He looks serious and mad but in an eerily calm way. We don't really know each other so I'm not sure what to expect but I'm waiting. I have a feeling we are in the same boat. We're used to being chased and not chasing anybody.

"I told you to answer it if you wanted to find out. Does that mean you like being punished, Angel?"

There's that name again. Biting my lip, I respond with a slow nod.

"So do you talk to X often?"

"I wouldn't say often, but he texted me after we ran into each other. But I don't initiate. I only respond." I don't know why I said that last part. "I honestly haven't thought about him since the party."

"Forgot about him, huh?" His muscles flex under his t-shirt, the ones in his arms moving like a wave as he pushes himself to sit at the edge of the couch cushion. "Do you make it a habit of getting drunk and forgetting people?" A look of disgust rests on his face.

What the fuck? Is he serious? "Wow! That's fucking rude, Kohen. You don't even know me." Tears well up in my eyes and I blink them away rapidly.

He scoffs. "It feels like I know enough."

"Well, you don't. You actually have no fucking idea. That party was the first party I have been to since my junior year of high school, thank you very much. I hadn't let loose like that in years, you asshole."

"Yeah. By the way you were acting, I doubt that."

I am so fucking furious! How dare he judge me like that. "I shouldn't have to fucking explain myself to you, but FYI, Kohen, I haven't let loose like that since I lost my best friend. She died at a house party two years ago in her sleep!"

"I thought Cora was your best friend?"

"She is, asshole. This was our third best friend, Cecille. We don't really talk about it but seeing as you think you know me so damn well. I had so much anxiety at your party since you weren't there. It triggered me. It's a huge part of the reason I don't like you. You weren't there and you are responsible for the people in your home. It's irresponsible. If someone had paid attention or been there, she might be here today, starting our freshman year of college together, being reckless. But she's gone."

Warm tears run down my cheeks, and he kneels in front of me. Much to my surprise, he wipes the tears from my face with his thumbs. His hands feel rough on my soft skin, calloused. I don't mind it, though. It just means he works hard at what he loves. This is unexpected. Sorrow is written all over his face as he looks at me.

"I'm sorry, Angel. You are right. I didn't know, I..."

My eyes meet his when I look up at him. He stares straight into my eyes, into the deep dark corners of my soul. It warms me like the sun warms the earth on a cool, gloomy day.

"I just...I don't know how to be around you. I barely know you and you make me crazy. You've taken over my thoughts since the moment I met you. You make me weak, Alex, and I'm not a weak guy. I don't like it." His fingers grace my cheek as he moves the hair on my face and tucks it behind my ear. "I'm sorry," he whispers.

"I'm sorry, too," I say, matching his tone.

"For what, Angel?"

"I don't know." I stare up at him, taking in his features. He is so handsome.

A few more tears fall from my eyes without permission, and that angers me. If only he knew he made me weak, too. But I won't give him that power over me.

I place my hand on his chest, not noticing how close we gravitated toward each other. Our lips are a breath away from touching. Chests heaving. Everything goes quiet.

I pull him into me and our lips meet. A fire ignites between us. The flames travel up my spine into my chest and spiral around my entire body. This kiss is deep and passionate, one that two strangers shouldn't be experiencing. We don't even know each other but the connection is tangible. Its elasticity bands us together. He lifts me into his arms and I wrap my legs around his waist. He stands with me, still tongue-tied and swallowing each other whole. He lays me on the couch and without any words, our bodies react to each other as lovers do. I lift his shirt and pull it over his head, tossing it onto the floor.

I pull back, breaking the place where our lips met, and take a second to take the image of him in. He has the body of a God, chiseled like a statue- all hard lines of muscle. Bless me. He is gorgeous.

It's then that the intrusive thought hits me like a ton of bricks. Why is he here? I start to overthink, and I can't even enjoy the kisses he is peppering on my lips, my cheek, and my neck, because I am sure this is some sort of cruel joke. A game of who can get into Alex's pants first.

I can't ever have anything good. My fight or flight kicks in and I want to push him away. I will not allow myself to be swallowed up in lust, thinking it's love, and end up with a broken heart. This feels like something uncontrollable and unexplainable. I need to run before I get run over. Right when I'm about to ask him to stop, he does.

"I'm sorry, I have to go." There is confusion in his tone.

"Wait, what? Why?" Panic takes over and the energy shifts. What did I do? Why am I asking? I was about to ask him to leave, but this catches me off guard.

"Yes, I forgot I had to do something. I have to leave."

He has to be lying. I can tell.

I feel a little abandoned and I don't know why. This is what I wanted. What does it matter who initiated it? He stands, picks up his shirt, and takes a long look at me.

“You are the most beautiful human being I have ever laid my eyes on, Alex. I just want you to know that.”

“Is everything okay...”

He interrupts me, leaning in for a kiss, and I’m speechless. I’m putty in his hands, but as he walks away, I’m reminded he doesn’t want me in his hands. “I have to go. I’m sorry.”

Just like that, he leaves me on the couch, confused about this whole situation. He walks out the front door and he takes all his sunshine with him, leaving me alone in the dark. Why did he leave? What the fuck did I do wrong? How can I feel so scared to lose him when I don't even have him yet?

So many questions run through my mind as I sit up, trying to get my thoughts together. I would call Cora but I don't want to ruin her date with Edward. I see Kohen’s headlights pull away and I feel empty. Used.

My phone rings. I run to grab it, hopeful that it's Kohen, but also feeling pathetic. Like a puppy making sad eyes at the people passing, hoping they will throw him a bone and take him home. That's me- a lost, homeless puppy no one wants. The name on the screen flashes and I let out a huff.

"Hello?"

"Hey, gorgeous. I know you said you were going to bed, but I just wanted to hear your voice."

"Thank you, X. Listen, I know you like me, and I just feel like I need to be honest."

"Mhhm?"

"I’m just not looking for a relationship right now. I just want to be friends. We can hang out and go do fun shit together, but just as friends. I just want to make sure we’re on the same page. I just need to focus on being the best me."

"No worries, gorgeous. I get it, and if all you want is to be friends for now that's cool. If it turns into something more later, I’ll be down for that, too. Listen, I know Kohen was there."

How the fuck would he know that? "How do you know Kohen was here? And even if he was, what does that matter? We’re only friends."

"No one is just friends with Kohen, Alex."

"Well, that really isn't any of your business. I said what I said. I got to go. Please don't call me again when I say I'm going to bed. Night."

Furious, I hang up. Why do these guys think they can just assume whatever they want?

I stomp up the stairs to actually go to bed before I do or say something I'll regret.

Not today, Satan. Not today.

Chapter 12

Alex

It's been a few weeks since I saw Kohen. He couldn't get away from me fast enough. I had a weak moment of being wine-drunk and I texted him. I just wanted to make sure he was okay, but he didn't respond. Xzavien texts me all the time but I made it clear that we were just friends and he respected that. I do like talking to him, but I'm just not attracted to him in that way. I mean, I was at first, but then Kohen happened. It isn't that he isn't cute or my type. It's just that Kohen is like a magnet.

I found a hidden folder of pictures in my phone when I was clearing out my storage from the night of the party. Sober me didn't remember everything drunk me did. That stupid line from that movie comes to mind. "It wasn't me, it was Patricia." That's what it feels like when I'm drunk, which is why I don't let myself get like that anymore. Tell-tale signs of my mom's addiction and alcoholic personality. I don't want to end up like her. I want to make something of myself. Make my name mean something in this world, and be a trailblazer.

Anyway, if my damn brain can stay on topic. The pictures are perfect. It makes him more human to me, not so God-like.

There are several pictures of us together and with our friends. I hate that I can't remember anything, another reason why I don't allow myself to have more than one drink. We really did spend most of the night together. I didn't believe him. The first image in the album is of me and him facing each other. My hands are moving like I'm explaining something or talking shit to him, and he has that cute smirk on his face as if he is unphased by what I'm saying. The rest of them that follow are of us laughing and taking shots. My favorite ones are the group shots. In every single one, his eyes are on me with a silly smile plastered across his face. My heart leaps and I do not like it. I don't want to like him at all. I want to hate him.

He is sarcastic, cocky, rude, and his friends are assholes. He is just a typical jock playboy and I want no part of him and his bullshit. I will not fall for Kohen Ventura. So why do I care so much about him ghosting me?

Classes are exhausting and I have a project to catch up on, but I can't focus on anything right now. He laid it on thick and was so persistent in talking to me that he showed up at my place when I blocked him, which is a red flag behavior. One thing about me is that I ignore the red flags. When I see them, I'm like, "oooo look, a circus, my favorite," then complain when the guy turns out to be a clown.

Cora walks into my room, bringing me out of my thoughts. "Hey, best friend. What are you up to?" Happy energy radiates from her.

"Ugh, I am looking through pictures I found on my phone from the party and driving myself crazy. You know, the normal stuff."

"What! Pictures? Why didn't you tell me? Am I in any of them?"

"Because I just found them, hello! And yes, you are in them and so is Edward. If anyone should be mad here it should be me because you remember everything."

"Well, not everything. There was a point after 2 am where everything just went fuzzy."

Handing her my phone, I plant my face into my pillows and scream. Dramatic, I know, but would I be me if I wasn't? Cora scrolls through the images, commentary included, as she swipes left through the album. I look up at her and her smile is huge. Her blue eyes glisten with fascination.

"Alex, these are freaking awesome. The blurry ones are hilarious! We were so drunk. Kohen is staring at you in every single one. He's obsessed!"

"Right! It's not just me then? I noticed that too, but it just doesn't make sense. Why ghost me? Clearly, there was something about me he liked. Like what the fuck?" I'm sitting up now, waiting patiently for her opinion. She hands me my phone, chewing her lip in thought.

"Has Edward said anything about it to you?" I feel pathetic and desperate asking her that but she's my best friend. She wouldn't make me feel like a loser for it like other people might. Waiting patiently for her response, I put my hair in a bun and grab the book I've been reading.

"Well, he did say that Kohen is pissed that you and X talk, but that's it. And that was just today, I promise. He said Kohen has been busy planning a fundraiser his gymnastics team is holding for the Special Olympics." A light smile touches her lips and I can't help the one that graces mine.

I did some more digging on him and he is active in the community here. He leads so many of the fundraisers and doesn't want credit for any of them. Sara has been a lifeline recently since she followed me on Instagram and messaged me apologizing for what Kohen did. She's the one who gave me a little rundown on him.

Like a ton of bricks, it hits me. "Wait! How can he be mad about me talking to X when he hasn't even talked to me since we made out on the couch?"

"What!" she shrieks at me. "You two made out on our couch? When?"

"That day when I blocked him, he showed up. We made out. It wasn't a big deal, Cora. Focus."

"Umm, it is a big deal! You didn't tell me all that. All you said was he ghosted you. I thought you were just texting and he stopped responding. What the hell, you have to tell me these things!"

"Well, he showed up, I was in a towel. He came inside and we talked, made out, and he ran away."

"See, if I knew that I would have hounded Edward to find out what the heck happened."

"Ugh, now I'm so embarrassed. Obviously, he thought, *"ew what am I doing here,"* and bounced."

"I doubt that. Maybe he got scared?"

"Scared of what, Cora? My big ass?" She spits out the water she just took a sip of with her laughter.

Our phones ping at the same time, and we look at each other, opening our messages.

"I just got a text inviting me to Kohen's fundraiser party tomorrow. You?" Cora asks, a worried look on her face.

"I got the same text but from Xzavien asking me to be his date."

I sit and think about it. I'm leaning towards a yes, but why didn't Kohen invite me? X has been consistent, I have to give him that, so I send a quick response saying yes and asking what time. My yes is also halfway because Kohen didn't send me an invite and going with X will bother him. It's Koehn's fault. The way he left and just hasn't responded is fucked up. Why make it seem like you're interested, tell me I make you weak and that I'm beautiful, and then just leave? I look over at Cora and she is texting away on her phone, smiling like an idiot. She must be talking to Edward, so I continue my mental spiral.

Maybe I'm wrong. Maybe going with X won't make him mad at all. Maybe I should just focus on X, have fun, and enjoy my time with him. He's the one trying after all. X has made it clear he wants to date me. He hasn't played any games like Kohen has. Actions speak louder than words and one make-out session means nothing. He didn't claim me like he said he would those two times at school.

Besides, I'm a single woman.

We're quiet as we get ready. She curls her silky blonde hair and I start in on my eyeshadow, going for a smokey look. I'm going to be bold tonight. Makeup is an art and my face is the canvas. A devilish smile graces my face and Cora's eyes meet mine. She knows what that means. My little devil wants to come out and play.

"Cora, let's go to the mall. I need to look like a fucking model at this party on Xzavien's arm."

I need something new to wear.

"You don't have to tell me twice, Hunny-buns. Let's go!"

We jump off the bed and head out the door.

I'm a queen and I wouldn't dare let him think he made my crown fall.

Chapter 13

Alex

We pull into the parking lot an hour later at the premium outlets in San Marcos. It's a popular shopping spot in Texas. There are restaurants as well. It really is a one-stop shop for any budget and style. They have stores ranging from Burlington and Papaya to Steve Madden, Guess, and Armani. There is a valet available, but we opt out. We aren't bougie like that. Instead, we head to the back of the parking lots where a few parking spots exist. It sucks being so far back, but Cora prefers it.

"It's good so we can get our steps in," she always says. Pfft! I'll stay chubby, thanks.

We get out and start walking to the center of the strip. The smell of fresh rain surrounds us, and moisture still lingers in the air. The rain bothers me. I like to listen to it, but I don't like to feel it, so I'm glad that it stopped. I also hate the aftermath of the humidity, the way it causes my hair to puff up. Hairspray is not a match for the humidity in South Texas.

"Where shall we start?" we ask each other at the same time.

"Let's go to Papaya first for old times' sake."

She smiles big and nods.

We link arms and make our way into what used to be our favorite store to shop at in high school. Granted we haven't been in here without Cecille, but that's why it feels right to go there. It's a small way to feel like she's here with us shopping. That's how it should have been. We walk around, the familiarity bringing tears to my eyes. It feels like such a long time ago. Walking in here, and picking some outfits for the night, is a way to include her.

We split up in the store as always. I want something that I'm going to break necks with. I want to feel like Cinderella when everyone stares at her as she makes her grand entrance to the ball. The difference between me and good little Cinderella is that I'm already a queen. I don't need a petty little prince to validate me.

I catch a glimpse of my best friend in my periphery and naturally, she is waiting for me before heading to the fitting rooms. She stands patiently with heaps of outfits in her arms. I laugh as I continue skimming everything on the racks, looking for the perfect thing to wear. It may be time to rethink the *wait for each other* clause.

"Go ahead and try them on, Cora. It's okay."

"Really?" Her smile is ear to ear.

"Yes, really."

She heads into the stall and it doesn't take long for my name to reach my ears. I turn to look in the direction of the fitting rooms and out walks my beautiful best friend. She looks stunning. Her eyes light up when she sees the approval on my face. Her long, toned legs in those high-heeled boots and short pleated skirt are going to get the attention of every guy at the party.

Edward better be careful. Cora is usually more modest, but I loved seeing her step out of her comfort zone since we started college.

"Cora, you look amazing. You're fucking hot!"

"Really?" she asks, smoothing out the skirt as she makes her way over to the 3-way mirror.

"Yes, bitch. You should know I wouldn't say something I didn't mean. If you looked like a trash bag, I would tell you."

"Savage," she laughs.

She really does look amazing. The plaid skirt is high-waisted, highlighting her tiny waist. She has it paired with a black strapless top that hugs her little body and pushes up her already huge boobs. When she turns around, I see the corset in the back and walk closer to tie it up for her. She runs her fingers up and down the ribbed bodice. It really is the perfect outfit for her body type.

"Promise you don't think it's too much?" A mark of uncertainty is on her beautiful face.

"No, Cora, I promise. It's perfect. I love it. You are stepping out of your comfort zone and that can be scary but do it!"

"Like Nike," she finishes, and we laugh.

I tie up the end and turn her around. "See, you look like a bad bitch. Wear it."

"What if Edward doesn't like-"

I cut her off, already knowing the last word of that sentence. "Fuck Edward."

She makes her way back into her dressing room. I'm a little discouraged since I still haven't found anything. Nothing feels right, like I've outgrown all of this.

"I'm going to go look around, nothing is catching my attention."

"Okay."

It's always so easy for Cora to find an outfit. I'm jelly but it takes me forever. Everything on the racks looks so unflattering for my body type. I wear a large, sometimes extra-large because of my curves but because I'm shorter it doesn't fit like it's supposed to length-wise. It's frustrating.

I turn a corner and decide to head back to the fitting rooms and see a gorgeous two-piece on a mannequin facing the wall. I don't know how I missed it before. I look at the tag and see it's my size. To my surprise, it's also on clearance. Jackpot!

The saleswoman, who seems to be everywhere I am, makes eye contact with me as I try to call her over for help. She puts her finger up, telling me to hold on, and walks away. Waiting impatiently, I see Cora out of the corner of my eye making her way up to the cash registers.

"Cora, come here. I found the perfect outfit!"

She walks up, eyes wide as her gaze reaches the place I'm pointing. "Holy cow. That's stunning. Definitely a head-turner with your body."

"I plan on breaking some necks with it on."

Finally, the sales lady shows up. I ask her if someone can get the outfit off so I can buy it.

"Someone put that on hold for pick up at 2:30." Her monotone voice and eye roll send me over the edge.

Taking my phone out of my bag, I check the time and it's 3:05. "Well, their time is up, so I would like to buy it please."

Cora steps closer, assuming I'm getting pissed, which would make her correct.

The sales lady rolls her eyes, making it extremely hard to keep my cool, so I take a step forward.

"I'll have to ask my manager."

She's walking away before I can even respond to her, so I follow.

"Are you serious? It's already been over thirty minutes. It should be completely up for grabs. If it was on hold, it shouldn't even be on the floor."

At this point, I'm chasing her as she touches up every single fucking thing she passes by on the way to the office behind the registers.

"If it wasn't for the mannequin, I would have just grabbed it myself, but God forbid you think I'm stealing it since you have been following me around the damn store this whole time!"

She finally looks back at me. "I wasn't following you," she says with her hand to her chest as if she is offended.

"Yes, you were. Every time I turned around there you were fixing or folding something. Give me that damn dress now or I want to talk to your manager to report you."

She holds eye contact with me for several seconds, thinking through what she is going to do next, I'm sure. Maybe I'm being immature but I *need* this outfit. It's perfect, and in this shitty life, small wins like this matter. They matter so much. I know I have money now and I can buy anything I want. I no longer have to live like I'm poor, shop at discount stores, or resale shops. But when you're raised that way, it becomes ingrained in who you are the same way traditions do. I don't have any traditions but shopping smart is good for any income bracket. That is one thing I think will always be a part of me.

A beeping noise comes from the walkie-talkie on her hip, and she responds in her earpiece so we can't hear her.

"My manager said you can have the outfit. Give me a few minutes to grab the step stool."

"Thank you," I respond, sarcasm dripping from every word.

She speeds past me, leaving trails of her cheap vanilla perfume behind her. I cringe. I hate the smell of vanilla stuff. I turn and watch her walk to the supply closet and she trips. I turn around fast so she doesn't see me laugh.

Karma is a bitch, isn't it?

"I'm going to check out. See you in a few."

I know Cora hates when I get upset and make a scene, but I can't help how I react to disrespect. The fact that the sales lady had already been following me pissed me off. She walks up with the step stool and takes a few steps up to reach the display. Cora could have grabbed it down easily and saved us all this trouble, but I didn't ask because she is always afraid to get in trouble. So I knew she would call a salesperson either way. Now we are here, dealing with this bitch. She looks to be about thirty. I hope when I'm thirty that I'm not as miserable in my life as she is.

She hands me the two-piece and I walk away before I get myself in trouble. I can't stand when employees are rude just because they can be.

Cora is waiting for me by the register with a scowl on her face. I hate upsetting her but I'm not going to let anyone treat me bad in any kind of way. I can tell she is embarrassed but I honestly don't think it's that big of a deal. I feel like I did better than usual.

"I still have to go try it on."

"Well, go try it on so you can see how it fits, and then we can leave."

I roll my eyes and do just that, hoping to God I don't need to ask anyone to give me a key or open the fitting room doors. I slip off my American Eagle jeans and pull my tank top over my shoulders. I stand there for a second, staring at my body in the mirror. I run my hand over my soft tummy, over each stretch mark and imperfection, hearing my mom's words echo in my head.

"You need to tone up, Alex. No man wants a chubby girl."

Fuck her. I had to learn to love myself. My parents didn't love me, and boys only loved me for one reason. Ironically, the reason she said they wouldn't want me is exactly why they do.

I continue scaling my body, looking at it through my mother's unforgiving eyes. My chest tightens, sadness washing over my features in the mirror. I stop myself. I run my fingers across my breasts, my cheeks, my butt, everywhere. I'm beautiful. Why didn't she think I was? I shake the thoughts from my head and refocus on the task at hand. I slip the skirt on, and its buttery material slips right over my thighs and hips. It sits perfectly at my waist, accentuating my curves there. I turn away from the mirror and check out how short it is in the back and how good my ass looks in it.

Excitement swirls around me now. The smile that graces my face could not be stolen at this moment. I look so damn good. I grab the top off the pillowed stool in the corner of the little room and pull it over my wide shoulders. My mother's voice possesses me again about my small breasts, but I don't pay any attention this time. I whisper in the mirror like I always do when she appears like a ghost haunting the halls of my mind. Not even Cora knows I do this.

I am strong.

I am worthy.

I am beautiful.

I deserve love.

I am NOT broken.

The last one is the hardest one to believe most days. I feel very broken.

Looking back at my reflection in the mirror, I am pleased. The right outfit can feel like magic. The top is like a tube top made of velvet material, but it has sheer sleeves with little diamonds placed sporadically starting at the chest and making their way down the arms. It's stretchy so it hugs exactly right following every curve and dip. The bottom is the same material on a high waist skin-tight skirt. It has gold chains around the waist that weave around the small of my waist gripping me in the sexiest way. The hem of the skirt sits mid-thigh, leaving the perfect parts of me to the imagination. I love that even though I show so much skin, there's so much left to explore. Kohen is going to eat his heart out wondering what lies underneath this soft velvet fabric.

I picture him running his hands over my body and I bite my lip. Heat rises up inside of me at the thought of him wanting me, desperate to be inside me. That kiss made me want him so badly, but I knew I had to push him away. Until he pushed first. Hopefully, it drives him crazy, the same way he has made me crazy wondering because he hasn't called or texted me since we made out. Now he will pay with the torture of him wanting me but not being able to have me because I will be there with his best friend.

I take one last look in the mirror before I take it off and pay for it. This outfit is fire.

Now to go find shoes.

Chapter 14

Alex

We walk down the rest of the strip mall after grabbing some pretzels. We needed to get a snack before getting hangry since neither of us ever eats breakfast. We decide on Steve Madden since Papaya didn't have the shoes Cora tried on in her size. Steve Madden has a big enough selection for the two of us and our polar opposite styles.

Walking into the store, I immediately see the shoes I want. It's like they beckon me, matte black with gold studs that wrap around the ankle and will flow up and around my calf. The heel is thick and chunky, which is good because they are extremely high. They are a statement piece all on their own, and I need them to complete this devilish outfit. Quickly finding the only pair in my size, I practically run to the checkout line, passing Cora on the way there with a bewildered look on her face. I pay for them as quickly as I can and let out a breath I didn't even know I was holding. Relief floods me. I'm going to look drop dead gorgeous.

Now I have to go find Cora. She knows if I can't find her, I will start shouting her name around the store like a little kid who lost his mom in the grocery store. She hates it. Doesn't take long to find her. She is looking at the nude pumps. I grab her wrist to pull her over to the ankle boots.

"You need a shiny black high-heeled combat boot for the outfit you picked. They are over here," I say, leading her to them.

"I know but maybe it was a little too risqué..."

"No, Cora you are doing this. You are wearing that outfit because you felt good in it. Stop second-guessing yourself. You looked so fucking good in it."

She sighs, giving into me, and I pull some options in her size so she doesn't have to think too much or talk herself out of anything. She's already removed her ballet slipper-style flats, so I shove a pair of boots at her. While she puts them on, I look around, admiring the simple beauty and elegance of this store. The hushed tones and nude colors make it so simple but become the staple of any outfit.

I snap out of my daydream when I see Cora standing in front of the mirror looking at the boots on her feet. They aren't the ones I tossed at her, but they look so good. They aren't glossy- they're matte, and they lace up the front of her foot and come up a little higher on the leg than most ankle boots do.

"I love those. Where did you find them?"

"Oh, the worker came up to me and said she actually saw us at Papaya and thought these would match. They just came in."

"She was right- they are perfect. Are you going to get them?"

"Yes. I'm going to rock the shit out of this outfit and I'm not going to feel bad about it."

I fake shock and gasp dramatically. "Oh, my word, Cora Rose. Language."

Giggling loudly and feeling content and excited about our choices, we leave the store happy and smiling. Much different than how the earlier part of the day went. It must have been the pretzels.

"Don't be mad."

We stop walking and I turn to look at her, worried. "Why would I be mad?"

"Well, I kind of have a surprise but I know you hate surprises. I don't want you to kill me, but I made us hair appointments..." She pauses. "At Mirror, Mirror."

"Breathe, Cora, that's fine. I don't know why you always think I'll get mad about little things I don't care about but then you don't register the things that *do* make me mad."

I roll my eyes, starting to walk towards the famous salon, which also happens to be one of the only ones for miles that keeps up with the newest techniques.

It's a one-stop shop for hair, skin, and nails. I used to go there all the time until the girl my ex cheated with started to work there. Hence why Cora would think I'm mad.

"So, you're not angry?"

"No. Anger would mean that I care and I don't. See?" I smile a huge toothy grin at her. "Happy as can be. Let's go."

"I don't believe you but okay, just don't set the place on fire. Besides, I made sure *she* wouldn't be there."

"Did you now? 'Cause that's not embarrassing."

"You *are* mad."

"I'm not but I would prefer if the whole salon didn't think that I was avoiding Crystal like the plague."

"Ugh, I'm sorry but it was just Leslie, so I'm sure she wouldn't have said anything."

"Drop it. Let's just do this."

"We can cancel," she practically yells. I don't know how else to reassure her other than walking in and sitting my ass in a chair.

"Cora, if you were that worried about me being mad, then why even make the damn appointment here?"

"Because it's the best. I was secretly hoping since you're basically in a love triangle now that you wouldn't care."

"I am NOT in a love triangle." Rolling my eyes, I see the sign from the salon and turn to walk right in without another word to my best friend.

"Hi, welcome to Mirror, Mirror." Just my luck. "Alex Monroe, is that you?"

Cora follows right behind, bumping into me, and I catch myself on the counter.

"Is that Cora, too? Oh my gosh- I haven't seen you girls in forever. How are y'all?"

I hate her stupid Minnie Mouse voice with her southern drawl. She moved to our small town of Lockhart, Texas halfway through our senior year and stole the love of my life from me. Granted he wasn't a very good person, but I thought I loved him. I thought he was forever. He got her pregnant and I never looked back. She was going to get my happily ever after and I accepted it and left that shitty town in my rearview.

"Hi, Crystal Anne. We are doing amazing. How are you?"

"Oh, I'm as sweet as a honeybee, graduated from beauty school as you well know. I may be a high school dropout, but I still made something of myself. You little ladies look just darling. Are you here for an appointment?"

I hate that she is so nice. It makes it hard to hate her. It really isn't her fault that we both fell for a piece of shit. Cora picks up the rest of the conversation as I sign our names into the book. I really am happy that Crystal has something good in her life. I'm a little irritated we ended up in the same city but everyone in Lockhart wants to move to the big city. Granted San Marcos isn't as big as Houston or Dallas, but it's an amazing place to begin life. Texas State put this city on the map, that's for sure.

Crystal makes eye contact with me and nods in the direction she wants me to follow.

I give Cora a death stare over my shoulder, and she mouths, "I'm sorry."

"Have you heard from Walker?" Crystal asks quietly.

My heart drops at the mention of his name. Like Voldemort in Harry Potter, we don't say his name.

"Umm no, I haven't talked to him since I found out y'all were having a baby and then you both left school, so..."

"Right." She pauses. "Well, I lost the baby, it was early on, but we had already dropped out. He booked it shortly after we found out. I was so embarrassed. I just couldn't show my face at school again."

"I understand and I'm sorry for your loss," is all I say.

"Listen, sugar. I know I'm probably one of the last people on God's green earth you want to see, but I just wanted to make my peace."

"Thank you, Crystal, but there really isn't any peace for you to make, at least not with me. I forgave you a long time ago and I thank you."

Confusion etches her perfect face. "Thank me? For what?"

"I'm thankful because, without you, I would have never given up on Walker. I would have let him keep coming back and taking every ounce of love, and forgiveness I had left. I emptied my heart and soul for him, and he was a vampire. I was his willing victim. I gave and gave, and he took and took."

"I just wanted to tell you to stay safe. I heard he's moving here and he's sober, trying to get his life back together. He got his GED." She winces a little as she drops the news on me.

"What! Here? Why?"

"I don't know but that's another reason why I had to see you, to warn you. I know he was abusive to you. I didn't get a chance for it to get that far but I heard about it. If it were me, I would want to know."

"Thank you."

"Now, on to better things... What do you want to do with this hair? It's so long and beautiful. Is it virgin hair?"

"Girl, it's the only virgin thing left on me."

We laugh hard for a while, and it feels good. I never hated her, I just hated that he made me feel like she somehow deserved him, like she was better than me. Maybe she was. Maybe that's why he never hurt her in the ways he hurt me. He hurt her in other ways, though. Trauma is trauma, hers isn't any less painful than mine just because it wasn't physical.

"Surprise me."

Her eyes go wide. "You shouldn't have said that, sugar. I'm gonna make you brand-spankin' new."

"I'm counting on it."

The rest of the evening is spent getting pampered. We feel like royalty. Cora got her nails done simply, a white and nude ombre with some accent rhinestones- short and ballerina shaped. My nails are extra-long stiletto shape, and they are sharp enough to stab someone in the eyes. They are glossy black, and I got one nail blinged out with Swarovski stones. They are perfect.

My hair couldn't have been more of a shock. Crystal is so talented, she added some blonde in my hair. I thought it was like highlights but she said it was a balayage and isn't as much maintenance. She took the color of my roots and smudged it down to blend my natural color into the blonde. It gives it more dimension and is not so drastic of a change because it all blends together beautifully. The biggest bonus is that my hair is still long and feels so soft and buttery. She didn't fry my hair like I have always been afraid of. Saying I'm happy with it is an understatement. I can't stop staring at myself in the mirror as I wait for Cora to be done.

Cora got a toner that turned her natural hair and made it an icy blonde color, almost platinum, then they curled the ends of it after giving her a little trim.

I walk around, taking in the atmosphere of the shop. They are so trendy, there is a floral wall on one side and lavender hanging from the ceilings. As I pass through more of the modern building, I see they have several themed walls, Instagram-ready. There's a wall covered in all different kinds of cool mirrors and another that has a huge neon sign that says *you are only as beautiful as you treat people.* I love it in here. I hadn't been in since I found out Crystal worked here and I don't know why. I regret all the time wasted, we could have been friends. She is actually so fucking awesome.

Making my way back to Cora, I take a detour to Crystal's station where she is cleaning. "Hey, Crys."

"Hey, sweetness. Is something wrong?"

"No, no, I absolutely love my hair. I just wanted to come and ask for your number. There's a party tomorrow off campus and I'd love for you to come with us."

"Really? Oh, my goodness, yes! Girl, I have wanted to be your friend since I first met you."

We exchange numbers and I make my way back to my best friend, smiling. I duck down to whisper in her ear. "Thank you for this, Bubbles." I use my childhood nickname for her. Making eye contact in the mirror, I blow her a kiss and she smiles big.

"Don't worry, I won't rub it in."

"Damn right, you won't."

We finish our pampering with pedicures, getting massages from the huge comfy chairs, and gossiping with Crystal and her coworker about college life. This was exactly what I needed to get my mind off of Kohen. Butterflies launch into flutters inside my belly. I can't wait for tomorrow.

Chapter 15

Kohen

This past week has been hectic. I've been killing myself at the gym. Training for the Olympics is no joke but my coach thinks I have what it takes to make it to the next level.

Gymnastics is my passion and it has saved my life. It has been a place to come and take out all my anger and aggression, so here I am on a weekend putting in work. It takes up most of my social time but that's fine. My specialty is the parallel bars and I'm good at it. My parents started me at the gym when I was only eight years old. Granted there were kids younger than me already on a strict regimen, but I feel like I didn't have a childhood. I see a sports psychologist regularly, but no one knows about that besides my family.

The sport grew on me and when the coaches and trainers saw the raw, natural talent and strength I possessed, they all poured into me. They started me on the Olympic track young.

I chalk up my hands and rub the bars above me so I can start training. I mount the apparatus and lift my body up and around several times, losing myself in the dizzying movements. My senses are overloaded and adrenaline rushes through me, the smell of the chalk and sweat running past my eyebrow. I'm not worried about it- I could do all this with my eyes closed, and sometimes I do. It's a rush.

Then Alex pops into my head. The way I left her, the look in her eye... My hand slips. I catch myself quickly. Someone watching probably wouldn't even have noticed the slip, but I know. I know the way Alex has crawled into my mind and taken up space there. Space that was not readily available. Space and time I don't have to dedicate to anyone or anything. That is why I left when we were making out, the energy was intense. Like nothing I've ever felt before. I had to walk away. As much as I want her, I know I can't have her. Like my father said, I could never make a woman happy. I don't have the time to. I need to learn to fuck 'em and dump 'em. That just isn't me, though.

The way my mother loved me and the admiration I had for her would guilt me so deeply. I know who they think I am, who everyone in this god-forsaken town thinks I am. Kohen Ventura- the campus playboy. I am far from that, but I let them think what they want and say what they want. Girls pretend they hook up with me, knowing they didn't and I don't correct them. I don't need to. Everyone wants to be the one who makes me fall in love. I vowed to never allow myself to fall in love again. The one time I did, she made me regret it. And I will regret it for the rest of my life because I almost gave up everything for her.

Luckily, as my father would like to remind me, I found out she was cheating. The time I had to dedicate to the gym was too much, hence the conversation about never being able to make a girl happy.

He left the gymnastics team for my mother and their young love. He resented her for it until the day she died. He wasted no time replacing her and that's okay. That's his cross to bear. I loved my mother dearly and I am glad she is no longer in the arms of his wrath.

I finish my routine and dismount the bars, wiping my hands on my gym shorts but it's no use. There is chalk everywhere, the same way sand blankets every crevice when leaving the beach. Hands on my hips, I pace the length of the mats, Alex consuming my mind again. Her luscious lips and curvy body, the way she felt so soft underneath me. Pulling me into her warm and welcoming arms... I crave her lavender-scented hair and tart perfume. That perfume has intoxicated me since the party. I need to find out what it is.

I sound absolutely batshit crazy.

Catching my breath, I walk up to my bag and grab my phone. I've been here for three hours. Time flies when you do what you love. I place the velour bag over my shoulder and wave goodbye to my team.

My team.

I wasn't sure if I would have gotten the leadership position since I almost lost my spot on this team altogether, but I pulled through. My hard work and dedication couldn't be wiped away by a few months of slack. I got this. Erica couldn't hold a candle to Alex, though, so I need to be very fucking careful. She was one of the worst women to walk this earth, but she's in the past and I hope she stays there. I don't see why she would come around again since she chases rich men. Money-hungry bitch. Her constant need for attention almost killed my season.

My phone pings and it's Alex. Like divine intervention, the universe is telling me it's okay to have her, to be happy to live a little. But I can't. I need to focus.

So, I ignore it. This is my dream, and I doubt this girl is serious about anything. I stuff my phone back in my bag and grab my keys so I can unlock my car. I have to run some errands before the fundraiser party tomorrow. My team is sponsoring a middle school gymnastics team so that they can travel to their final meet of the year. Some of them are heading into their high school teams so this is a pivotal time in their life and I'm happy to help. My phone pings again and suddenly I see stars. Alex Monroe sent me a naughty little picture. I want to open it but then she would know I read it and so I settle for the little thumbnail in the message preview window.

"God damn, Angel." It takes all the willpower I have to ignore it, but I do, I have to. Focusing on training is detrimental to my success this season. I promised myself I'd stay on task.

Plugging the phone into the charging dock of my car, I see message unsent in place of where the image used to be, and I laugh.

This girl is going to be nothing but trouble. I can tell.

Chapter 16

Alex

The sun beams on my face through the window as the alarm goes off for the hundredth time, and it won't let me snooze anymore. If I want to snooze one hundred times, I should be able to. I roll onto my side away from the blinding sun and check the time. Noon. I blink a few times to clear the fuzziness there so that I can scroll through my notifications. I manage to sneak a peek at my phone through one eye and see I have several texts from X, but still zero from Kohen. I'm annoyed but also not surprised.

Sitting up to try and wake myself up so I don't fall back asleep, I catch a glimpse of myself in the mirror and jump. I didn't recognize myself with this hair. My laughter brings Cora into the room, which only scares me again. She has a pastel green clay mask on her face and self-tanner all over her body. I laugh even harder, snorting in the process.

Her confusion is adorable. "What's so funny?"

"First of all, you look like an alien. Second, what the hell are you doing?"

"I'm prepping. I might have decided I'm going to have sex with Edward." She exits the room quickly and I launch off my mattress to follow her. Did she say what I think she just said?

"I think I heard you incorrectly. Cora, you're losing your virginity tonight?" I'm a little angry and I won't let that show yet, but Edward does not deserve to take her motherfucking v card. Following her into the restroom, I see the counter cluttered with waxing products, makeup, that hideous facemask, scrubs, and lotions.

"You heard correctly."

"What the fuck is all this? Do you have twenty other girls hidden in here somewhere? Because this is enough beauty products to prepare a whole cheer squad for you to lose your virginity."

"You know I like to be prepared. I want everything perfect."

"It isn't going to be perfect because Edward is an asshole."

"He treats me good and he's nice."

"But do you love him, Cora? You always said you wanted to wait until you were going to get married. Why change your mind now? Is he pressuring you? I'll kick his fucking ass."

"No, it is my decision. He doesn't even know yet."

"*Pfft.*"

"Listen, Alex, I'm a big girl and I can handle this. Trust me. I have been researching it. I know it isn't going to feel good, it's going to hurt, and I'm going to probably bleed, but I'm prepared. I have a little bag."

"Oh, okay, Cora. My bad- you have a little bag. What was I thinking? That fixes everything?" sarcasm and anger drip from my tongue like toxic waste. I love her and I just want what's best for her. "I told you before, losing my virginity was the biggest mistake of my life. I thought it didn't matter, it was just sex, nothing would change. But it does change Cora, you will change. I don't want you to regret this."

"I won't. I know you think you control everything and everyone, but I have decided, and you will just have to accept this."

"Fine. Accepted," I spit back as I turn to walk away. "When that fuckboy breaks your heart, I'm not even going to say I told you so. Because when he does, not *if* but *when*, you are going to hear them echoing in your mind when you're all alone and empty, and I won't be there to pick up the fucking pieces of the mess he is guaranteed to leave behind."

"Good, because I don't want you there." I know she is crying. I can hear it in her voice.

I slam my door, tears sliding down my cheeks. I don't want to fight with her, and I'm already feeling guilty for being mean, but this is a mistake. I just know it. I take a few deep breaths and walk over to the window seat. I open one of the small windows on top to let some fresh air in and gather my thoughts. The front door slams and I see her walking over to the little bench under the trees in our small backyard.

I don't want her to do this, but she is right, and it isn't my choice. I suck it up and gather all the strength in the universe to go apologize. Cecille pops into my head and her words run through my head.

"*Go apologize, Alex. She is softer than you, and you're coming at her hard. You have to remember that you catch more flies with honey. Just go say sorry.*"

Cecille was always the voice of reason in our friendship. The balance between us. It's funny that she became my own personal Jiminy Cricket.

We shouldn't be arguing at all. Life is way too short, and friends are much too important.

Making my way downstairs as slow as possible so I don't look like a little bitch, I catch a glimpse of a car that looks like Kohen's parked outside. Sleek and black, that isn't the type of car that belongs in this neighborhood. I rush down the stairs faster now, so I can stare out of the little window at the top of our bright red door. The car is gone now so I chuck it up to my imagination. Cora is in the kitchen gulping down a bottle of water with tears in her eyes. I feel bad.

"I'm sorry, Cora. You're right. I heard Cecille in my head telling me to chill the fuck out. I don't run your life and I shouldn't. I can't protect you from everything. We need to live our lives, make mistakes, love, and lose love. We are young!"

"I forgive you. I heard Cecille tell me to remember that you just care so much about us and would do anything to keep us safe, even if it meant putting yourself in harm's way."

She walks up and pulls me into a hug. These quick little fights are a norm between us because we are so different. Love keeps us close, though. Love is a promise to never leave, never give up and never judge. And I need to do a better job of it.

"Okay now, let's go prepare your vagina to get pounded!"

"Oh my gosh, you are relentless."

"But you love me?"

"Yes, you little hussy. I love you."

I hold my pinky out and she wraps hers around mine. "Promise, promise?"

"Promise, promise."

We seal it with a kiss and rush upstairs to get ready for the night ahead.

Chapter 17

Alex

Waiting for Xzavien to pick me up, I figure I have thirty minutes before he gets here. Men are always late, so I do some last-minute touch-ups on my hair and lipstick, before popping a piece of gum in my mouth.

Lights flash into the living room and I rush to look through the fuzzy windows. He's here. What the fuck? He's early. Instead of being grateful that he's on time, my dumb ass is annoyed. This is why I never end up with the good ones. I roll my eyes as I see him walk up the sidewalk.

Knocks echo throughout the hallway. Taking one last look in the mirror, I fix the placement of my outfit, even though I'm sure I'll have to fix it at least a hundred more times tonight since everything rides up, because of my body shape, thank you mother nature.

I yank open the old red door and he steps inside without invitation. More annoyance radiates through me. He shouldn't have done that.

"Hey, gorgeous. Are you ready?"

"Yes, let's go." His hand wraps around my wrist, pulling me into him. This guy is relentless. When will he give it up? "What are you doing?"

"Just showing my gratitude for this date you agreed to go on."

"This isn't a date, X. I told you we are..."

He cuts me off, "Just friends, I know. But if I can be honest with you, I think you're just scared. Scared that you might find something real with me."

Who the fuck does this guy think he is? I'm not scared. I'll admit I'm a little scared of Kohen. "Xzavien, trust me. Take my word for what it is. The truth is, I wouldn't lead you on that way."

"Alright, alright, let's just go have some fun. Either way, I'm proud to be the man that has you on his arm."

"I'm not a prized hog."

"I didn't mean it like that. I just meant you will be the most beautiful girl there."

Just then, Cora comes down the stairs like a bat out of hell. "Can I ride with you guys? Don't ask, Alex. Please, I'm already upset."

"I won't ask, but it isn't up to me. It's up to X."

"Of course, any friend of Alex is a friend of mine."

I want to scream. I don't know why he is making me so frustrated, but he is. I know I should be excited but if I'm being honest, I just want to see Kohen.

I want to see his face the moment he spots me, and his jaw drops to the floor.

It's a short ride to his huge three-story brick house, it's so luxurious with black brick and white pillars that adorn the front of the entryway. The driveway is lined with lights that seem to be placed inside the cement. I have never seen anything like it and don't remember any of this from the last time I was here. The flowers and shrubs are pristine. I don't fit in here. Butterflies begin to flutter, causing a riot inside me.

X pulls into the drop-off zone and assures me he will be back. As soon as he drives off, I let out a sigh and Cora looks at me like I'm being rude.

"What?"

"Be nice, Alex."

"I am being nice."

"Mhmm."

"Does Edward know you are here? Where is he?"

"Yes, I texted him when we pulled up," she says, a hint of bitterness lining her tone. I wonder what he did now.

"Okay, is he coming out to walk you in?"

"No, and I don't need him to."

"Don't get smart with me. You're right- you don't need him. You have me and I'm sure X is okay with walking us both. He'll love it."

We giggle, locking arms. She smiles but I know it bothers her that Edward doesn't take the initiative to do the little things. He is all about showing off and being extravagant, but he always has a motive. He is a little older so being young isn't an excuse anymore. He's a senior, he is supposed to be a man and a man should know how to cater to his woman no matter how strong, beautiful, and independent she is.

X is walking up to us right on time and he smiles. He looks so handsome, and every time I take a second to really look at him, I'm reminded of why I was so attracted to him the first time I met him. He has a simple yet sexy style, different from most of the guys he surrounds himself with. It's like he doesn't have to try as hard as them. He is wearing a black button-up long-sleeve shirt rolled up to the elbow, with black jeans and gray Air Maxes. I try not to stare because I don't want him to think I'm checking him out as anything more than a friend.

Xzavien extends his hand to me and I grab it, hesitating. I am overthinking every single action now, hoping that he doesn't read into anything. He extends his other hand to Cora, and I release a breath I didn't realize I was holding. His gaze rakes up and down my body and he makes direct eye contact with me. I look at Cora and she looks away when our eyes meet.

"You look gorgeous, Alex." A blush rushes over his cheeks. "And so do you, Cora."

"Why thank you. X is such a gentleman. Right, Alex?"

"Yes, thank you." I tuck a curl behind my ear and hope to God I'm not blushing, because it wouldn't be for the reason he thinks it is. He needs to know there is no hope for him here. I'm here as his friend, better yet I'm here for Kohen.

We start up the walkway to the door which proves to be difficult since it's made of tons of gray river rock, and these heels are a little too chunky for this. The one thing I do know is Xzavien would never let me fall, so I feel safe in his grip. He has a firm hold on me and I know I can trust him to keep me steady. He truly is a great guy and I know he could easily become my best friend.

Arms intertwined, we walk into the party. Instead of pulling my arm away like I want to, I force myself to keep it there. Part of me wants Kohen to see me and X together, to eat his fucking heart out knowing he ghosted me, but the other part of me doesn't want to be seen, doesn't want to be here at all, doesn't want Kohen to see me on someone else's arm... Stupid brain.

Making our way into the crowd, I start to feel a panic arise in my chest, a small vibration of worry crawling up my body until it starts to churn negative thoughts in my mind. I release Xzavien and move to the middle so I can grab Cora's hand. We don't like to be separated at parties.

Anything can happen in a split second and since Edward isn't with her, I need to make sure she is safe. I know it's a slim to none chance that what happened to Cecille will ever happen again, but when you lose someone so close to you at such an early age, it becomes a permanent scar on your brain and in your heart. It's a loss that will never dull. She should be here and sometimes I still feel like it's my fault that she's not.

I rein in my thoughts and reroute them to more positive things. X leads us further into Kohen's incredible house. I gawk at the black walls and silver accents. There is new furniture in every room, like he remodeled since the last time we were here. That was only about a month ago. I feel a little crazy, like maybe time has warped and somehow more time has passed than I realize. There is no way he re-did all of this. One more reason why I can never be with someone like him. I bet they just tossed all the old furniture out, not thinking that there are families that are in need of bare minimum household furniture, like a couch.

The entryway is as big as our living room, and because there are crowds of people standing all around, it takes us a while before we get to the grand hall that leads to the kitchen. The ceilings are over twenty feet high. I feel like a mouse in a mansion. Small and insignificant, unworthy of walking through this luxurious house. We make it to the kitchen, and I release Cora's hand to wipe the sweat away. X leaves us to get drinks.

"Are you okay? Your hands are sweaty."

"Yes, I was anxious, but I pushed through."

"Me too."

It brings me comfort that I'm not going through the motions of anxiety alone. Cora busies herself texting Edward to find out where he is, and I take the opportunity to scan the room for Kohen. Having no luck, I bring my attention back to my best friend. She looks stressed and I'm sure it's because Edward is being a little bitch. I hope for his sake that he doesn't leave her hanging.

The kitchen is huge, and the marble countertops are gorgeous- white with gold flakes throughout the glossy surface. I run my fingers across the top and shiver at its coolness. My body temperature runs hot for a woman. Whenever Cora and I share a bed, she brings a separate cover for herself because she says I'm a space heater.

Xzavien makes his way back to us, smiling. He has three red solo cups. I'll admit, he couldn't be more perfect. The simple gesture speaks volumes about the kind of guy he is, the kind of guy I should fall for.

"Here you go, ladies. I got you some Malibu and pineapple juice."

"Thank you so much. You are too sweet." I give him a peck on the cheek as I grab my cup. I see a flush of pink spread across his tan skin and it makes me smile.

Cora widens her eyes at me, trying to send a message with the gesture, but it isn't what she thinks.

"Yes, thank you so, so much. I feel like a third wheel, especially because my dickhead boyfriend isn't here to serve me himself," Cora says, her voice lined with disappointment.

"No thanks needed. We are all friends here."

My mind wanders as I take my first sip. I think about how I was so attracted to Xzavien first, and just like the last time, Kohen is nowhere to be found. My head must have been shaking on its own accord because when I look up, Cora and X are both staring.

"What's wrong?" they ask in unison. Maybe they should date each other. God knows Cora needs a good man and X is amazing.

"Oh, nothing. Just having conversations with all the personalities in my brain." We laugh and some of X's other friends come up to chat with him.

Suddenly warning signs go off in my head. Anxiousness sets in but not like how it did before.

I shake the feeling off, blaming the alcohol. My thoughts pull me away as X, his friends, and Cora turn into background noise. I don't know why I'm here in this huge house, waiting for a guy who doesn't even want me while on the arm of his best friend. Why am I falling for the bad boy again? I feel bad for X, like I led him on without meaning to. Sure, I wanted to make Kohen jealous, but I like X. He's a good guy. Maybe I should choose X- he is here and Kohen isn't. He makes an effort to talk and hang out, he wouldn't have left that night...

Standing here quietly, listening to the people talking in this little huddle, a familiar scent invades my nose. I feel stuck in place like stone. I can't move a single muscle, my body tensing up in anticipation of the man that scent is attached to. It's heavenly. I hear a whisper in my ear, the slight smell of sweet mint follows, and I quiver. Chills roll down my spine and goosebumps erupt all over my skin. Kohen.

My body must have been warning me that he was near. Responding to him the way it does only for him, he makes my skin feel like it's on fire in the best way. The words that hit my ear make me tighten my legs together.

"You look so fucking delicious in this skirt, Angel." His hand slides down my body from my waist to my hip, and he lightly runs his fingers over the mounds of my ass. "I want to rip this off right here, right now, and fuck you for all these people to see."

I gulp. Everything about him awakens my senses and my body is tingling from head to toe in response to the closeness of his body. He is close enough that I feel the heat off his body but not enough that he is touching me. I wish he would.

I'm terrified to turn around and face him, but I want to see him so badly. He probably looks drop-dead fucking gorgeous and that's precisely why I am torn about looking. I hate that I feel this way, that he does this to me. Why does my body betray me and respond to his filthy words? This is why I'm here, though, right? For him, to see me, to want me. Shit!

I'm pulled out of my little trance when X pops into my head. I completely forgot about him. Did he see us? What the hell is wrong with me? I'm such a bitch. I shake my head at Kohen, still not looking at him, and walk away without saying a word. I pretend like there is no way he noticed how my body reacted and that I am completely uninterested. I move away and look over at Xzavien, relieved to see him and Cora engaged in deep conversation. They didn't seem to notice whatever the hell that was between me and Kohen.

Kohen makes his presence noticed. "Hey X, what's up man? Where is Edward?"

Cora is caught up in another conversation with the girl from her class and I'm grateful. They are talking about Edward. I know she is embarrassed to be here alone. Especially because he lives here, too.

"I don't know, bro. He was supposed to pick her up. We talked earlier and he had a plan to get her before I picked up Alex. We actually came here together. So, we are just hanging out until he gets here. I didn't want to leave her alone, so she walked in with us."

I feel X's arm run behind my back, his touch gracing the skin that peeks between the two pieces of my outfit. It makes me shiver, but not in a good way. It feels wrong. His touch isn't meant for my skin.

Kohen's eyes follow the movement of his arm and he clenches his jaw. "Oh yeah, so you three came together, huh?"

X places his arm around my shoulder as he responds. "Yeah, man. Just being a gentleman." He rubs his thumb back and forth on my shoulder.

I shoot a glance at Cora and she is already staring at me with wide eyes. No words are needed, that's all it took for Kohen's smirk to disappear. The look on his face lights a fire inside me. There's a flash of jealousy in his eyes, making them darker than usual. I'm glad. Who does he think he is? He can't just pick up where we left off after he left me there alone with no explanation, no calls, no texts. Hell, he didn't even respond to me, so he has no right to come and claim me now.

But damn do I want him to. I know it's immature and I don't give a single fuck. If looks could kill, I'm sure I would be dead, because I lean into X like I want this. Kohen is shooting daggers at me. I can feel the intensity of his stare on my skin and everywhere he looks sends sparks of electricity through me. He breaks the small moment of silence.

"Wait, you and Alex? When did that become a thing? I thought you were dating someone?"

Dating someone? What the fuck? If X is dating someone, how has he had so much time to pursue my ass? My eyes grow wide. Unless it's me he thinks he is dating? Fuck!

"Nah, man. I'm not dating anyone. Alex and I are just friends, but I wish she would be mine," he says, staring down at me from his 6'2" standpoint with that beautiful smile of his. It makes me feel small. I smile back to be polite but deep down I'm sick to my stomach. I can't believe he just said that in front of everyone. Worse than that- to Kohen. I want to disappear.

"Well, that's crazy. I could have sworn I heard you were seeing someone."

"Nah, like I..."

Kohen cuts him off mid-sentence making eye contact with me directly. "Not you, X. I'm talking about Alex. Aren't you seeing someone?"

He knows damn well we haven't made anything official and that we haven't talked since he left me on the couch, wanting to be fucked.

"I'm not. I haven't dated anyone in years. I was trying to get into something with this one guy, but he ended up being a flake. We kissed and he got scared and ran away," I deadpan, looking straight back into his eyes, not backing down. All the nerves were now gone from my body and replaced with my signature bitch attitude. If he wants to play, we can play.

"Even better for me," X jokes, and we laugh. I like that he isn't afraid or intimidated by Kohen.

Cora hasn't said a word and I wish she would give her Miss Perfect two cents right about now. I wonder if something is wrong.

"Cora, is Edward coming?" I ask, hoping she will get the hint that I need her right now. I need her to stick her nose where it doesn't belong so I'm not in the middle of this awkward conversation. So, I'm not in the middle of these two boys who seem to be fighting over whose turn it is to play with the broken doll.

"Alex, do you want to dance?" Kohen really has the audacity to not only interrupt everyone talking, but to also ask me while his best friend's arm is around my waist. He's brave, especially because X just said he is interested in me as more than friends and that we are here together. I'm such a stupid girl because I want to say yes right now, but I won't. I can't. I refuse to give him the satisfaction.

"No. I'm good," I respond flatly. "Cora? Edward?" I repeat to my best friend who seems to be in some sort of trance.

"Yes, he is coming over here now. He was playing beer pong." Her phone rings and she has a hushed conversation and then hangs up. "Actually, I'm going to go meet him upstairs." This makes me anxious, but she seems excited, so I let it go. I'm only glad the asshole didn't fully flake on her.

I take a moment while everyone is distracted saying bye to Cora and look at Kohen. He is wearing a black Armani sweater that is fitted to his body frame with tan Armani joggers that fit exactly right. He looks delicious, the perfect mix of casual and dapper. My favorite part is the pristine shoes on his feet- classic white high-top Nikes that have touches of black and tan that match the colors of his outfit perfectly. My mouth waters and I fucking hate it. I hate him. I hate the way he fucking makes me feel things I don't want to feel and I don't even fucking know him.

He catches me staring. I look away, asking Cora if she wants me to walk her. She doesn't, so I let her go. If she needed me, I trust that she would let me know.

"Have fun, Bubbles."

She smiles big and that's all the reassurance I need. I kiss her on the cheek and watch her float out of the room. The next time I see her, she will be a changed woman.

"Hey, X. Do you want to dance?"

"Yes," he responds immediately and with no hesitation, so I grab his hand and lead him onto the dance floor, leaving Kohen all alone. Just like he left me after our kiss.

The dance floor is buzzing with life, bodies are moving to the rhythm of the beat and the vibe is immaculate. Dancing is so freeing. You can let go, let go of the past, let go of who hurt you, and just connect to the music. I love it. I always wanted to major in dance, but my mom said I was too chubby. I joined in high school, but the voice of doubt ate away at me. She placed that voice there and it's loud.

As soon as we reach the middle of the dance floor where all the life is, X grabs my waist, leading me into his body. He starts to move to the music and I'm shocked. He knows how to dance. I can't contain my excitement. The smile on my face is so huge that I can feel it. I love when a guy knows how to dance. It's the biggest turn-on. If he can move his body on the dance floor, he can move it in the bed. I don't know if that's true but I heard it once and I'll always remember it.

I don't even know what song is on, all I know is I feel the vibrations enter my ears and flow through my body like the blood flows through my veins. My body follows his and I let everything go. Nothing matters here. I can dance to anything and if X keeps this up, I think I found my dance partner. Finding a dance partner is like finding a soulmate.

The song transitions to an old nineties jam I remember my neighbor teaching me, called "*This is How We Do It.*" Expecting X to walk us off the dance floor since it's a group dance, he surprises me again. He grabs my hand, and we line up with everyone. Before we know it, we are sweaty and panting while we laugh hard. This feels so good, natural, and easy. The bass pounds against the walls and the energy surges throughout the entire house. It's a powerful feeling. This is probably why so many dance partners end up in intimate relationships. Dancing is sensual and intimate and when you share it with someone, it connects you.

Dances like this are my favorite. I turn to look at X and my stomach drops. This is a new side of him I didn't expect to see. I like it but guilt hits me at the same time. I slow down and X must notice because he grabs me, turns me, and starts to put a twist of his own on this shit, pulling me back into the moment. I love this. X is so fun. I forget about Kohen for a minute, just living in this moment, until I catch a glimpse of him on a turn. His back is to me, and a thin bleach blonde slut is rubbing his arm while she talks to him. His face is hidden, so I don't know how he is reacting. Is he smiling? Annoyed? I look down at her feet and see her black flats. What a basic bitch.

Surges of jealousy run through me, mixed with adrenaline and alcohol. I'm riding a high, and in this situation, it isn't a good thing. I can't show him that jealousy, though. The song ends and it fades into a slower country song. I recognize the song as "I Don't Dance" by Lee Brice. I wrap my arms around Xzavien's neck and tell him to lead.

"A real man always leads," he whispers, a little smirk playing on his lips. He spins me around and my arm brushes his lower back as I make my way back around his body. He really is such a good dancer. I glance back at the space where Kohen just was and see he is gone. X spins me again as the song ends and I giggle.

"What's so funny, gorgeous?"

"I don't know. I just didn't know you could dance. I like it. I'm having a good time."

"Well, that's good. That's the whole point. I have to say, I'm disappointed you don't remember the first time we danced together."

"What do you mean?" We take a seat at one of the tables set up around the room.

"We danced the first time I met you. I know you probably don't remember, it's cool. I know you were a little buzzed."

"Oh my gosh, Kohen. I'm so sorry. I really was so drunk that night... I hardly remember anything after my first drink."

"Well, are you drunk now, too? Because you just called me Kohen." A hurt look spreads across his handsome face and my gut wrenches. Even though I don't want anything romantic to do with him, he is still my friend. He has been so patient and kind over this month of getting to know each other. I wouldn't call him Kohen.

"No, I didn't," I laugh, trying to play it off like he heard me wrong. There is no way I would have called him Kohen.

"You did. Trust me, I would give anything to hear my name grace those beautiful lips." He brushes his thumb across my bottom lip, and I am stuck like a statue, afraid to even breathe. The giant room suddenly feels so small. What is he doing?

"If I did, I'm sorry, I didn't mean to. He just gets under my skin."

"It's okay, every girl I know likes Kohen. I just thought you were different." That hits me wrong.

"Just because I like someone, doesn't make me like everyone else." I stare at him intently, wanting to catch every response written on his face.

"Wow, so you admit that you like him. I thought you just said he got under your skin?"

"I'm a little confused here, X. Where is all this coming from? I thought we were friends. And yes, Kohen gets under my skin, but trust me when I say I don't want him to."

"Friends. Right! My bad. I have to go to the restroom. I'll be right back." He scoots his chair out loudly catching the attention of several tables around us and stomps off to the restroom without another word. I don't know how to act, I want to be pissed and talk shit, but I did this. I used him to make Kohen jealous, but it was all innocent fun.

Things were clear about our friendship from the beginning. I know X likes me, but I can't help that. I walk over to the bar and order a drink. I look around for X and can feel the hairs on the back of my neck rise, my senses are tingling, knowing Kohen is close. His breath brushes my ear and I feel his chest press to my back. His lips grace the spot behind my ear and flames ignite inside me, my body warming.

"Kohen," I say, barely audible.

His hand comes around my waist and he grips my love handle before moving to the front of my soft belly, lightly moving his thumb back and forth. My head falls back onto his shoulder and I sigh. His hand moves down my belly and toward the valley between my thighs. His fingers play with my hemline, and I spread my legs, wanting his touch. His fingers breach the lining of my lace thong, and he groans, pushing his hard dick against my ass. I grind my ass against it in circular motions that also push his fingers deeper between my lips. The friction from all sides is tantalizing.

"You're so wet, Angel. I just hope it's for me."

He pushes a finger into me and pulls it back out, slowly sliding up and down my slickness, gently passing it over my clit and back into me again and again.

"Yes," the word slips past my lips in a breathy sigh of pleasure.

Then he pulls away from me completely. Coldness takes over the space where he brought warmth.

"Why did you do that?" I ask, anger and annoyance lacing my tone.

"Only good girls get public affection," he smirks.

"Asshole."

He laughs his deep godly laugh. I melt and can't help but join in.

"I didn't want you to stop."

He pulls me into him, his arms sitting on the small of my back, and my hands on his chest. I stare up at him through my lashes and he kisses my nose. A small but intimate act that has my stomach turning.

"You didn't, huh?"

"Nope," I pop like the little brat I am.

He removes one of his palms from my back to grab my hand and he brings it to his face. The stubble on his cheek feels good as he rubs the back of my hand over it, his eyes shut for a split second and the feelings running through me scare me. What the fuck is happening right now? I was just with his best friend. My mind is reeling. He looks at me and smiles.

"Come on, Angel. Let's go upstairs."

Chapter 18

Kohen

(Chapter 17 POV)

Watching her dance with my best friend is launching me to a new level of jealousy I've never dealt with. I want to rip her curvy body out of his hands. Every moment I see them together pisses me off more and more. I feel like a stalker lurking in the shadows. The only reason I don't scoop her away is because I enjoy watching her. Seeing her body move, her eyes scanning the room for me. I know she's looking for me because she's with him. The sight of her in the small moments, where she doesn't feel like she has to impress anyone, when she thinks no one is looking. She'll look at herself in the reflection, or brush her hair out of her face. Even when she aimlessly plays with the chain belt on her waist. Simple moments where her guard doesn't have a reason to be sky high and her features are soft and relaxed. Those little things make my dick rock hard for her.

The fact that a girl I barely know has my attention this way blows my mind and I have a feeling it is the exact same way for her. The way she told me off the first time she met me and never backed down got under my skin. She doesn't chase me or beg me for time and attention. I like it, but the flip side is it makes me want to follow her around like a little lost puppy. That's the part I don't like-being so fucking intoxicated by her that I need a little hit. It's just lust, it has to be. The moment we fuck, it will dissipate.

As the night goes on, I entertain guests, show my face where it needs to be seen, make my donations, and finally grab a drink. It's only one drink, I won't overdo it. I want to be sober for the moment I swoop in and save her from Xzavien's boring ass.

I walk to where I saw them last and they aren't there. The long halls in my home don't help the anticipation I feel to get to her. There she is- the sight of her freezes me in my tracks, her luscious body sways to the rhythm of the beat where she stands... It's fucking teasing. No one around her notices, they are too busy chatting.

But I notice.

Sneaking up behind them slowly, I swear her body knows I'm nearby. The swaying stops and her demeanor shifts, her body now tense. She looks around discreetly but doesn't look in the direction I'm coming from. I scoot as close to her as I can without touching her and whisper in her ear. I try to get her attention so we can leave this shit show, but she stays at Xzavien's side, which makes me want to rock his shit. He knows I like her, he knows I'm interested, but he always has to try and take what's mine.

She rejects me at every point and even denies my offer to dance and ends up on the dance floor with him. I let it happen. If I wanted to stop it, I would. I'm the king of this fucking castle.

X is acting real brave tonight with her on his arm. He'll regret this, I'll make sure he remembers. My jaw hits the floor when she asks him to dance. I'll watch them dance, I want to see his hands on her, see if she likes it, if she wants him, too.

I watch them dance for a few songs and it's all good fun. They don't get too close or grind, but she looks to be having so much fun. Her face is lit up like a star in the sky. No, not a star. A star isn't worthy enough. Alex is the sun.

Everything is fine until she wraps her arms around his fucking neck. I walk away before I do something I'll regret and X would love to make a fool out of me. I need a fucking drink. I set my sights on the bar and make a beeline for it. I know I said I'd only have one, but I can't take much more of this shit. Why does she play so many fucking games? I know I left her house without a legit explanation, and I haven't had the time to text her or respond to the texts she sent me, but I told X to let her know what was going on. I'm training for the Olympic team and I don't have much time, and any time I do have is spent training. I refuse to drop out like most gymnasts. I'm guessing he didn't tell her if she is all over his dick like this.

I take several shots of El Jimador tequila, it's the best. My uncle Ruben swore by it, he would talk about it like it was gold. He could probably sell it to the distributor. I keep it stocked, even though I don't drink often because it reminds me of him. I keep seeing images of Alex dancing, she looks so free with him. Sexy as fuck regardless. Fuck!

I feel a hand rub my back and I look over my shoulder. I deflate when I see it's not Alex.

"Hey, Ko, how's it going? Drinking alone, I see. Want me to keep you company?"

"No, Sasha. I don't. I'm waiting for someone."

She rubs my shoulder, one hand on my chest leaning in with her big juicy tits practically in my face. It does nothing for me. Alex is all I want, and I want her now.

"Get the fuck away from me, Sasha. Go find some poor freshman to fuck. I'm sure there are plenty living off daddy's wallet. Hell, maybe you can fuck them both and double-dip. I don't give a fuck. All I know is I want you far away from me and fast." I take another shot and shove her hand off my shoulder. "Don't ever fucking touch me again."

It's harsh but I hate when girls just think they can touch me, not every man wants to be used as a sexual fucking toy, believe it or not. I know I'm in the minority, despite what the people in this tiny city believe. I do not fuck *nearly* as many girls as they think I do. Fuck around yes, but not all these women deserve what I have to offer and I don't mean sex.

Not even bothering to look in the direction of X and Alex, I run to the restroom. All these shots have me needing to piss.

I come back buzzed, not drunk. My alcohol tolerance is too high to be drunk off a few shots. A few people stop me to talk but I just want to get back to the bar. I'm sure Alex left with X by now.

I look up and couldn't be happier that I'm wrong. That sexy crazy girl is sitting at the bar, *my* bar, as if she is waiting for me. Because I'm buzzed, I'm brave, braver than I already am on a regular basis because my lips touch her skin and *fuckkk*. She feels good, her skin is soft underneath my lips. She smells like fucking heaven. I need to know what that perfume is, it drives me crazy. My arm wraps around her and things escalate quickly between us right here in front of everybody. I need her now. She is so wet.

I stop, her frustration is written on her face and laced in her tone but I don't care. This little brat is going to learn to be a good girl. I pull her into me and I don't know what fucking possesses me, but I kiss her nose. I kiss her fucking nose! I bring her hand to my face and rub the back of it across my midnight shadow. My eyes close unwillingly because her skin feels so fucking delicious against mine. My dick is so hard, I think it will explode. The feeling of skin on skin never felt so fucking good. Better than sex, if possible. It comforts me like something I've never felt before.

I don't know what the fuck I'm doing but I know I'm doing it with her.

"Come on, Angel. Let's go upstairs." I take her hand and lead her to the stairway at the end of the grand hall. She follows close, one of her hands wrapped in mine and the other holding my arm. We make our way to the second floor and then the third. We're both out of breath and buzzed. I place my finger on the pad and it beeps, letting us know it's open. Her eyes are wide and wandering. I push the door open, and she passes in front of me to get through the doorway, smelling fucking amazing.

Chapter 19

Alex

The size of Kohen's bedroom is mind-blowing. It's like a whole apartment set inside the middle of this huge fucking house. He has an open living room with black leather couches and a huge glass coffee table set in front of it- also black. There are touches of gold everywhere but I can see the theme of this entire room is black on black. It's sleek and gorgeous like him.

"Is this all yours?"

"Yep, like it?"

I do but I won't admit it. "You have another kitchen up here?" I scoff.

"Yes, this is my private quarters, two bedrooms, a game room, office, and kitchen."

"And no bathroom?" I ask, one eyebrow up in question. He smooths it with his thumb and the simple touch ignites me. I can feel my breath speeding up, my chest rising and falling a little faster.

"Of course, I have a restroom, Angel. Want me to show you?"

"Yes," I say without thinking. Why the fuck do I want to see the restroom? In my head, I heard him ask me if I wanted to do something much dirtier.

Taking my hand in his, he walks me through a short hallway and we pass the kitchen. Surprise- black marble and black appliances. We reach the door of the restroom, and he uses his hand as if to show me the way. I turn the knob, push it open, and my jaw drops. I think I even drool on the floor and I'll gladly lick it up.

The bathroom is one huge room. There's a glass box in the far corner with a huge platform showerhead. I bet it's one of those rain ones. Making my way further in, there's a bidet and a toilet, and his and hers sinks. My stomach drops at the thought of him sharing this space with someone, but I snuff those emotions away because we are nothing but an infatuation to each other. There is a garden tub with eucalyptus and lavender, the same thing I have in my restroom.

I look over my shoulder at him and he is brushing his teeth. What an odd thing to do at a time like this. I run my fingers over the smooth counter. I am pleasantly surprised that this room is actually all white. The gold accents still litter the space, from the handles on the sink and toilet, to the little specks embedded in the counters.

"This is gorgeous, Kohen. I know this is going to sound weird, but I love bathrooms. Like, I am obsessed with them. I have *Better Home* magazines that focus primarily on restrooms. If I ever do anything in my life to where I can own my own home, I want a bathroom just like this."

I turn around and see he is leaning against the sink, ankles and arms crossed, just looking at me. A huge smile adorns his gorgeous face.

"What?"

"Nothing, I just think it's cute that you are so happy about a restroom."

"This is NOT a restroom, this is a bathroom."

"Okay, bathroom," he chuckles.

"It's not funny. There is definitely a difference."

Something strange possesses me and before I know it, I'm moving toward him. I plant myself directly in front of him. He uncrosses his legs and his arms and pulls me against his body. My small feet sit in the middle of his big ones. I wrap my arms around his neck, my fingertips barely touching because he is so tall. He leans down and kisses me. Something about the kiss sends a vibration of warmth through my body. The kiss isn't sexual- it's soft and intimate. I pull away and look up at him.

"Why did you do that?"

"Do what? Kiss you?" Confusion etches his face.

"Yeah."

"Because I wanted to."

"Well, don't." I walk out of the restroom and back out to the living room, eyeing the front door. I look back and he isn't following me. Pausing to calm my racing mind, I sit on the couch, waiting for him to walk in here.

"Why don't you want me to kiss you?"

Is he really talking to me all the way from the bathroom? I take my heels off and walk back over there on a mission to talk shit when I see him standing in front of the mirror in just his boxers. I'm a little shocked because I wasn't expecting him to be brave enough to just be walking around almost naked. It takes a few moments to register all the tattoos I never noticed before. He has several big pieces on his back and chest, as well as some trailing down his arms. How did I miss them?

"Why don't you want me to kiss you?" he asks with floss in his hand, pulling me out of my trance.

"Why are you brushing your teeth and flossing right now?"

"Answer me first." He tosses the floss in the small metal trash can and I roll my eyes.

"Because you kissed me all nice and soft and I didn't like it?"

"How do you want me to kiss you?"

"I don't know, Kohen, like normal, but don't change the subject. Why are you going through your whole dental routine right at this moment?"

"Because I drank."

"And?"

"And I struggle with alcohol, so I want the flavor out of my mouth."

"Oh."

"Yeah, oh."

"Sorry, I didn't know."

"It's cool, I'm done anyway. Let's go watch a movie and I promise I won't kiss you nice or soft." He chuckles again and I melt.

"Fine, but only if you pinky promise."

"Oooh a pinky promise, huh? Okay."

Sticking his pinky in the air, I wrap my little one around it and my pussy just about purrs out loud because he kisses it. He fucking kisses it. I quickly let go as if his touch burns me. Grabbing my hand, he wraps his pinky around mine and puts it to my lips. I kiss it softly without a word and he pulls me by our connected pinkies and leads me back into the living room.

"You have cute feet."

I look down at my feet. "Oh, sorry. My feet hurt so I took the heels off before I walked back to your restroom."

"Don't apologize, babe. Mi casa es su casa." He throws himself back on the couch and I join him. He instantly places his huge hand on my thigh and it feels so good.

"I had no idea this was up here, or that you even had a third floor. It's beautiful."

"Thank you, there is one more floor but the only access is through my room. There are no other doors on this floor."

"What is it? Another apartment?"

"No, no, it's a rooftop patio."

"But you have a huge backyard. Why do you need a patio on the roof?"

"I needed space that was just mine since X and the guys live here. I am wealthy enough and don't want any of them to have to pay rent or worry about anything other than school, so I let them all live here with me. That was always the plan when we had it built."

"Right when I think I have you figured out, you shock me again."

"What do you mean?"

"I expected you to be a rich pretentious asshole like all the others I've met, but money doesn't seem to faze you or affect who you are."

"Well, my mom had a big part to do with that. She was poor and her family worked for my father's family. She went to high school with him because they lived in our area and my grandfather paid for her and her brother's education. He says she was the most beautiful woman he had ever met, he was a jock, and she was a cheerleader. She didn't have to be rich to fit in because she was an amazing human being. She wanted to be a model and an actress, and she was for a while, until she got pregnant with me."

I notice he talks about her as if she isn't here anymore, but I don't ask.

"Well, she did an amazing job because, other than you ghosting me, it looks like you're a pretty good guy."

"I try, and I didn't ghost you. I just got really busy. I'm a gymnast and I'm training for the Olympics. Usually, when you're training, you quit school pretty young to train full-time, but I wanted to finish. I want a career to fall back on."

"You could have just told me. It would have saved me from a lot of toxic behavior."

"You toxic? No!" I smack him on the shoulder, and he pulls me closer to him. "I'm sorry you thought I ghosted you, I am just a very busy guy. And you, Alex Monroe, were unexpected."

I smile, and before I know it his lips are on mine. I'm not sure who kisses who first, but I decide I don't care. I grab his head and pull him deeper into our kiss and I feel his hands in my hair tugging gently on the long locks. I climb on his lap, and I feel his hard length under me. I quiver, squeezing him between my thighs.

Before we can get any further, a knock sounds on the door. Kohen huffs in frustration.

"Hey, Kohen, are you in there, bro?"

It's Xzavien. Guilt hits me like a Mack truck and nausea follows. Kohen stands up, heading to the door and I follow. Might as well rip the band-aid off. I told him we were just friends. Kohen can't turn the door knob any slower. I don't know how X will react, but I really don't give a fuck. The door opens.

"Hey, have you seen Alex..." Before he finishes his sentence, X's eyes meet mine, and devastation is written all over his face.

"Yeah, bro. She's here. What's up?"

"Nah, it's good. I was just making sure she was safe. Y'all have a good night."

He walks away without another word, head hanging low. I hate to admit that I don't want to chase him. I know that's fucked up, but Kohen closes the door, deciding for me.

"Should we go after him?" I ask, following him back to the couch.

"Not unless you want to go home with him. He knows I like you. I told him a few weeks ago, which brings me back to this past week. Did he not tell you what I was up to?"

"No, he never mentioned you, and we texted a lot." He raises a brow, a touch of jealousy in his eyes. "Was he supposed to tell me? Because that should have been you."

"I told him to tell you that I was training."

"What? He never told me anything." That pisses me off and now I'm glad that I didn't go after him. Fuck him. That's fucked up.

"It doesn't surprise me that he didn't tell you, but like you said, I should have just done it myself. He is my best friend, and I should be able to trust him. But then he does shit like this. I don't know if it's jealousy or what, but we are fucking grown now."

"Enough about him." I slowly climb back on his lap.

"Fine with me." He tugs at my hair gently, causing my head to roll back.

"So do you bring all your little girlfriends to this sexy bachelor pad?" I have a playful tone, but I find myself seriously wanting to know and I hate it.

"Nope, I've never brought a girl up here before. My ex came close, but it never happened."

"Shut up, you don't have to lie. I'm a big girl and we aren't together, so you can stop with all that." I start to climb off, turned off by the bullshit he's spewing to try and get in my pants.

"I'm not fucking around. We were about to fuck before X knocked on the door. So, I'm being honest, but I do have a question for you- do you like him? Because you showed up to my party with him."

"Yes, I came here with X, but I told him we were just friends from the beginning. If you wanted me to come here alone, you should have invited me yourself."

"That's where you're wrong, Angel. I think you very much wanted to know. I think it bothers your pretty little fucked up head to think of me inside another girl. I'll tell you right here, right now- I don't want you with X. I don't want you with anyone other than me, and I don't need any other woman. I'm... selective."

"Well, I can show you the texts that I have nothing to hide. X and I will never be a thing, even if you didn't exist. Besides..." I hesitate, choosing my next words wisely. "The reason I was at the bar in the first place was because I called him Kohen." Rolling my eyes, I look away, embarrassed by my own admission. I just gave him a little bit of ammo against me and I don't like it.

"You called him by my name?" he asks, his smirk quickly turning into a huge radiant smile, dimples on full display. My heart fucking melts.

He pulls me back down roughly on top of him and grinds upward into me, his big hands kneading my ass like Play-Doh. It hurts a little but in the best way, making me tingle all over. He peppers kisses on my skin, setting little fires with each peck.

"I'm telling you right now, no other woman has graced this fucking room but the maid."

"How do I know you didn't fuck her in here?" My lips are a whisper from his.

"Because she's my aunt."

Thank fuck. I roll my back and grind my pussy onto his hard dick, moaning at the contact.

"Fuuuck, Angel." He licks his thick lips and looks down at where our bodies make contact.

"You make me feel crazy, Kohen Ventura."

"Same to you, Alex Monroe. You awakened a monster in me, and I don't know what it is about you, but I don't think I have it in me to let you go now. Can I take this off?"

It's about damn time he asks. "Yes, please, I want to feel your skin on mine."

Butterflies fill me as he removes my top, my heart is pounding, and my mind is reeling. Every sense is alive like a live wire waiting to make contact with something or someone. Him. We kiss a deep, electrifying kiss.

Coming up for breath, I whisper without thinking, "I want you, Kohen."

He pulls back and looks into my eyes. I don't know what he sees there but he smirks a little. "You want me, Angel?"

My hands fly up to my face in embarrassment. He leans forward, trying to pull them away from my face. I'm so stupid- why the fuck did I say that?

"What's the matter- cat got your tongue?" he laughs, tickling me. "What did you say, Angel? I didn't hear you."

I cave. "I want you!" I'm practically yelling it, our laughter filling the room.

"I never wanted anything more in my life and it scares the shit out of me. We don't even know each other, but...something about you just draws me to you. I'm not used to it." His face is serious now, something I don't recognize in his hazel eyes. They are darker than they were before. I bite my lip, waiting for the next words to grace his lips. "Fuck, Alex. I want you too, baby. You are so fucking beautiful." He grabs my face in his palm.

"You have no idea how fucking happy you just made me."

He pulls my face to his, our lips collide, and it's euphoric. This thing we have, it feels like we have been fighting against it, trying to pull apart like magnets but giving in feels so good, so easy. So, I do. I fully let myself give in just this once hoping to God or whoever that it doesn't crash and burn.

"Fuck me," I say in between kisses, my hands buried in his curly hair, tugging at the short strands. "Please, Kohen. Fuck me."

I stand up again so he can remove my skirt. Seconds feel like minutes as he does, and my body misses the warmth of his. He examines my body like a piece of art, staring at me, his hands running down my hips, to my thighs... He slaps my thigh and shock runs through me, pain and then pleasure. Heat spreads through me and I know I'm soaking wet. He traces a thick, white stretch mark that runs along my hip, and then brings his face to it, kissing it. I take a deep breath, the feeling foreign. His hot tongue traces the line back down and then he bites my inner thigh, pain, then pleasure. What the fuck is he doing?

He pulls off my black lace thong and tosses it on the floor behind me, then follows up by removing my bra and tosses that, too.

"Turn around, baby." I listen without pause. Wanting him to see my round ass. "Holy fucking shit, Angel, you are fucking perfect."

Smack.

His palm hits my ass and I whimper from the little sting.

"Sit down, baby."

I turn to sit on him. He pushes me back the other way and pulls me down, my ass on his lap. The only thing between us is his boxers. I feel him hard under me and I want nothing more than to have him inside me. I lay back and open my legs, and as if he reads my mind, his hands snake around me and run down my body. He stares at my breasts. Pinching each nipple and circling his finger around, making goosebumps erupt around them. He makes his way down, grazing over my soft belly, his touch becoming a little firmer when he runs his fingers over it, making his way to the valley between my legs. His fingers reach the soft skin of my pussy, and he spreads my lips with his fingers. I grind into him, the simple pleasure causing waves to roll through me. I want him inside me now!

"God damn, Angel, you are so fucking wet."

In a breathy voice, I respond, "For you, yes. You make me feel so good, Kohen."

"Say my name again, baby."

"Kohen, please."

His fingers circle my clit and a spasm runs through my legs, making them tighten in response. He runs them through my wetness. He finds my entrance and uses his middle finger to fuck me. As he glides in and out of me, his palm rubs my clit at the right moment each time, making me feel like I'm losing control. Then something happens inside me I have never felt before- his middle finger reaches a spot that makes me come almost instantly. A gush of fluid comes with it. I don't know what the fuck it is, but I love it. The waves slow down and Kohen pulls his finger out of me.

"I'm sorry," I say shyly. "That's never happened before."

"What are you sorry for? I fucking loved it, and I love it even more now that I know you have never done it before."

He pulls down his boxers and his cock bounces freely from the confines of them. It's big and thick, and although I'm no virgin, it has been a while. I hope it doesn't hurt. I want so badly for him to make me feel good. He licks his finger and spits it in his palm rubbing it around his dick.

"You're mine now, Alex. Do you hear me?"

"I hear you, but you have to show me because I don't listen well."

"Fucking brat, get up."

He stands up and turns me to face him, then picks me up and I wrap my legs around him instinctively, placing my hands around his neck. I've never fucked like this, because let's face it, I'm a thick girl.

"Am I too heavy?"

"No, baby. You are perfect, and all this ass and thighs make fucking you even better. One, because it's something to hold onto, two it feels good in my fucking hands, and three it makes my dick so hard thinking about what it will sound like to pound into this tight little pussy. How hard I can fuck you with all this plump cushion..."

I reach down between us and grab his thickness in my hand, leading it to my entrance. I watch his eyes as I place him in the perfect spot to enter me and he pushes into me.

We both gasp audibly and instantly our lips meet. His hands are holding me up by my ass, grasping me hard as he drives into me. His massive cock tears through my tight walls, and it feels fucking delicious.

"Ruin me, Kohen. Make me yours and only yours."

He grunts as he fucks me harder and faster. He is so strong and fucks me like a ragdoll, like I am as light as the air surrounding us. My pussy clenches around him, grasping him tighter and he lets me know he likes it by the way his dick pulses inside me, reaching deeper and deeper with each thrust.

"Fuckkk, baby, you feel so fucking good."

The noises our bodies are making because of my wetness dripping between us.

"You are so fucking wet, I love it. This. Pussy. Is. Mine."

"Yes, it's yours now. Keep going, harder."

I use the grasp I have around his neck as a counterweight and grind my pussy into him every time he thrusts back in. "Let's go to your bed. I know I have to be getting heavy."

He isn't complaining but I want him to enjoy fucking me and to be able to completely let go. I also don't want to worry about how heavy I must be.

"No, I'm gonna fuck you right here until we both come, then we are going to take a bath and go to bed and fuck again." He turns and my back hits the wall. I lean back and he groans. "That pretty pussy looks so good swallowing up my cock. You're such a good girl."

Oh my god. This man is fucking heaven-sent, or maybe it's hell that sent him. My karma for breaking men's hearts. He pounds into me hard. Since my weight is on the wall, he releases one ass cheek and starts to play with my clit with delicious circle motions as he grinds his pelvic bone into me. He rolls his body into me like waves into the sand.

"Come for me, baby. Show me how good I make you feel."

My body listens like he is in charge of her, and she comes. She comes harder than she has ever come before, tears rolling down my face as my body releases.

"Oh my god, Kohen. I'm coming, I'm coming."

With one hand on my ass and one reaching up behind my neck, he pushes me down onto him hard and I half whimper, half moan. What the fuck?

"Ahhh, fuck yes. This pussy feels so fucking good."

Thrust. Grind. *This is heaven.*

Black spots cloud my vision and he grunts, his forehead meeting the top of my head. His chest heaves while his cock pulses inside me. Hot come fills me. I can feel the mixture of us running down my thighs.

"Fuck, Angel. That felt so good. It's like you were made for me."

"Same. Sex has never felt like that."

I unwrap my legs from his waist, and he removes himself from me. I'm still pinned to the wall in front of him and he just stares at me. Both hands are on the sides of my head as he cranes his neck and kisses me softly on the lips.

"You are going to be trouble aren't you, Angel? I just know it."

I smirk. "If you know it, then why ask?"

I stand on my tiptoes to kiss him and he pulls back. I smack his arm and he laughs, reaching down to kiss me. When our lips meet, a little shock electrifies us both and we pull back at the same time, looking at each other suspiciously, but neither of us mention it. He kisses me again as if to see if it happens again, and it doesn't.

"Let's go shower, baby."

Giddy emotions overtake me. He smacks my ass and I lead him to the bathroom, excited to get under that shower, and even more excited that it will be with him.

Chapter 20

Alex

We climb in the hot shower and the scent of the eucalyptus and lavender engulfs us. The shower head above us pours down on our bodies like a rainstorm. The space between us is less than a foot but it's too much. I reach out and touch him. Loving his muscular body, I run my hands down his abs.

I look up at him and he's already staring at me. My heart flutters, releasing butterflies in my stomach. I bite my lip, withholding a smile.

He's smiling, the dimple in his cheek that drives me crazy on full display. He takes a step closer to me, causing my hand to rest on his chest instead of his abs. His heart is pounding hard beneath my palm. It's like a fortune telling me he wants me as bad as I want him. His hands find my waist, squeezing the soft flesh there. He pulls me to his body. One of his large hands slaps my ass, causing me to yelp, while the other finds my lips. They part for him and he runs his thumb over my bottom lip. Water runs down my face as I stare up at this man, no not a man, a God. He pushes his thumb into my mouth and like it's second nature, my lips wrap around it to suck on it gently. His dick is rock hard and pressing up against my belly. I wrap my small hand around it, pumping gently, and his head rolls back.

"Fuck, Angel," leaves his lips in a whisper. So quiet that I almost didn't hear it with the sound of the water.

His thumb leaves my mouth as his body goes a little slack. I keep pumping as I stare at him. I study his chest rising and falling as he leans against the shower wall. His eyes are closed but the expression on his face tells me enough. I slowly move down to the tiled floor so that he doesn't know what I'm about to do. I keep my eyes on his face as I take him into my mouth and his eyes shoot open.

"Oh my god, baby. You look so sexy on your knees for me."

I clench my thighs together, feeling the rush of my body reacting to his praise. His hands find my hair and he moves it from my face.

"I want to see you, while you suck my dick. Such a pretty girl."

My pussy must be dripping now and his words just make me want to please him more. I swirl my tongue around his tip as I bob my head up and down, making sure I place close attention to the sensitive skin at the tip. His dick twitches in my mouth every time my tongue runs over it and I fucking love it. I feel in control here, powerful.

I cup his balls as I run my tongue down the side of his length and he sighs.

"Yes, Angel. Take my cock like a good girl." He bucks his hips into my mouth, and his eyes widen in surprise when I don't gag. "Oh, you're a filthy little slut. Aren't you, Angel?"

I nod in agreement, continuing my assault. He pumps into my throat faster and I moan around his dick.

"Fuckkk, Alex. I need to fuck you right fucking now."

He slaps my ass hard and turns me around. I place my hands on the bench in front of us and spread my legs open for him. I look over my shoulder at him and he pumps his cock a few times, examining my most intimate parts displayed for him like a piece of art.

He steps forward and inserts his fingers into me all the way to the knuckle and swirls them around inside me. "So wet for me, Angel." He removes his fingers and replaces them with his thick cock, stretching me open for him.

"Oh my God," I say as he fills me up.

He pumps in and out of me deliciously. I thrust my ass towards him, meeting him thrust for thrust and it feels so fucking good. I feel his hands gripping my ass and spreading my cheeks apart as he pulls me into him so he is in the deepest part of my core.

"I want to fill every pretty hole you have, Alex. I want every single part of you to be marked by me, to belong to me. Do you understand, Angel?" I tighten around him, gripping him with how turned on I am right now. He slaps my ass. "Do. You. Understand?" Each thrust is a delicious punishment for not answering quickly.

"Yes."

"Yes, *what,* Angel?"

"I understand." I moan in pleasure.

"Good girl."

I feel his fingers circle the last place he has yet to fill. If I'm honest, no one has fucked me there.

He pushes a finger just past the surface and thrusts forward. He's still fucking me when he pushes into my ass. Although it's uncomfortable for a second, the sensation is different. It makes the way he's fucking me feel... Even better?

"Oh my god, Kohen. Why does it feel so good?"

I push into his hand and dick simultaneously, causing rolls of pleasure to roll through my body. "Fuck me harder, Kohen," I beg and he does. He fucks me like a rag doll as he uses his angle and his grasp on my body to pound into me. Grinding his pelvis into me as his finger fucks my ass, I come. I come the hardest I ever have in my life. My legs are shaking and my pussy must have his dick in a chokehold with how hard I'm coming.

"Oh, fuck yeah, baby. Your pussy is so tight." He thrusts into me a few more times, moving the hand holding my waist to my hair, and he pulls me into him as he comes inside me. I feel his cock throbbing as my pussy milks every drop. He leaves himself inside me as we catch our breath. He removes his finger from my ass and places both hands on either side of me. He kisses my shoulder and moves back, removing himself from inside me. I feel the emptiness immediately but I try not to let it bother me.

The first intrusive thought hits. *You were too easy, he's going to hit it and quit it.* I don't let it settle. I get up and move to wrap my arms around him. He kisses my forehead and then my lips. That's the small security I needed at the moment.

"That felt so fucking good, Angel," he smiles at me as he backs away to grab some soap.

"I know it did, huh?" I ask playfully.

We laugh and he holds the soap out to me. I open my hand so he can squirt some in my palm. We spend the rest of the time just rinsing the sex off our bodies quietly. A few kisses and smiles are exchanged. What was supposed to be a quick shower turned into a second round of sex but neither one of us is complaining.

Chapter 21

Kohen

My thoughts keep circling back to Alex. I can't even focus on training, so I give up, heading for the locker room. I just know this girl is going to drive me fucking nuts. I'm okay with it, though. She is different and so fucking beautiful. I'm unsure what my next move looks like, but I know I want her to be a part of it.

It's been a week since the party, the first time we fucked. She let me fuck her, not just once but three times in one night. I didn't expect to fuck her pretty mouth in the shower but she seemed so turned on by the rain and the jets, and the fact that we both had lavender and eucalyptus in our bathrooms. I didn't get the fascination, but she sucked my dick so good that I thought she drained every ounce of come, swallowing it like a pretty little slut.

She finally unblocked me, and we have been texting, although X still tries to text as well. He has been giving me the cold shoulder and I don't understand why. He knew I fucking liked her and he was pursuing her behind my back. Shit's fucked up. I'm sick of him wanting what I have and trying to take what's mine. He can't have Alex- he will ruin her. Everyone thinks Xzavien is this good guy, but they will see his truth eventually. Fucking snake.

I can tell Alex is loyal, though, and probably to a fault. She is guarded as well and doesn't get too emotional or close. She pushes a little and I like it. Submission is a privilege and I want to earn it.

My phone pings while I shower and decide it can wait. I want to finish quickly and get to Alex's house. I'm going to surprise her with our first date. I yank my sweatpants up my legs and around my waist. My deodorant falls to the floor and X steps up, grabbing it.

"Hey, bro. What's up?"

Pulling a white T over my head, I nod, grabbing my deodorant from him so I can put some on. "Just getting ready to go see Alex."

"With a wrinkled shirt like that?" I could smack the smirk off his fucking face.

"It probably won't stay on long anyway."

His eyes widen and I see the shock hit his face for a moment. He wasn't expecting me to be so forward. I don't give a fuck. "Well, she's outside of the locker room waiting, so it may be a little hard to fuck her in front of everybody out there," he laughs. I grab my shit and jet for the exit.

Looks like neither of us is playing when it comes to this girl, but I never lose. X knows that.

I see her hustling away from the locker room doors.

"Alex, wait!"

She looks over her shoulder at me and quickens her pace, but it doesn't take long for my long legs to catch up.

"What the fuck, Angel? I was calling you. Where are you going?"

"I heard what you said to X. Your shirt won't stay on long?" The anger in her eyes is tangible, her chest is heaving and she's shaking under my hand. "I'm not some slut you can just fuck whenever or wherever you want."

"You're not." I push her body against the wall, closing her in. There's nowhere for her to run and she has backed herself into a corner. I kiss her and she turns her face away from me. She's breathing even harder now.

"No, I'm not! Let me go."

"No."

"Why?"

"Because you want me to fuck you, right here, right now, in front of all these dick heads, so they get a little taste of what it's like to fuck a queen like you." She smiles like I thought she would and I try to kiss her again. This time, she lets me. She makes me pay, though, biting my lip hard, pulling blood. "I promise I didn't mean it like it sounded. He was being a dick, and I wanted him to know that pussy is mine."

"Just because I let you fuck me once doesn't make it yours. It was yours for the moment."

"For three moments," I correct her. "Wait. My bad- one of those moments, it was your mouth that was mine." I rub my chin as if trying to remember, and she smacks me on the arm.

"You're an asshole."

"A sexy asshole who you like inside your juicy wet cunt."

She bites her lip and pushes her body against me. She rubs her hand over my hard cock and smacks it. It knocks a little air out of me and she laughs.

"Stop being a dick."

"You are going to pay for that one, Angel."

"Oh yeah?"

"Hell yeah."

"Well, can I pay for it later? We have somewhere to be."

That triggers the question I had for her. I step back and take in her appearance. She looks like she is dressed for a date. X must have seen her out here looking so fucking delicious. I look like I just got some wrinkly clothes out of my bag. Well, I did. I was going to surprise her with a date night in, Netflix and chill, but it seems like she has other plans.

"What are you doing here?" I ask.

"If you don't want me here, I'll leave." She turns to walk away. Goddamn, this girl is going to be the death of me.

"I just mean I was headed to your house to surprise you, and you are here surprising me... So I'm just wondering."

She smiles, I love seeing her smile. "Well, I'm glad you didn't make it because I hate surprises."

I laugh so loud, it echoes through the gym. "But you are here to surprise me. Right now. Make it make sense, babe."

"Just shut up and come with me."

"I'll follow you anywhere, Alex Monroe." For dramatic effect, I place my hand over my heart, and she rolls her eyes.

"Just shut up and come on."

I follow her because I'm just glad she is here. She came here, wanted to surprise me and hang out. Great minds really do think alike. I'll take this as a sign that I'm headed in the right direction with her.

Chapter 22

Alex

We climb into Kohen's car. I'm nervous as fuck. I wanted to surprise him while he was in the shower, but I ran into X and he assured me Kohen was busy with the trainers. I'm having a hard time believing he has any bad intentions with our friendship but maybe I'm just being naive. I never trust anyone, but X has been a good friend to me. He has been patient and earned my trust to an extent.

I shake away thoughts of him. I'm with Kohen right now and I want to focus on that. He terrifies me- that's for damn sure. My usual scare tactics don't work with him. I've been a stressed-out raging bitch this week and he has taken everything I've thrown at him and spun it around on me, making me laugh and forget why I was even upset in the first place.

I like him but I fucking hate that I like him. I don't want to. I wanted to show him he couldn't have me, that I wouldn't fall for his playboy ways...and then I fucked him. I shake my head and that catches his attention.

"What's wrong?"

"Nothing. I'm just mad."

"At me? What did I do now?" he laughs, and I roll my eyes and look out the window so he doesn't see my smile.

"I'm mad at myself." Crossing my arms and wiping the smile from my face, I look his way. He's so gorgeous. It isn't fair that he gets to look that good in a wrinkled white t-shirt and gray sweatpants. My mother's little voice of doubt enters my mind and I shudder.

"Men like him don't like chubby girls like you. I'm not being mean- it's just the truth. Ask anyone."

"Taking accountability today, are we?" he laughs.

I shake her voice from my mind and look into his eyes. He is staring out at the road, one hand on the steering wheel and the other running over the stubble on his chin. I watch the way his chest rises and falls. Why the fuck is it making me feel...peaceful? What's wrong with me? He catches me staring and switches hands on the wheel, now placing his free hand on my thigh and squeezing lightly.

"What's up, Angel? You look like you're going to be sick. Need me to pull into the next store for some water or something?"

"No, I'm okay. I just felt a little lightheaded."

"Let's go grab some food, huh? What do you want?"

Deciding that's how I'm going to say *fuck you* to the voice in my head, I'm going to pig the fuck out. If Kohen doesn't like it, he can kick fucking rocks.

"Let's go to 54th Street DraftHouse."

"Hell yeah. Burgers and beers. You're a woman after my own heart."

He's suddenly staring at me so intently that it's making me uncomfortable. Is he mad?

"What?" I say rudely.

"Put your seatbelt on."

"What? Why?"

"Safety first, babe. If you don't buckle up, I'm pulling over."

"Are you serious? No, I hate my seatbelt."

"Well, that's just careless. Put it on- I'm serious."

"No," I laugh.

I'm shocked when he actually hits the blinker, gets in his right lane, and pulls onto the side of the road.

"Oh my god! Okay, I'll put it on." I pull the stupid strap over my body and click the buckle into place, making a big dramatic show of it. "There, happy?"

"Ecstatic," he says.

"You don't even know what ecstatic means."

"I heard that."

"I meant for you to hear it."

We make eye contact and I have every intention of giving attitude, but when I see the pride on his face from getting me to put on my seatbelt, I smile. We break out into laughter.

Only Kohen Ventura can make me so fucking giddy and stupid. I just don't know if that's a good thing or not.

He puts his other blinker on and merges into the lane, continuing our trek to the restaurant. I turn to look out the window and close my eyes, listening to the tires on the pavement. Suddenly, I hear him shift in his seat, so I look at him in the reflection of the window. I see him staring at me, contemplating whatever it is he wants to do. Then he softly rests his hand on my thigh, palm open, eyes back on the road. He quietly releases a breath that he was holding.

I don't know why, but at that moment, my stomach turns upside down and inside out. The butterflies release into my chest, and my heart feels funny. Even though it isn't sexual, something about the simple touch feels so much more intimate than anything I've ever experienced. Something inside of me shifted when I just saw the way he was looking at me and didn't know I was watching.

This date is a bad idea. I close my eyes again, hoping that I'm just imagining all of this. It's an illusion in my head just like my mom's voice. I zone back in on the sounds outside my window, and he raises the volume of the song on the radio, quietly singing along.

Please, God. I don't want to fall for this man. He will be the end of me, I just know it.

The car slows down and I open my eyes. Sure enough, 54th Street Draft House is coming up on the right of us. He pulls in and I unbuckle my seatbelt early, earning a side eye from him.

"Calm down, daddy. I won't fly out of the windshield while you're going five miles an hour."

"Mmm, call me daddy one more time."

"Ew no. I mean to each their own, but daddy kink is not my thing, so get that shit out of your head right now."

"What about papi then?" He laughs and I want to kiss his stupid face so bad.

The car turns off and he gets out and runs around to open my door, like he has the few times I've been in his car. That's something I'll have to get used to. He grabs my hand, and our fingers intertwine, ripples of energy reverberate through my body at his simple touch. He leads us into the restaurant, opening every door like a perfect gentleman but I know he isn't. I know what words leave that filthy mouth and how those fingers feel inside me.

The hostess flirts with him and he doesn't even pay attention to her. I love it. Also, something I'll have to get used to. Even though he isn't paying any attention to her, I want to knock her the fuck out for trying while she clearly sees we are together. She seats us and when she walks away, she places her hand on his arm and I pretend not to notice.

"Let me know if you need anything, anything at all."

Desperate, much? I watch him out of the corner of my eye as he removes her hand from his shoulder a little aggressively.

"Don't touch me again. Don't pretend like you can't see my girlfriend sitting right next to me. That is very disrespectful. Now walk away before I call your manager over and report you."

"I'm sorry, sir. I was just being kind."

"No, you were being a thirsty slut. Now go."

My jaw must be on the floor because he stares at me like I have two heads.

"What's wrong?"

"I can't believe you just did that."

"She was disrespecting you and I don't play that shit."

"I've just never experienced anything like that before. Every guy I have been with ALWAYS hits on the waitress."

"Not this one. Even if we were just here as friends, she wouldn't know that, so I'm not about to entertain it."

He picks up his menu, not giving it another thought, and my stomach drops. Suddenly it doesn't feel as special, he said he would do it even if he was here with someone as friends. That's fine. It's stupid that I thought I was a little bit special.

Picking up my menu to hide the disappointment on my face, I skim, not really able to focus. I look around the restaurant at the decor that's placed all over the walls. There are vintage signs and art everywhere. There are statues of the Blues Brothers dancing on one of the half walls, and I remember watching that with Cora and her brother because we didn't have a tv. I look back at the menu, but I feel too overwhelmed to choose, so I stare at the ceiling where there is a huge box car hanging next to a canoe and some tires. What the hell would happen if those fell? Damn intrusive thoughts, it's all I can imagine now. Thanks, brain.

The waitress comes up and asks if we are ready to order. I have no idea where I mentally went for the last however many minutes.

"Do you know what you want, Angel?"

"No, sorry, can we have some more time?"

"Yes, of course. Take your time. I'll be back in about ten minutes to check on y'all again," she smiles at me and then at Kohen and walks away.

"What's the matter, babe?"

"Nothing. I'm just in my own head."

"I can tell."

"How can you tell? You barely know me."

"I know enough. Besides, I can feel your energy. It's been off since I told the hostess to fuck off. Did you think that was rude?"

"No, nothing like that. I guess I just couldn't focus."

"Well here- let's make it a game."

"A game? How?"

"What's your favorite drink?"

"Root beer."

"Favorite food?"

"I can't pick- there's too many." I reach for the menu to see again, and he raises it out of my reach. "Kohen, give it."

"Pizza, wings, or burgers?" he asks.

"Not pizza. That's too much bread."

"Wings or burgers?"

"A burger."

"Okay, fries or tots?"

"Fries," I smile. He just keeps surprising me.

"See? Done. I got you, Angel."

I lean in and kiss him without thinking. His hands run through my hair and we got lost in the moment. I feel the moisture between my legs and move my hand to check if he's hard. He is. I moan into his mouth. He bites me.

"I can come back in five minutes if you need more time."

Pulling away, lips swollen, hair a mess, I smile, and my cheeks burn with embarrassment. "It's okay. We're ready."

Kohen places our order and the waitress leaves to put it in.

"Can I ask you something?"

"Sure, baby, what's up?"

"What are we doing, Kohen? This is weird isn't it?"

"What's weird about it?"

"I feel like we barely know each other, but at the same time it's like I've known you forever."

"I feel the same way, but I have felt that way since the moment I first met you."

"What? That's impossible."

"Why is it impossible? Things go unexplained in the world every day. Why can't I feel an instant attraction or connection with a beautiful girl who doesn't take my shit?"

"I don't know."

"Exactly. You don't know, and neither do I, but that's why it's okay. There doesn't need to be an explanation for everything. If there was, we wouldn't have the wonders of the world, right?"

His logic is crazy but makes sense and I feel silly for thinking otherwise. People fall in love in weirder ways, I'm sure. I think of the instant connection that my favorite characters make in my books. It's possible, like Everlynne and Seph from *Beautiful Graves* by LJ Shen, or Hardin and Tessa from *After* by Anna Todd. They weren't in love or anything right away, but it was an instant pull to the other for unknown reasons neither could explain. I feel like that could be scientifically possible. I can't be this fucking crazy.

Those are books, though, the little devil on my shoulder reminds me.

That's not possible for you.

You aren't that special, my mom's voice echoes in my head.

Maybe she's right. I don't deserve someone like Kohen. He deserves better than me, the broken doll. My phone vibrates in my purse, but I ignore it. The only person I want to talk to is here with me and Cora should be with Edward. So whoever it is doesn't matter right now. I'm busy having a mental breakdown internally.

Like he knew what I was thinking, Kohen pulls me into him, lifting my leg over his muscular thigh. "What's up, beautiful? You're quiet tonight."

"I was just thinking about what you said, about a connection that is unexplainable, and I agreed but..."

"But what?"

"But I don't deserve that, Kohen. I'm broken. Damaged, no good. I don't know if I deserve someone like you."

"Woah woah woah, where is the badass girl I know you to be?" He knocks gently on my forehead. "Hello, Alex, are you in there? Because the girl running your body right now is tripping."

I smile weakly.

"Come on, Angel, let's just enjoy the moment. Tell all the voices in your head to shut up." He leans in to kiss my forehead, my nose, and then my lips. Just like that, my demons are silenced.

In perfect timing, our food is delivered, and we begin to consume every bite in front of us.

We finish eating. Kohen grabs the check and we make our way out to the car. I feel the heat of his hand when he intertwines his fingers with mine. My breath hitches. It's such a simple act but almost more intimate than sex. Sex is easy. Find a hot guy, make him want you, let him fuck you. For me, it's always about making men want me, letting them have me then driving them fucking crazy.

I've never held anyone's hand, even my ex didn't like it. He said it made him look weak. That's part of the reason I don't look for anything but a quick fuck. He taught me that the most intimate parts of a relationship made me weak. Like my mother, and I never want to be like her. So, I don't seek out anything but some good dick in my pussy and go on about my day.

My phone rings and I take it out of my bag to look at it. It's Cora but I already missed the call. I call her back and get no answer, so I text her while climbing into his car.

Me: hey C whats up? Sorry I didn't answer. I was at dinner with Kohen.

I still don't get a response, so I call one more time. Something in the pit of my stomach makes me feel a tinge of worry. Still no answer, so I decide to check her location. Right at that moment, I get a text, and my stomach drops.

Cora: SOS

I call her and again no answer, so I go back to the location app, worried as fuck at this point.

It looks like she is at Kohen's. What the hell?

"You okay, Angel? You're so quiet all of a sudden."

"It's Cora. She needs me. Can you take me to your place like ASAP?"

"Yeah, it shouldn't take too long if I get on the freeway. What's going on? You look like you have seen a ghost."

It feels like I *have* seen a ghost, like I could be losing another best friend. The SOS text is something we came up with in case one of us was uncomfortable on a date and needed saving.

"I don't know. She sent an SOS, which she would never do if she was safe. Can you just please hurry?"

He grabs my hand and brings it to his lips for a kiss. "Your hands are shaking, babe. Don't worry, I'll get you there."

The car accelerates with a hum, and the scenery starts to blur. I close my eyes, sending a silent prayer up. I don't know if I believe in prayer but Cora does and for her, I'll do anything.

"I thought she was with Edward. Her location shows her at your place. I'm hoping it was an accident or something, but she isn't answering her phone." I know it's probably not an emergency because she would have called 911, but it is urgent. My anxiety is going to the worst-case scenario, the scars from Cecille's death run deep.

I text back.

Me: SOS 5

So she knows I'm five minutes out. That gives her time to let whoever is bothering her know that I'm on the way, she has to go.

"It's going to be okay, Alex. Whatever is happening, I will make sure it's okay."

"You don't fucking understand. I can't lose her."

"You won't." I fully expect him to pull his hand from mine because of how I snapped at him as punishment. Withdrawing affection, but he doesn't. Instead, he squeezes it gently and brings it to his lips for a kiss. "It's gonna be okay. Trust me."

So, I do something that is completely out of the ordinary for me. I trust him.

Chapter 23

Alex

We pull into the driveway, and I text her letting her know that we are here.

No response.

I call again and her phone goes straight to voicemail.

Come on, Cora.

"I'm going to check inside, okay?" Kohen says.

"Okay, thank you. I'm going to wait here." I call her a few more times and it goes straight to voicemail.

What the fuck?

My phone rings and I answer it without looking. "Hello?"

"Hey, she isn't here. No one has seen her. They said her and Edward were here earlier but that was around eight. Edward is passed out in his room."

"What the fuck? That dick! It's past midnight."

"I know, baby. I tried waking him up, but he must have taken something because he wouldn't budge. I'm coming back out and I'll drive you to look for her."

"No, I'll get an Uber. don't worry about it. This isn't your problem."

I hang up and pull the Uber app up on my phone. I know I'm being rude but I don't care. My best friend comes first.

I walk to the end of the driveway to wait for my ride, and then I check Cora's location again just in case. The little red circle is moving. It's almost right on top of where I am and I refresh, making sure it isn't lagging or something. If her phone dies, it would be gray. I don't even think twice. I chunk my heels into the grass and run.

I run in the direction of that little red dot because she is less than five minutes away and her dot is moving slowly, so she has to be walking, or with someone who is driving extra slow. I feel rocks under my feet and it hurts, but absolutely nothing will stop me.

My heart drops when I see her, my feet speed up and my strides become longer as I just need to get to her. Make sure she's okay. Her arms are wrapped around her little body as if she is cold or in pain.

Hot tears spill from my eyes. I was having fun, laughing and kissing and talking with Kohen while my best friend needed me.

I call out to her, and she stops walking and turns slowly in my direction. I shout again and she sees me. She stands still and I couldn't get to her any slower. It's as if years pass before I reach her. Like everything is in a slow-motion time warp.

As I get closer, I see mascara running down her face. She has been crying. There's blood running down her leg and it takes everything in me not to throw up. Not because blood makes me queasy but because something happened to my best friend.

"Oh my god, Cora. Are you okay?" I wrap my arms around her. Painful sobs leave her as I hold her tight and safe in my arms. "What the fuck happened? Why are you walking?"

"It hurts," is all that leaves her mouth.

"What hurts?"

She just sobs into my shoulder.

I pull my phone from my pocket. My Uber left. "I'm going to call an ambulance."

"No, Alex. Please, no."

"Okay, babe."

Fuck. I dial Kohen and he answers on the first ring.

"Are you okay? Did you find Cora?"

"No, Kohen, we are not okay. I'm on 5th and Holland. Please come get us. Something happened to Cora and I need you," my voice cracks as tears spill down my face uncontrollably.

"On my way."

I hang up and feel so numb, so helpless standing here with her in the middle of the street. So much is going through my head right now, but I have to focus. I have to keep all my questions to myself for now.

I notice Cora straightens up and she reaches for my hand. I don't hesitate and place my hand in hers. The moment with Kohen holding my hand in the car flashes through my mind from earlier.

"I'm here, Cora. Are you okay? I feel so bad that I wasn't with you."

Her face contorts and she whimpers a little from whatever pain she is feeling.

"We need to go to a hospital. Can you tell me what happened?"

She stares blankly into the night sky as she clutches her stomach.

"Cora? What happened? You're bleeding. I'm freaking out here!"

"I..." she pauses, tears streaming down her face as little sniffles leave her nose.

"Did Edward hurt you, Cora?"

"I'll go to the hospital, but please just don't ask me any questions, okay?"

I want to argue, I want to make her explain. I know I shouldn't, but I feel like if I know what happened, then I can take care of it.

"Cora, please. I'm going to lose my mind."

She sighs and squeezes her arms tighter around her stomach. Now I feel bad for pushing. Sobs leave her loudly this time and I wrap my arms around her, pulling her into a hug. I'm thinking about the worst-case scenario right now.

"Edward and I had sex," she blurts. Releasing her stomach, she brings her hands to her face, crying hysterically now.

"I thought you guys had sex at the party a couple weeks ago?"

"We didn't."

"Well, what the fuck? Did he force you? Should I be calling the cops?"

"No!" she practically shouts. "Please, don't call the cops. It hurt but I don't think he meant for that to happen."

"Did it hurt because he was rough or do you think it was because it was your first time?"

I want to bitch him out. Why the fuck is she out here alone walking, instead of cuddling up to the boyfriend she just lost her v-card to? He is just home asleep, not a worry in the world after fucking my best friend and letting her walk home. I'm going to kill him.

"Did he know it was your first time?" I already know the answer but I want to make sure. "Kohen is on the way to get us."

"Why, where is the car?" she asks, confused.

"We were on a date," I say softly, knowing she will beat herself up about disturbing us.

"Oh, my god. I didn't know." Sadness washes over her features.

"Don't ever be sorry."

Right then she doubles over, clutching her stomach, and falls to her knees. "I think I'm going to be sick."

I'm pulling her hair out of her face right as I see the bright, almost blue headlights of Kohen's car. Thank god. I am so fucking thankful for this man right now.

Chapter 24

Alex

Kohen is on the phone all the way to the hospital. I can't make out what he's saying because my anxiety is reeling. My heartbeat is the only thing I can focus on. I have so many questions I want to ask but this isn't the time. I remember how it felt when I went to get a rape kit done. It was the most horrific thing to relive the trauma over and over to each cop, detective, nurse, doctor, and social worker. It was devastating. I won't do that to Cora.

I hear my name far off in the distance, bringing my attention back to the real world and out of my flashback. The lights seem brighter, the air thicker, and I find my chest tight from holding my breath. I look down at Cora's head in my lap and she has her eyes closed. I run my fingers through her hair and she stirs. I feel Kohen's eyes on me, so I look at him, but he is staring forward. I look at the rearview mirror and his hazel eyes meet mine. Butterflies.

"Are you okay, Angel?"

I gulp, not wanting him to know where I went in my head, or what happened to me. "I was just in my own head about what the fuck could have possibly happened to her tonight."

"I'm sorry, Alex. I wish there was more I can do. We are almost at the hospital. How is she doing back there?"

"She's sleeping, I think," I whisper like it makes any difference.

"We're here."

The fluorescent lights of the hospital's emergency room sign come into view and I can breathe easier, knowing she will be okay soon.

We are never really okay, the little devil whispers.

And she is right, we never fully heal. No matter what.

Kohen pulls up to the big sliding doors of the ER where the ambulance dock is.

"Kohen, this is for ambulances. We can't park here."

"I got you. My family owns part of the hospital." He jumps out of the car, meeting some nurses with a wheelchair on the other side of the car. "Come on, let's get Cora checked out."

This man keeps surprising me. Just when I think he can't get any better, he does something like this. A big part of me doesn't fucking like it.

Imagine what you'll owe him for this, the little voice of doubt says.

The nurses wheel her into the E.R. and ask us to wait in the lobby while they get her settled into her room. I know what they are really doing, though. It's clear where she is bleeding from, and they want to make sure she wasn't raped.

Could that have happened?

I shake the thoughts from my head because she would have told me if she was. It's impossible. Her and Edward must have just gotten a little too rough and she just lost her v-card.

I make myself stop pacing the hallways and sit with Kohen. He has his head lowered and his hands together in front of his lips like he's praying or something, so I don't bother him.

My eyes search the room for a distraction, my senses heighten, and I can hear everything around me. The buzzing of the snack machine, the hum of the computer at the triage desk. It's too much and my leg begins to bounce. This hospital is huge, the area opens up in front of me like reverse claustrophobia, and everything is just too much. The scent of cleaning products, the chill in the air. Goosebumps erupt on my skin, and I close my eyes to try and refocus. I just want my best friend to be okay.

I feel a warm hand on my thigh and my eyes open. They're met by the most intense, beautiful hazel eyes known to man.

And like a breath of fresh air, I crash my lips to his.

I don't know what made me need to feel his lips on mine at that moment. It's like I'm a dementor in *Harry Potter* and I can suck what strength I need from him through that kiss, and he offers it up like a sacrifice. His lips warm me in ways that I've never experienced. Like a fireplace in winter. I bathe in this warmth, this moment, in this disgusting hospital. He makes it feel warm and safe like it's all going to be okay.

I don't like it one fucking bit.

"You okay, Angel?"

I look at him, studying his stupid face. I hate that he always asks me if I'm okay. I'm fine. I'm always fine. "Yes, I'm okay. I'm sorry, I don't know why I kissed you."

He smirks. "It's okay, I know why you did."

"You don't know anything about me."

He hums. "I don't need to know your life story to know you feel something for me. You feel something and you're scared. So, you're going to fight it, push it away, sabotage it. And that's okay. I'll still be here. Making sure you know that I, Kohen Ventura, am not going any-fucking-where."

He kisses me gently and I have no words. Instead, I cross my arms and feign annoyance. This man has bewitched me, I don't know why or how, and it all feels too fast but I like it just as much as I hate it.

"So you're some big shot here, huh?"

He laughs. "No, I'm just the son of the people who invest in this hospital. My father is a doctor."

I don't miss the way he looks away when he mentions his dad and the way he called him father so formally. I wonder what the story is.

Wait. No, I don't because I have way too much on my mental plate right now to give an actual fuck.

We wait for what seems like days when the nurse calls my name into the lobby. I jump up and rush to her.

"Ms. Cora is requesting you in her room. Follow me."

I glance over at Kohen. He gives me a little smile as if approving of me going in. I roll my eyes when I turn around because I do not need his approval. I was going in no matter what.

We walk down the long white-washed hallway and take a right into a big room. A16 the door panel reads. I walk into the room and past the curtains just as Cora is bringing her legs down from the stirrups.

This is the rape kit room. My heart begins to race and panic rises in my chest. I know I need to keep calm but I will fucking kill whoever hurt her. Her hand finds mine as if I'm the one who needs comforting. I risk a glance at her and I'm met with big blue glazed eyes. She's been crying.

"It's okay, Alex. This was just an exam."

A tear falls down my cheek. Like always, my selfish ass makes this about me. I can't speak, my throat feels tight, and I can feel the blood rushing from my heart, up my neck, and to my throbbing temple. I'm trying to keep it together.

"Alex."

"What?" is all I manage to croak.

"I wasn't raped, I promise. Let the doctor explain."

The doctor. Right. I sneak a glance to where he stands with the nurse, looking at me as if I'm about to shatter. I'm not.

I was broken a long time ago. I couldn't shatter anymore. If I did, I simply wouldn't exist.

"Are you okay, Miss?" the nurse asks me.

"I'm fine."

The doctor comes up and places a hand on my shoulder, causing me to flinch. His heavy hand on my shoulder in this room is too much to deal with right now. Anxiety courses through my body like adrenaline.

"Get your hand off me, please," I say it a little louder than intended but he needs to understand it's taking every ounce of me to be in here. I'm here for my best friend.

"My apologies."

"What, um, what's wrong? What happened? Why is she in here?"

Dr. Malcolm- that's what his name tag says- begins to explain and it takes all my strength to hyperfocus on the words he's saying. "She has a broken hymen, so we have some blood from that." I glance over at her, confused. She smiles weakly to reassure me, so I stay quiet and listen. "But the pain she was experiencing was not normal, so we ran some tests and she had a pathologic cyst that ruptured. If you hadn't brought her in as quickly as you did, it may have been much worse."

"A cyst?"

"Yes. It's rare but sometimes they rupture after intercourse and flood the pelvic area, causing pain and nausea as well as some confusion and fever. Like I said, it's very rare."

He shakes my hand and offers a small smile as he makes eye contact with me. I examine his face, the wrinkles around his kind eyes, making me feel guilty for my frustration earlier. "She is lucky to have a friend like you."

One single tear runs down my cheek. I swipe it away before Cora sees. I don't feel like a good friend. I don't feel like I'm a friend worth having. I should have been there, but there is no time for self-deprecation, so I suck it up and let it the fuck go because this isn't about me. I head over to kiss her forehead so I can go wait in the lobby again while she has the IV removed and gets dressed.

"I'll be waiting for you in the lobby, bestie," I say with a small smile.

"Okay. Is Kohen still out there?" Her voice is small and she sounds exhausted.

"Yeah, yeah he's still out there."

Her smile grows and her expression lights up.

"What?" I ask, rolling my eyes.

"He's a keeper, Alex. I think he loves you."

"Shut up, Cora, or I'll leave you here! He doesn't love me and he isn't even mine, so how can I keep him? Besides, he has girls falling at his feet on a daily basis. Why would he want me?"

He wouldn't, the little voice in my head whispers.

My hand is on the handle of the door when I hear her clear her throat to say something else, so I turn to look at her over my shoulder.

"Do not ruin this, Alex Monroe. He's here with you. He could be anywhere else but he is here waiting in the lobby of a hospital his parents basically own, waiting for your best friend to be okay."

I scoff. "Yeah, probably because he wants more pussy."

"Ugh, do you always have to be so crass?" We both laugh, knowing damn well that I do. "Seriously, best friend, hear me when I say this. Tell the voice in your head to shut the eff up and go and claim that man because you deserve it."

Without saying another word, I walk out of the room. I can't think about anything else right now. It has been a long night and I just want to get her home. I thought my best friend was raped tonight. I'm glad that she wasn't but I still want to know why she was dealing with all of this by herself.

I'm going to kill Edward.

Chapter 25

Alex

I walk into the lobby with a thousand thoughts running through my mind, but then I see him. He is sitting in the same chair in the corner of the room. He has his head down and he is looking at the floor. His otherwise perfect hair is a disheveled mess, but he looks sexier than ever. Right as I'm about to say his name to get his attention, he looks up. His eyes immediately meet mine and it takes my breath away. He looks so sleepy and worry etches his face. Cora's words from earlier ring in my head.

"He is here with you," she says, trying to encourage me.

He could be anywhere else.

She's right, she is fucking right.

He stands as I approach and pulls me into a hug. "You okay, Angel?" He kisses my cheek and tightens his hold around my body.

"No, I'm not. I'm not okay but you're making it better."

He pulls away to look down at me. He kisses my lips so softly that I'm not even sure I feel it. He brings me back into his body and rests his chin on my head.

"Sit down and rest. I'm going to talk to the receptionist and make sure everything is squared away with Cora."

I listen. I sit my big ass down and rest. I don't know how much time has passed when I open my eyes, but it feels like seconds. I didn't even realize I fell asleep, but a warm blanket covers me and I'm in the car. Kohen's car. I panic, checking the back seat and I see my best friend peacefully sleeping. I feel a large hand rest on my thigh and my body relaxes, feeling safe. Safe. That's not a word I throw around, but it feels right. I look over at him and I'm fucking terrified. I don't want to feel safe. No, I don't want him to make me feel safe, because then when I don't have him the safety is gone. I just need me, myself, and I, and Cora.

I try to fall back asleep, but I can't, his hand is so heavy on my thigh now.

"You awake, Angel?" I smile at his voice. It's like a knife cutting through butter, so smooth and deep and it's just another stupid thing about him that comforts me. Another thing I hate to love.

"I can't fall back asleep. Where are we?"

"I took the long way home. I figured you guys could use the rest so I've just been driving around so that you can sleep. I didn't want to get to the house and have to wake you up again when we got there."

"So you drove us around for hours like babies that can't sleep?" I laugh quietly, not wanting to wake Cora.

"I guess I did. Although it sounds stupid when you word it like that," he laughs and runs his hand through his hair, rubbing it over his sleepy eyes.

I unbuckle my seatbelt so I can lean over to kiss him.

"What are you doing, Alex?" he asks with a hint of anger in his tone.

"Kissing you," I say, confused.

"Put your damn seatbelt on. What if we get into an accident?"

"It's okay, Kohen, I trust you."

"You shouldn't. Put it back on, please."

"I shouldn't, got it," I say sarcastically, nodding my head. I buckle back up, my throat tight from embarrassment.

"That's not what I meant and you know it. I need you safe, okay?"

"Okay, safe. Got it." Only now I don't feel safe. I'm guarded and my walls went right back up. I move his hand from my thigh and turn to face the window. "Keep both hands on the wheel, Kohen, it's unsafe. 10 and 2 and all that jazz."

Cora's voice rings through the silence, "Stop being a bitch, Alex. Keep your damn seatbelt on and relax. He wasn't trying to be mean- you're just overreacting."

Eyes wide, I turn to look at her. "Cora! Oh my god, did you just cuss at me?" Half shocked and half proud, I wait for her response.

"Yes, bitch. I did because you're not going to fuck this up with your damn trust issues. Kohen, please pull over and kiss my hoe-ass best friend so she can calm her tits please."

Kohen and I look at each other. He does as he's told, pulling over onto the side of the road.

"Oh, and also thank you for driving us around like babies."

He puts the car in park and I look over at him through my lashes. I can feel heat spreading over my face and neck. What the fuck is this guy doing to me? I peek over my shoulder to see Cora resting with her eyes closed, and when I look back at Kohen, he has moved closer. His thumb grazes my bottom lip.

"So fucking beautiful."

I melt in my seat, my insides mush at the sweet words he makes sound so filthy. He kisses me deeply and everything around us fades away. My subconscious fights for reality to stay but it slips and slips away as he kisses me. My lips open wider to make room for him to take every broken piece of me. Consume me.

I look up at him as I pull myself away. Confusion is written across his features.

"What's wrong?" he asks quietly.

Still staring at him, I drink in and learn every single detail of his face.

"Ruin me, Kohen. Make me yours."

I reach up and run my fingers through the short hair at the nape of his neck and he groans quietly.

I pull him back into me for one more kiss. It's just a soft peck on the lips but just as magnetic as any of the other kisses we have shared.

"Let's get Cora home."

"Whatever you say, Angel, you're the boss."

I smile at that little comment. "Damn right, I am." We both laugh.

We pull into the driveway of our quaint little house. I'm not embarrassed of it at all. I prefer it over Kohen's gigantic unwelcoming mansion. His little section of it is perfect but the rest can go. It's too much space for one person and that's why he allows all his friends to live there like it's some frat house.

The car turns off and Kohen opens his door. A part of me hopes he stays over but a bigger part of me knows he should go so I can spend time with Cora after this crazy night. I should be alone in case there is anything else she wants to tell me that she didn't feel comfortable enough to at the hospital.

He runs around the car to open my door for me and helps me out. He must be so tired, but he isn't even showing it. There is no complaint on his face, no attitude or huffing and puffing for us to hurry. He closes my door and I'm just standing there observing him like he is some sort of alien.

"Angel, why don't you go get the door open so I can help Cora inside, instead of checking me out?"

"Oh, okay," I say, rushing up the walkway and digging through my purse for the house key. So embarrassing.

I unlock the door and swing the heavy wood open and go back out on the porch to wait for them. Normally, other women might be jealous of the guy they like paying attention to their best friend but I know it's innocent. I may be toxic but Cora is an extension of me. My God-given sister and I would do anything for her so the fact that he is so attentive to her means he cares for me.

Whoa.

Number one- I just said *the guy I like.*

Number two- I just admitted to knowing he cares for me.

The sound of their footsteps on the bottom steps pulls me from my thoughts. I'm thankful for it because I know my mind was about to spiral. We help her into the house. She requests to be in the living room. I guess she doesn't want to be in her room tonight. That's fine, we can binge movies and eat snacks. Total girls' night.

We get her onto the sofa. I run upstairs to get her blankets and pillow, and as I'm about to make my way down the stairs, I stop, listening to the words floating up the stairs.

"She is hard to love, but she is worth it. I know you have feelings for her, I can tell."

I hear him laugh quietly, and the sound fills me with warmth the same way a cup of coffee does on a cold day.

"Oh, I know she is probably hard in every way, but I also feel she's worth it in every way, too. I can't really explain it."

"Explain what?" she asks.

"The way I feel. I have felt it since the first day I met her. There's a light around her, a magnetic pull that draws me to her. I can't help it."

"Oh my god, Kohen, you have to tell her."

"Nah. If I could ask you for one thing, it's let me tell her when I'm ready. She doesn't seem very open or receptive to me. I don't want to push her or scare her away."

"I get that, and okay you have my word."

"Get some rest. I'm sorry that the night went down this way, Cora."

"It's okay. I'm sorry for interrupting y'alls night."

"No way, anyone that's important to Alex must be amazing. Make sure Edward knows that, too."

I hear his feet making their way to the front door, so I begin to descend the steps before he leaves.

"Kohen?"

"Yeah?"

"Don't give up on her, as hard as she gets, if she is giving you a hard time it's because she is having a hard time and probably scared as fuck for another person to break her heart."

"I don't plan on it, Cora. Goodnight."

I hit the bottom step as he opens the front door. "Wait for me, Kohen. I'm just going to give her this and I'll walk you to your car."

He nods and I cover Cora with her blanket and toss the pillows at her face.

She giggles and tosses one back at me. I hop out of the way and it misses me. I stick my tongue out at her and she mirrors me. It's like we never left kindergarten.

I come up behind Kohen on the porch and wrap my hands around his waist from the back. I feel him tense up, not knowing how to react to the vulnerable act. I don't know why but it feels right and maybe it's because he is looking away and can't see me. I rest my head on his back, and even though my head only reaches the middle of his back, I close my eyes and listen to his heart. It comforts me. His hands come up to meet mine where they wrap around his abdomen, rubbing his fingers up and down my arms gently.

"Want me to walk you to your car?"

Say no, say no. Stay.

"Yeah, Angel. I'm exhausted."

I want to ask him to stay but I don't, and I won't. My brain won't allow me to be that vulnerable.

He removes my hands from around him and the smallest sting of rejection hits me. Why am I like this? I'm confident, beautiful, and sexy, and guys always want me. What the fuck is it about this guy that makes me feel inadequate? Is it because he's good?

He grabs my hand and holds it while we walk. I stare at the ground, hoping he doesn't see the little bouts of insecurity growing from the seeds of doubt my mother buried in me. We don't say anything on the walk, the only noise coming from the crickets in the grass and the cool breeze making its way through the leaves in the trees around us.

It's peaceful.

I'm glad for the large front yard we have as we make our way to the car. I sneak a peek at his face in the moonlight and, as always, his eyes meet mine. He was already looking at me, waiting for me to look at him. We pause our walk and laugh. His hands wrap around the small frame of my face and we just stare at each other for a few moments before he finally speaks.

"This feels good, Alex. I really like you, but..."

Butterflies erupt in my belly. I feel like I could throw up. I wonder if he's going to say anything after his little talk with Cora. "But?" I ask nervously. My hands hold his forearm, anchoring myself to him as I wait for the next words to leave his mouth.

"I'm terrified that you are going to rip me to pieces."

I scoff. "Me? Rip *you* to pieces?"

"Yes, you- Alex Monroe- the toughest girl I have ever met. You may rip me to pieces." I follow his line of sight to the place where our hands now meet. "Just the simple touch of our skin, your hand in mine feels so good. Is that weird?"

"It's not weird at all. I was thinking the same thing. I think that every time. It feels so...calming, it almost makes me sleepy."

"Yes! That's exactly how I feel too, Alex. I'll be honest, you confuse the fuck out of me."

I don't know what to say. I feel like this is too good to be true. He is a player, a cocky asshole who just wants to say he tamed me. I'm just a challenge to him. A conquest- once won, he will tire of me.

He stares at me, waiting for a response, and moves a piece of hair behind my ear.

Why is he so good? There has to be some kind of catch. I feel so confused and scared, he is nothing like I thought he would be and that scares me even more.

"I don't know, Kohen. Do we even know each other enough to say we like each other? I like hanging out and this..." I say and then kiss him.

He kisses me back, tugging softly on the hair that hangs down my back.

He pulls away. "Tell me you'll be mine."

"I don't want you to break my heart. I didn't expect any of this. I don't want to like you. Everyone said..."

He interrupts me before I can finish the sentence.

"I don't give a fuck what anyone said, Alex, and I don't want to hear it. I let people think and say what they want. They don't know me. Things aren't always as they seem. But you, *you* can know me, you can know me like no one else knows me. Me and you, I think we are the same. The feeling I get when I'm around you, and when I first saw you..." His facial expressions are telling the story his heart wants it to. I feel my heart beating rapidly in my chest, pounding at the walls surrounding it to be near his.

I interrupted his speech with another kiss, jumping up and wrapping my legs around him. I already know he can handle carrying me easily. The embrace feels like fire, the flames licking at every inch of my skin. My body lights up for him- he is the light to my darkness. His light is a flame, it may consume me whole. That's where my fears lie- in the fact that he could incinerate my heart and soul to ash. There will be nothing left.

Don't fall for any of this, the little voice whispers.

I don't plan on it. This is just sex, just surface level, it isn't going anywhere. Even if I wanted it to, it's too good to be true. He must have something up his sleeve. Some game he is playing with me. I'll be damned if he wins.

A little spark of pain travels down my arm, and it brings me out of my intrusive thoughts. He's biting my shoulder. But then peppers kisses over the area he just brought pain to.

That feels like a foreshadow of things to come but I don't let that thought run. I want to feel every single thing that's about to happen. So I pull myself into the moment. Sex. Just sex.

He pulls my body to him, grabbing handfuls of my ass, and tits as his hands roam over my body. "Fuck, your skin feels so good." I hear him inhale a deep breath taking in the scent of me. His fingers reach my waistband and I unwrap my legs from his torso. My feet touch the ground and I open the door to his car and slide into the backseat. He watches me with a hunger in his eyes I've never seen, pupils dilated, lips swollen, he's gorgeous.

I pull my sleep shorts down my legs and toss them to the floorboard. His eyes widen as he realizes I'm not wearing any panties. I place the heel of my feet on the edge of the seat and spread my legs for him.

"Fuck, baby. That's a pretty pussy. Tell me it's mine."

I slip my fingers in between my legs and dip one inside of me, watching him watch me and I'm dripping wet for him. The way he watches me makes me feel like a goddess.

"This pussy?" I tease as I continue the little show for him.

"Yes, that's MY pussy." I see his resistance slipping and he moves a little closer.

"Nah ah ah." I remove my fingers and start to close my legs. "Don't come any closer, Kohen, not until I say."

He feigns shock. "Come on, baby, don't tease me. Let me slip in the backseat with you." He dips his head inside the door frame and I put my foot out to stop him.

"No, sir, if you want me to show you MY pussy, you play MY way."

"Fuck, Alex, okay. Angel, just let me see that juicy peach, baby."

He backs up like a good boy and I open up for him again. My clit is throbbing and even though I want him to take me right now and fuck me like I'm his greatest sin, I stay patient. This is my game and he will fuck me on my terms. I rub circles around my clit, dropping my head back as I picture his strong calloused hands in between my legs instead of mine.

"Tell me, Alex, I'm begging you, tell me it's mine."

I make direct eye contact with him as I slip two fingers inside. "It's yours," is all I say and he pulls his shirt over his head, the bulge in his sweats making me ache for him to fill me. He rushes in the back seat and rips my shirt in half, my tits bouncing free, my nipples pebbled from my arousal and the cool air.

"No bra either? You have been a bad girl, Angel."

"So punish me then," I tell him with a smirk.

His head dips down between my legs and I freeze. No one has ever been there, not like that. It's too personal.

"What's wrong?" I hate that he's noticed.

"No one has ever done that."

"Ever?" he asks, surprised.

"Ever."

"Let me take this first from you, Angel."

"I don't know, Kohen. It's weird."

His fingers assault my clit, melting my anxiety. Our lips meet and he dips his fingers inside of me.

"You are so wet. I fucking love it. Let me show you how a king treats his queen." He moves in between my legs again, his eyes meeting mine. "I got you, Angel." He takes a deep breath. "Smells fucking delicious."

His fingers move to my hips as he gets ready to devour the most intimate part of me. It seems silly that someone eating me out makes me so shy when I'm sex confident. I guess because I have no control there. I've never thought about it long enough, every time a guy tried, they took the easy way out because they just wanted to fuck me.

His mouth is on me and an explosion of energy radiates from my clit. My core clenches as it moves up my thighs and into my belly. Like butterflies, only much more potent. My thighs clench his head and I try and wriggle away from the overstimulating sensation. Not because I don't like it but because it's too much. This shouldn't be any different than when I'm getting played with or fingered, but holy shit it does. It's so much different. Like I could say or do anything. He licks and sucks and spreads me open so he can feast on my pussy. The juices mix with his spit. Nothing could turn me on more as I watch him wreak havoc on me. Rolls of pleasure flow through me and pressure builds inside, making me dizzy. I drop my weight back and bring my hands to his hair, pulling and tugging at it.

"Please, Kohen."

He moans against me and the vibrations set me off.

I come so fucking hard, I see stars. I pull him up and kiss him feverishly. The pleasure this man just bestowed upon me is like nothing I have ever felt before and I want to make him feel just as good. I tug his sweatpants down. He moves off me to pull his boxers down, too. The small space he put between us feels like too much. I need him closer and I fucking hate it.

He looks at me with his cock in his hand. Pumping it a few times, he moves on top of me, pulling me up towards him as he whispers, "Ride me, Angel. Show me who this cock belongs to."

Me. That's who.

I switch positions and climb on top of his lean body and my thick thighs sit on either side of him. He grabs, them squeezing. "Fuck, I love this."

"What?" I ask.

"Your fucking body, your skin, everything, it's intoxicating, a drug I just want to keep taking hit after hit, even if it brings me to my knees."

I plunge his dick inside of me, dropping myself on it. He groans, squeezing my thighs even harder. I know it will bruise but I don't care. I want him to mark me, to ruin me, to make me his.

I grind my pussy on his dick in slow circular motions, and my eyes drift closed.

Chapter 26

Kohen

Her eyes are closed as I stare at her riding me. She's so fucking sexy. She is seducing me with her body. It's like there is a song playing that nobody else can hear and her body is moving to the rhythm. She grinds her pussy on me as her walls tighten around my throbbing dick. I'm so hard for her. I reach up and pinch her nipple between my thumb and my forefinger, rolling it, and her luscious lips part, releasing a breathy moan just for me. *Mine.*

I take it greedily like I want to take all her breaths. I want her heart to beat for me. Just me. What the fuck am I doing? What is she doing to me? She bobs her pussy up and down and she rolls her hips and it's fucking heavenly. The pressure building at the base of my spine lets me know I'm about to come and I know we aren't protected. I don't want to be protected. I want my come to fill her up, to see it run down her legs when she pulls me out of her delicious pussy. It's not that I want to get her pregnant, I mean we are in college, and I'm sure neither of us is ready for that. We barely know each other, but the carnal urge to make every fucking cell on her body mine is overpowering every logical thought my mind possesses.

I thrust up into her, wanting to make sure she comes before I do. I grind as I come back down and she yelps. I grab her waist and pull her pussy into me, not wanting a single space between us.

"Kohen, please," she says, lust lacing her voice.

"Please what, Angel?" I know what she wants but I want to hear her say it.

"Make me come."

"Say please, like a good girl." I thrust up into her with each word. She's holding herself up, one hand on the back seat and one hand on the headrest of the front seat, her body floating over me as I fuck her from the bottom.

"Fuck, Kohen."

"Say please, like a good girl."

She begs and that's all it takes. It's like she passed go and collected $200. I spin her around and she's under me. I fuck her relentlessly, hard, and furiously because she fucking said *please.*

"Fuck yes, Angel. I love it when you beg for me."

My cock glides in and out of her wetness as she lifts her legs to my shoulders, reaching down to spread herself open for me. The sight is fucking glorious.

"That pretty pussy looks delicious. You're such a good fucking girl."

"I'm your good fucking girl."

She moans as her pussy convulses around me. Her sweet, sweet climax spills around my dick. The sounds of our bodies meeting make me fucking crazy.

I come hard inside her beautiful pussy, the aftershocks like electricity between us. She lays there spent, eyes closed, breaths ragged, hair a mess. Still, she is the most beautiful thing I have ever seen. I pull out of her and immediately regret it. I want to stay inside her forever. My heaven.

The one thing that drives me batshit crazy for this girl is her confidence. She lays there bare for me, every single part of her on display for me like art. She is a masterpiece and makes no apologies for it. Absolute perfection. I look over her body, taking in each part of it, her breasts, the mounds of perfection, her dark nipples pebbled with the cool breeze flowing through the car. We didn't bother to close the door. My eyes move down to her soft tummy and the light stretch marks that are displayed there. There are only a few but my fingers itch to trace them down the curve where her waist meets her hip. And those thick fucking thighs... I want to squeeze them and bite them so I can see where she belongs to me. And then my eyes meet the valley between her legs, that little slice of heaven my angel gives only to me.

I stare at it and watch how our juices glisten together in the moonlight as the mixture escapes her. This feeling takes over me, one I'm not familiar with, but before I know what I'm doing, I have two fingers in her pussy, pushing everything seeping out of her back in. She stirs and her eyes fly open and meet mine.

"What are you doing?" she asks, her breasts moving up and down as she breathes.

"I don't know," I tell her honestly. "Do you like it?"

I push my fingers to the knuckles inside her and twirl them around, feeling the mixture inside her covering them. I move them in and out of her slowly and she starts to grind her pussy into them.

"Yes," she says simply. Both of us are navigating unknown territory here. Not just with this or the sex, but everything. Us.

My dick is hard all over again, "Want some more?"

"Yes," she moans.

"Say please."

"Please."

"That's a good girl, turn around."

She does as she's told and my dick swells in my hand, pre-come already on the tip.

I thrust inside her in one deep stroke and her body jerks forward as she says my name.

"What, Angel?"

"Fuck me hard."

"Oh, I plan to." I stick the fingers I had in her pussy into her mouth and she cleans them up nicely, sucking our mess into her warm mouth. I grab her by the back of the neck and fuck her like she wants me to. Hard, fast, and deep. Her moans are proof of her pleasure. Her pussy clamping around my cock is a sign she's close. I keep going, a second wave of energy hitting me, even though I haven't slept a wink. I am an addict and she is my drug.

I slap her ass and she yelps.

"Fuckkk, yesss, Kohen." The soft gleam of sweat covering her body is fucking beautiful. How much more obsessed can I become with her?

"I'm coming," she screams. "Don't stop."

Wasn't planning on it.

Just then, I feel a gush of liquid release from her pussy. It's like my cock gets the message and I come right along with her. I release her and her face drops to the seat, her luscious ass in the air as my cock still sits inside her while I finish filling her glorious pussy up for the second time tonight. She bounces herself gently on it, milking me as I come. I slap her ass again and she jumps a little at the contact.

"Damn, Angel, your pussy is fucking magical."

She smiles. "I'm sorry about your seat. That's never happened before."

I lean in to kiss her cheek. "Don't apologize, baby, that was a fucking honor. Besides, I'll just get it detailed later this week."

We adjust ourselves in the backseat and I give her my t-shirt to wear since I tore what she was wearing in half. She hasn't spoken at all, and I wonder if I should say something first, but I wait. The key to this woman is patience.

She slips into my shirt and I pull my boxers up my thighs. I see her inhale my scent from it out of the corner of my eye. Why is she acting so shy now? How can the confident sexy girl I have started to get to know also be so shy and quiet? Such an oxymoron, yet here she sits.

"You okay, Angel?" I see the little smile tugging at the corner of her lips. She loves it when I ask her that, this I know for sure.

"Yeah, Kohen. I'm fine."

"Okay, I'm just making sure since you're being awfully quiet. Did I hurt you?"

She scoffs. "Don't flatter yourself." We burst out in laughter.

"I just meant like...I wasn't too rough?"

She tucks her hair behind her ear and looks up at me through her dark lashes. "No, I... loved it."

"Yeah?"

"Yeah!" she confirms, biting her lip.

"Okay, stop looking at me like that or we will end up in round three."

"No, we need a shower."

"I'm so fucking tired," I admit. "What time is it?"

"Will you stay?" she spits out.

"You want me to stay?" I'm surprised, but in a good way. I would love to fucking stay.

"Yeah, I mean if you want to, if you don't it's fine. I'll see you whenever."

I bend down to kiss her gently on the lips and whisper, "I would love to fucking stay."

She kisses me back and whispers, "Okay good, I want you to."

There is vulnerability. And even though it's small, it feels like a win.

"Then I'm staying." She smiles up at me, it's a simple smile. The truth is in her eyes though when I look into those gorgeous honey-brown irises, I see the secrets she holds there. The honesty, the excitement. This is why I need Alex Monroe to be mine. She's fucking special. The way she looks at me is special, she won't admit it, but her eyes do. I'll fight for the truth they tell me, even if it kills me in the process.

Chapter 27

Alex

We walk back across the huge yard I was just admiring, and now wish it was smaller so we could get inside faster. Dark clouds take up the sky with little pops of light flashing in the far distance.

The door closes louder than expected as a burst of wind blows against it forcefully, making it harder to close. A storm must be rolling in.

"Well, that was quicker than I expected. Y'all must fuck like animals," Cora shouts from the living room just past the entryway.

"Oh, hush, he's still here, you little witch," she laughs from the living room where I can hear the courtyard lunch scene from *Grease* playing in the background.

"Oh, I know he is. I knew he would tell you how he felt and you would NOT tell him, but show him in other...ways," she laughs even harder at that one, and Kohen and I join in as we head over to the couch with her.

"I hope it's okay that he stays, C." I plop myself on the cushion next to her and wait patiently for a response while focusing my gaze on the tv.

"Of course, he can stay. Besides, there were some tornado warnings on the tv a second ago, so it's better this way so that your precious knight in shining armor doesn't get swooped up to OZ with Dorothy. God knows you will find a way to get there and murder anyone who's looked at him, including the Wicked Witch. Phsss, she ain't got nothing on you."

"Ha ha ha, so very funny. Really, you should look into participating in stand-up comedy. Your future is bright my friend."

She rolls her eyes and continues watching Sandy pining after the bad boy everyone wants, and she can't have. This movie always got to me because I never understood why, in the end, Sandy had to be the one to change. He tried and failed and so what, that's good enough? Hell no. He better work for it, too. He doesn't grovel, doesn't fight, and he's a fucking pussy. Now Kenickie is a guy I can get behind, or better yet, let behind me.

"Stop being a ho for Kenickie and pay attention to your man," Cora says, interrupting my thoughts. I hate how she knows me so well, but I ignore it and look over at the space I felt Kohen's weight settle in. He's fast asleep, as he should be.

I watch him, the way his chest rises and falls slowly as he breathes. The quiet snores coming from the small space between his lips, his long thick lashes, way too long for a guy I might add, it's definitely not fair. And the way the tips of them cast shadows on his cheeks. He stirs and I freeze. I don't want him to catch me staring at him like a creeper. His hand reaches out and he feels around him sloppily and I move my thigh closer to see if it's me he's searching for. He feels the skin on my leg with his pinky and moves his hand over my thigh and lightly squeezes, a small groan leaving him. My heart swells. He was feeling for *me,* my mind can't comprehend this. It's fucking weird. Time feels like it's been altered- like it's a tangible flexible thing that makes it feel like we have known each other much longer than we have because this isn't normal.

"Alex?" Cora's voice breaks me from my hypnotizing thoughts.

"Mmm, yeah?" Turning my head to look at her, I see the movie is paused and I didn't even realize it was so quiet.

"Are you okay? I said your name twice and you didn't respond."

I think about that for a few seconds before saying anything. "I'm sorry, I'm so tired. I must have been daydreaming or something." A strike of lightning lights up the entire yard and a loud boom of thunder shakes the window right as it hits the tree across the street. Kohen pops up so fucking fast, it scares me.

"It's just thunder and lightning from the incoming storm. Cora said there were some tornado warnings." I rub his thigh to comfort him. I don't know why because that's not something I do. Why the fuck am I doing that? I remove it and look over at Cora as she stares at me, then my hand, and at the place on his body I removed it from. Her eyes dart right back to mine and I look away.

"Oh, damn it scared the shit out of me. It sounded like a gunshot," Kohen says. His eyes are so sleepy and he rubs them as if trying to force himself to stay up even longer. Rain begins to tap the roof and I decide it is time to head to bed.

"Let's go to bed, Kohen. Cora, do you want us to help you upstairs?" I stand and look down at where she sits.

"No, babe. You guys go to bed and I'll sleep here. I love falling asleep to the sound of the rain."

"Kohen, let's go upstairs." I grab his hand and pull. He gets up slowly like his body weighs as much as an elephant's. We turn to make our way upstairs, and just when my foot hits the bottom step, I hear Cora clear her throat.

"Alex, can you help me real quick?" She clears her throat again and I look up at Kohen who is already at the top step.

"Go ahead, lay down. I'll be right in."

Walking over to Cora, I pick up a water glass off the end table and hand it to her.

"What's up? What do you need?" She smiles softly, her eyes filled with tears.

"Are you okay? Need Tylenol or something?" Panic fills my chest.

"No, I'm just... I've never seen you like that." She wipes a tear from her cheek.

"Like what? I'm just being myself."

"I don't know, Alex, but you are different with him. I know you can't possibly love him, because you barely know him but...it's... something, something different."

"I don't know. What could be different? He was nice to us so I'm being nice to him, that's it." I don't even believe myself. *Fuck! What the fuck do I do?*

"If you say so, Alex Monroe. You can lie to me all you want, but stop lying to yourself, babe. You deserve better than that...*Angel.*" She busts out laughing and I grab a pillow and throw it at her face.

"Goodnight, Cora. I love you, don't scream for me when Ghostface comes to kill you."

"Oh, don't worry. I won't. He can stab me with his dagger any day, so hot."

We truly are fucked up. I just don't know which one of us is more fucked up-her for loving a fictional character who murders people, or me for falling for a real guy, who's good to me.

I walk up the stairs smiling. I can't wait to sleep. The bedroom door is cracked open, the light from the hall hitting the center of my bed perfectly. I have a small fear of the dark, so I always leave it cracked like that and I placed my bed strategically for the light to hit the center. I stand in the doorway and admire the strong sexy man in my bed. I hate him.

He is so handsome and kind that it pisses me off. I thought he was just a playboy. The vibe check was wrong as it sometimes can be. Some small part of me still thinks he has to be too good to be true. I pull my shirt over my head as I enter the room, freeing my breasts from any and all confinement. I pull down my shorts and open the bathroom door. I feel sticky from the car sex, so I grab an oversized t-shirt and head to the shower.

I freeze as I hear Kohen stir in the bed and groan. Walking over to him naked, I reach out and run my finger across his exposed thigh. He is under my blanket but has one leg sticking out of it all the way up to his thigh.

I slowly move the blanket and find him in his birthday suit. I giggle and he stirs again. Backing up toward the door slowly to make my escape, I hear him say something. I wait a few seconds to see if he speaks again, and when he doesn't, I turn into the hall.

"Angel?"

I freeze. Did he just say, Angel? As in the nickname he calls me?

"Kohen?" I whisper, looking over my shoulder at him. There's no response, so I continue into the hall closet for a clean towel and grab him one for the morning, too. I tiptoe into the restroom and close the door, being careful not to wake him. I run the hot water and throw my hair in a bun since wash day isn't until tomorrow. Steam fills up the small space and reality hits me like a ton of bricks.

Suddenly I remember we haven't been using a condom. Shit. I will need to send him for the morning-after pill. He is the one who didn't want to use a condom, so he can go pay for it. I wonder if I should get on birth control if he's going to want to fuck me without one.

Fuck.

We need to get tested, too. If there is one thing I don't fuck around with, it's my sexual health. He has me being careless and I don't like it, not one bit. Anger surges through me. I step into the scalding hot water, loving the burn of it on my skin. I let it run down my body and the tension releases making me feel weightless. I roll my neck side to side underneath the water. I haven't started my dance rehearsals yet because of my regular classes. I feel like I'm so behind. I know I'm going to feel sore from head to toe. I don't tell too many people I'm a dancer because they look at me like I'm an alien. Thicker dancers have always been frowned upon.

The door *clicks* and I see a shadow approach the outside of the curtain. My heart races, not from fear but from excitement. The thought of him excites me, and I don't know how to fully comprehend that, but I'm going to roll with it for now. I watch his hand reach to pull the curtain back, and I rush to face away from the curtain so he doesn't know I saw him coming. I let the water run over my face and try to hold back my laughter.

He's quiet as can be as he steps in, his energy powerful. It exudes from him like an expensive cologne. Filling up my senses.

His arms wrap around me and I fake a little jump.

"I'm sorry, Angel, I didn't mean to scare you. I must have dozed off. Why didn't you wake me up?"

I turn to face him and wrap my arms around his neck. He cranes his neck and our lips meet for a quick peck.

"You looked so peaceful sleeping, so I wanted you to rest. You did so much for me tonight."

He tugs at the bottom of my hair, making my head roll back. Then he brings his mouth to my ear, biting it softly before speaking.

"I wanted to see you get naked for me." His lips move from my ear, down to my neck, as he follows the trail to my collarbone that only he can see. I've given this man the map to my body and soul unwillingly. I don't mind it, but I'm scared shitless. I'm going to hate loving him because loving him means he can hurt me and break me in ways I haven't let anyone close enough to do in so long.

My only hope is that he cherishes the fact that I'm giving him the honor to know me. My only solace is that he is doing the same exact thing for me. I feel aligned with him somehow, and as crazy as it sounds, I trust him.

We finish up the shower. He washes my body, moving slowly over the most intimate part, teasing me. As many times as I try to engage, he shuts me down. Usually, that would bother me, eat away at me, and make me feel unwanted. Hashtag *sex trauma,* but with him, it doesn't hit that way. The intimacy he shows me outside of fucking me is weird and rare, but enough to make me feel secure. *Security isn't real,* the little voice reminds me. I believe her and pull back.

"You need to go get the morning-after pill for me tomorrow. I think you should grab it because you are the one who didn't use a condom." I look into his eyes as he responds, seeing if any flashes of anger pass there.

"Okay, Angel, no problem. I'll grab it on the way home, and then bring it back so we can go on another date."

"Another date," I ask, smiling like the idiot I am.

"Yeah, I want to spend as much time with you as I can before training gets too crazy." He shuts off the water and I scramble to find another topic to argue about because I wouldn't be me if I just accepted he's good.

"Also, we need to go get tested." I exit the restroom, knowing that's the one thing he will probably disagree with like most guys do.

"I just got tested when my ex and I broke shit off. I haven't been with anyone but you since then, so I can either show you the results or go again. Whatever makes you feel comfortable."

I sigh in frustration. "I want a new test." I'm short with him and climb into the bed.

"If you got enough rest, you don't have to stay here if you don't want to," I say, pulling the blanket over my bare legs.

"Alex, stop," he says while climbing in. "Stop sabotaging. I'm fine with everything. I'm not going to disagree, now stop being a fucking brat and let me hold you."

I stare at him incredulously. The fucking audacity of this man. He's right, though.

"Don't talk to me like that," I say, rolling my eyes, hoping he takes the bait.

"Oh, you don't like being told to be a good girl?"

"Nope, I sure don't."

"Bullshit, Angel. Bring that sexy little ass over here and kiss me before I fuck all that attitude out of this curvy little body."

"Hmph." I turn away, making sure I rub my ass on his thigh.

"Oh, you want this dick, don't you Alex Monroe?"

"No, I don't. I'm going to sleep."

"The fuck you are, rubbing that juicy ass all over my leg. I think you know exactly what you're doing."

I stay still, a smile as wide as the sky on my face. I'm not giving in, so I ignore him and fake it like I'm going to sleep. But before I know it, his big body is above me. He grabs my wrists in one of his hands and uses his hold to maneuver my body to face him. He pins them over my head and dips his head to suck my nipple in his mouth through the oversized shirt. His other hand reaches underneath to tease my nipples as his lips attack mine.

My core is aching for him. I feel the wetness from my pussy gathering between my legs. He grinds his knee into me, applying pressure in the most delicious way. I moan into his mouth and he growls.

"You're going to regret being a little brat."

"Oh, am I? Because I don't think I am."

He laughs, a darkness in his eyes I haven't seen yet. It's as if I'm dealing with another man altogether. My pulse quickens and I wonder if he can feel it thrumming underneath his fingertips. I've never been handled this way, but I fucking love it. He isn't intimated or phased by my confidence.

"Hurry up with it. I'm getting bored." He lifts his head from my neck where he was lightly sucking and looks straight into my eyes.

"Shut the fuck up and take this dick like a good little slut."

His free hand reaches down between us to release himself from his boxers. Then he moves it to my uncovered pussy and begins his assault. It's heavenly. He rubs my clit and brings me to the edge and then slides two fingers inside of me until I'm grinding into them.

"Fuck me, Kohen."

"What was that, Angel? You want me to do what?"

"Fuck me," I say louder.

"I don't know. I don't think Cora can hear you downstairs. You've been a mouthy little brat, so if you want this cock inside that pretty pussy, you better say it where I can hear it."

He removes his hand and circles around my slit as he kisses me deeply. I buck my hips into his hand because I will take anything from him I can get.

"Such a thirsty girl," he teases.

"Fuck me now, Kohen," I say so loud that I'm sure Cora hears me.

He thrusts into my pussy which is dripping wet for him. My hands are still restrained as he pounds into me. They are numb now, but I don't fucking care. He fucks me unapologetically, R.I.P. to my pussy. He hits deep inside me, causing the lines of pain and pleasure to blur. My hands are released and I move them to his curly jet-black hair. I tug at the strands at the base of his neck.

"Tell me this pussy is mine, Alex." His hazel eyes meet mine and I melt.

"It's yours, all of me is yours. You own my mind, body, and soul. I don't want you to but you do."

He doesn't pause, he fucks me even harder, forcing me up toward the headboard and I fucking love it. His kisses are desperate. With each one he takes more of me in, his drug, his addiction. He grinds his pelvis up into mine, rolling his hips at the same time and I explode. My pleasure ripples down my body and into my center as my pussy grips him.

He groans loudly into my mouth and I feel the throbbing and pulsing of his cock as I milk him. He falls over me, the weight of his body a comfort. He rolls off of me and slaps my thigh. That was fucking heaven. I could die right now, and I would be the happiest woman entering hell.

I laugh and he joins in on the laughter.

"That was okay." I roll over and rest my head on his chest.

"I'm just kidding. I've never been fucked like that and I loved it." I move to kiss him and like clockwork, his fingers find my hair and he tugs at it, forcing me to look at him longer, not allowing me to move in for the kiss just yet. He stares at me so intently, like I'm something he needs to study, or something he isn't sure is real. Like I'm going to disappear into thin air. Like I'm a masterpiece.

Finally, without a word, he lets go and our lips meet gently now. He rubs his hand thoughtlessly down my back until it stops, and light snores leave his tired mouth.

I can't sleep, so I just lay there, staring at the stars outside my window, listening to his heart. My heart, the heart he is giving me, the one I'm trusting with mine. Somewhere between his shallow breaths and heartbeats, I drift to sleep. Safe, with Kohen Ventura.

Chapter 28

Alex

I wake up and immediately notice the warmth beside me missing. My hand flies to the spot where he should be and just like I thought… Empty. My eyes fly open, and panic ensues. He wouldn't just leave like that, would he? I check my phone and it's 11 am with no calls and no messages. My eyes dart around the room for a note, but again, nothing. My stomach drops.

I jump up and rush around the room looking for something to put on under this t-shirt so I can run to Cora's room and bitch about this. I can't believe he fucking left. I grab my phone on the way to her room so I can text Xzavien. Kohen doesn't know I will fuck his best friend to hurt his feelings, and I plan to do it.

Right when my hand touches the doorknob, I take a step back so it doesn't hit me. The first thing I see is a coffee cup, and the tattooed arm it's attached to is not Cora's. I toss my phone on the bed and relief washes over me. I'm glad I didn't text Xzavien. That would have been a mess.

"You okay, Angel?" I hate the way I love for him to ask me that. His phone rings before I can tell him I thought he left. I think I'll take that as a sign that I should keep it to myself. He doesn't answer, but instead ignores it and shuts it off. Hmm, shady much?

"You aren't going to answer that?" I'm genuinely curious.

"No, wasn't anybody important. Want a sip of my coffee?"

"No thanks, but I see you made yourself at home. Why did you turn it off?" He sips his coffee carefully and I sit patiently waiting for his response. His eyes meet mine as he slurps.

"My phone?" I nod. "Well, because it's dying and I already told you I want to spend as much time with you as possible before I have to start training." Such a good excuse, but he did tell me.

I need to fucking chill, I'm still reeling from thinking he left. This anger is pointless, so I decide to let it go. I move closer to him and lay my head on his shoulder and hand on his thigh. He kisses my forehead and I melt. I fucking melt. Why the fuck am I like this? I was ready to throw all of this away just because I thought he left. I grab his coffee cup and put it on the end table.

I climb into his lap and he wraps his arms around me. His fingers find the ends of my hair and I feel him tugging at the strands lightly. "Why do you do that?"

"Why do I do what?" he asks, looking puzzled.

"Tug at my hair or play with it anytime it's down. I mean I'm not complaining, I was just wondering. It's cute."

A laugh leaves him as he continues to twist the ends in his fingers. "I don't know. I guess I didn't realize I'm doing it, or that I had ever done it before."

"You're doing it right now." We laugh. He kisses me and pulls it harder. "And what, you don't like it?"

"Oh, I fucking love it. I was just wondering why." I grind into him and he tugs it back harder exposing my neck. He starts gently sucking on the skin there and I can feel his dick rock hard between us. I palm it and he groans as he pushes the solid flesh into my hand.

"Fuck, Angel, we can't." He releases my hair and I look at him.

"Why, you don't want me?" I say, batting my lashes and pouting my lip, hoping he gives in to me.

"Exact opposite. I want you so fucking bad, but we need to get ready." That's right- our date.

"Okay, fine. But you're missing out." I walk away and sway my hips for extra effect.

"Oh, I know it. That pussy is pristine and it's all mine, but I want to enjoy other parts of you today. I want us to get to know each other on a deeper level."

He stands and makes his way over to me, trapping me between his body and my dresser. The air leaves me, no matter how much time I spend around him, he takes my breath away. He is absolutely fucking breathtaking.

His eyes are a deep green, with gold in the middle that flows out to blend with the green, like an artist took a paintbrush and strategically placed golden streaks of gold there as if to make a sunflower. The outer ring of his eye is such a thick band of black, it's like nothing I have ever seen and almost looks fake. My hands move to touch his face on their own accord, and I couldn't stop them if I wanted to. It's as if my mind and body need him, for my senses to be filled with the sight, scent, and touch of him.

These feelings are overwhelming, mostly because I've never wanted this. It feels inevitable, written in the stars, or like fate.

Star-crossed.

I pepper kisses along his chiseled jaw. Before I know it, the words leave my mouth. "I like your face."

He laughs and so do I. I love laughing with him. "I like your face too, Angel. You are absolutely beautiful." I feel myself blushing and I look away. "Look at me," he tells me.

"No, I have to get dressed, remember?"

"Look at me now, Angel." My eyes dart to him responding without my permission to his command.

"You are so fucking beautiful, inside and out."

"Are you sure?" I ask, desperate for his praise. I've never been talked to like that before him and now I crave it. Don't get me wrong, I've been told my pussy feels good, it's tight and I'm hot. But Kohen's words pierce through me, infecting me with his toxic poison that possesses me and I welcome it. Giving myself over to it, to him.

"Yes, Angel, in every way that counts." Our lips meet and he grabs my waist, squeezing gently. "Now get that sexy little ass dressed," he says, slapping my ass to get me going. "Chop, chop, baby. We are wasting daylight."

Chapter 29

Kohen

We pull into the theme park and I head into the VIP parking area and pick a spot. I look at Alex. Wonder fills her eyes as she stares at all the rides out of the window.

"Is this where we are going on our date?" Excitement laces her voice and joy fills me up in return.

"I never got to go to a theme park before. We couldn't afford it growing up and when the school went on field trips, my mom never signed my permission slip."

"So I did good? You're excited." She kisses me hard, her tiny hand landing on my shoulder and squeezing it.

"You did so good, babe! One time I forged her signature and halfway there, the bus pulled over and the principal picked me up to drive me back. I got in so much trouble. I just wanted to have fun like every other kid."

She called me *babe* but didn't even notice. I'm chipping away at the walls she's built up. She's guarded, but I won't let that phase me. Despite what people think, I'm a patient man. It helps that she's worth it. I'm playing the long game here. So far so good.

Alex

I feel giddy, like a little girl. Butterflies flutter around inside me with excitement. I have always wanted to come here. I look over at Kohen's handsome face and he unbuckles his seatbelt and leans over, twirling the ends of my hair around his fingers for a second before he gently tugs on them to bring me closer to him. I shift my body to face him, biting my lip trying to contain my excitement.

No words are spoken as I look into his hazel irises. I see what he wants from me. I cup his face in my hands. Placing both palms on either side of his cheeks, shock rushes across his features at the gentle gesture. I pretend not to notice and lean in for a kiss. Our lips touch gently at first and then he pulls me into him with desperation. Like I'm the air he needs to breathe in and fill his lungs with to survive. I get it since he is my air, too. I hate that he is, but I can't help it anymore. I want this. I want *him*.

I pull back. "Okay, Kohen. If we keep this up, you're going to be the only ride I get on today." I place a quick peck on his lips and a sigh escapes me. "Thank you for bringing me here."

His smile spreads from ear to ear and the dimple I love is on display. I poke it.

"I love this dimple."

"You love it, huh?" he teases.

"Yes, I do."

"Good, I'm glad. And you are welcome. I love this place, it grounds me. Brings me back to my childhood, a time when I could just have fun and be free. You know?"

"I don't, my childhood wasn't the best. My mom was... Well, she was something special and not in a good way."

His hand grazes my cheek as he pushes the hair away from my face, causing me to look up at him. "I'm sorry, Angel."

"Anyway," I say, pulling away. "Enough of that, let's have some fun. Show me the childhood I never had!"

"Okay, bet! I'm going to make this the best day ever."

Reaching over to open my door, I see him running around to beat me to it, so I act like I dropped something on the floor to let him. Look at me being kind. Cora would be so proud.

My door opens just as I'm straightening up, and he holds his hand out for me to grab. "Oh, we have a gentleman. Chivalry isn't dead after all."

He laughs the most beautiful laugh. It's deep and grainy and it does things to my insides.

"You have a funny sense of humor," he says, lacing his fingers in mine. We begin to walk hand in hand to the ticket booths. I look at him out of the corner of my eye several times, wishing this was a dream. Most women want a man like him, he is the dream for them. Me, I only see all the ways letting him treat me right could hurt me. I battle with myself constantly. Wanting him, hating him for making me want him, and being scared of being hurt by him. That's where self-sabotage comes in. *Hurt him before he hurts you.*

I suck in all the negative thoughts and push them to the back of my mind. Determined to enjoy this day, I squeeze his hand gently and tug so he moves closer to me. I rest my head on his arm as we walk, and he brings his free hand up to tug at the ends of my hair, causing me to look up at him. He winks. I smile as butterflies explode inside me.

Ticket booth in sight, I begin to take my purse out and ask how much tickets are so I can pay for myself. He stops dead in his tracks, causing me to pause and look back at him. Disbelief stretches across his face, his left eyebrow raises in question, his head slightly slanting like a confused puppy.

"What? Why are you just standing there?"

He scoffs. "Put your wallet up, I'm buying. This is going to be the best night of your life, and I want to be fully responsible for giving it to you."

I giggle. "Yes, Sir," I say playfully, batting my eyelashes dramatically as I walk up to him, placing my palms on his chest. "I'll let you give me the best night of my life." He wraps his fingers around the back of my neck, forcing me closer.

"Keep teasing me and I'm going to bend you over one of these cars and fuck you." I gasp at his words as he brings his lips close to mine without touching them. "Right here in the parking lot for everyone to see, would you like that, Angel?"

"Yes," is all I can manage to get out. If I was wearing panties they would melt. I love this side of him. He is kind and sweet to me and I love it, but this dark side of him that is rough, possessive, and commanding is such a turn-on.

"Well, my sexy little slut, you're going to have to wait until we get home. Right now, we're going to have fun."

"Fine," I say, smirking. "We have too much sex anyway." Pulling away first, I make my way up to the guy selling tickets and his eyes widen, taking note of my pebbled nipples underneath this tank top. "We want two tickets," I say. He has yet to make eye contact with me.

Kohen clears his throat and I move over, giving him space. "She has eyes, bro. Stop fucking staring at my girl's tits or I'm going to go in there and rip your eyes out of your fucking head, got it?"

I look up at him, shocked, my jaw on the cement. What the fuck? I mean don't get me wrong- I fucking love that shit, but it was extremely unexpected. I cross my arms over my chest to cover up what I can. Kohen keeps eye contact with the guy the entire time he's paying. He grabs our wristbands and we head through the iron gates. I have officially checked an item off my bucket list.

"What do you want to ride first?" he asks nonchalantly as if he didn't just go all caveman.

"Nah ah, don't try and slide past what just happened? What was that back there?"

"Nothing, I just..."

"Just...what?"

"I don't know, I don't want anyone looking at what's mine?" He bites his lip nervously, and it makes me giddy, the two extremes this man has for me make me feel good.

"Okay, I got you. Let's get on The Rattler first. I've always wanted to ride it because they say it's the only coaster built of wood, is that true?"

"Yes, it's true. They tried to reinforce it with steel recently, but the company's original owner went to court to object to it. As far as I know, it's still the OG."

"Fuck yes!" I'm excited.

We walk up several flights of stairs and get in line. Luckily, Kohen also got what's called a fast pass, so we can skip ahead and not have to wait at the end of the line. They call us up to the first car and my body is radiating with energy and excitement. We climb in and the bar settles across our laps. Kohen's hand is on my thigh, his pinky rubbing the softness there. The man buckles the last strap for us and helps the rest of the riders get settled in safely. The horn blows and we begin to move. The slow and steady climb up the coaster gives us a moment to talk.

His hand has shifted closer to the inner part of my thigh. His pinky is a hair away from my pussy and it causes me to hold my breath. I want him to touch me there so badly. The rumble of the coaster beneath us and the clicking noises of the car making its way to the top, combined with this surge of energy, are making me feel hot and bothered. I spread my legs and he rubs the lips of my pussy with three fingers, his middle one making its way through my lips. I jump a little at the sensation.

His lips meet my ear and the soft warmth of his breath as he speaks drives me wild. My pussy is dripping wet and I thrust my hips up into his hand. "Shhh baby, don't make a scene." His tongue grazes my ear and his middle finger enters me at the same time. Cool air blows through my hair. I hadn't even noticed we reached the top. His palm presses into my clit as his fingers fuck me, and it feels so *fucking* good. I close my eyes, trying to conceal the secret pleasure I'm receiving.

A rush of wind whips through me, eyes still closed, and the rumble of the wild coaster aids in the sensation of this finger fucking session.

"Oh my god!" I shout, throwing caution to the wind. No one can hear me anyway. I buck into his fingers every moment I get. My abdomen is tight from pleasure, my core clenching the delicious feeling of his fingers inside me, fucking me.

"That's right, Angel. Come for me, baby. You look so sexy."

I moan loudly, opening my eyes to find his, a whirlwind of trees, mountains, and scenery from the park flashing by. Finally, my eyes meet his, and the darkness within his irises, while he watches me, brings me to the edge. He shoves his fingers down to the knuckle and I grip them. My orgasm rocks through me like nothing I have ever felt in my life.

"Good girl, you are so fucking beautiful." He removes his fingers from me and I watch him, thinking he is going to wipe them on his jeans, the coaster still knocking us around. I gasp when I see him close his eyes and smell them. "Mmmm, you smell so fucking sweet, Angel." Then he puts them in his mouth, sucking my juices off his fingers. My eyes widen as he slides them out slowly. "Tastes sweet, too," he smirks. "I told you I would make this the best night of your life."

He is so fucking right. This is absolutely the best night of my life. We spend the rest of the time riding every single ride here and playing every game. His treat.

I think I could get used to being his.

Chapter 30

Alex

The last few weeks have blown by in a blur. It's as if I've been driving full speed on this racetrack called life and the world outside is either standing still or following suit. Kohen has been the sweetest through all my mood swings and I couldn't like him more than I already do. Aunt Flow is currently visiting, and it feels like somebody is repeatedly stabbing my uterus with a knife. He's supposed to come over tonight so we can snack and watch tv. I refuse to say Netflix and chill, which Kohen constantly teases me about.

I expected him to disappear while I had my period, but like every other time, he proves me wrong. Just like every other time I refuse to believe he is this good. There has to be something, right? For now, I've stopped looking because I'm enjoying the now. I still can't even believe I'm saying this. Subconsciously, I'm waiting for the other shoe to drop. I like him- a lot- but my heart remains locked away, and the key has been swallowed by the beast inside my soul. Not letting anything or anyone close enough to break it further. To be honest, it isn't even a whole heart. Only shattered pieces reside in its place. Does a shattered heart still beat? I guess we will find out.

My phone pings.

Kohen: I can't wait to see you, Angel.

Me: me too, see you soon

Kohen: I got all the goods, but I can't find those galaxy cubes you keep asking for anywhere.

Me: ugh it's okay. I know they are a pain in the ass to find, thanks.

I silence my phone as I enter the dance studio. I haven't told Kohen I dance yet. I don't tell many people. Sometimes the goal to be a dancer seems far-fetched. I love all types of dance. Salsa, cumbias, line dancing, ballet, everything. My favorite is freestyle, though. I like hip hop, but there's just something about sensual dancing. It's empowering to dress sexy and wear some heels. I love seeing women build their self-esteem and confidence while taking the classes. Expressing your individuality through art, with your body... It's sexy as fuck. I'm thicker, so I get all the eyes on me from people assuming I can't go as hard as they do. Shit, I go harder. Dance runs through me like blood runs through my veins.

Dance isn't a realistic career goal, but I love it. I put my heels on over my fishnet-covered feet and look around to see if anyone is here yet. To my surprise, it's empty. The mirror-lined walls reflect the broken doll back to me. She is beautiful but broken. I turn to look at my ass and it looks amazing if I do say so myself. My black daisy dukes hug every curve. The fishnet hose come up to my curvy waist and meets the edge of my black crop top.

I grab the remote from the table and press play. "Under the Influence" by Chris Brown blasts through the speakers. I place the remote back down and begin to sway to the music, my hips winding back and forth like a boat sailing through a stormy ocean. My arms lift and hit each beat, and then I run them down my breast and abdomen until I'm bent over and reach my toes. I drop down to the floor, on my hands and knees crawling toward the mirror slowly. My hair is a disheveled mess, but damn I feel sexy. I roll my body, face down ass up until my body is upright and I'm on my knees. I run my hands through my long hair as I bounce up and down on my knees to the beat. In one swift motion, I pop up to my feet and walk away from the mirror as if I'm a model on a runway. I see some of the girls from class watching and recording. I don't mind it, I'm not shy.

One of the guys from the hip-hop class walks by and pauses to watch. He leans against the door frame, a smirk playing on his lips. I'll admit before I met Kohen, I had a huge crush on him. I only wanted to fuck, though. Nothing serious for me.

I whip my hair around and my body follows to face the mirror again. To my surprise, right as I sway my hip to the right, a large hand splays across my abdomen, and the crowd roars. His body moves in rhythmic sync with mine. My core clenches and guilt makes my stomach flip flop. We continue to mirror each other's freestyle motions. It's as if it's something we've choreographed, the guilty thoughts run rampant in my head. Why the fuck should I feel guilty? The dancer's hands are in my hair and I roll my head, following his lead. I love a man who can dance. We move like we're one person, a battle we are both winning. He runs his hands gently over my ass as we spin slowly and he's behind me. My body follows his, so I bend forward as his hand runs down my spine. I drop to the floor again and the music cuts suddenly.

I look up to the place on the table where I left the remote and see the last person I ever thought would show up here. Kohen.

Kohen

My chest is fucking heaving and my heart is beating so fucking hard. What the fuck is Alex doing here, and why the fuck is she dressed like that? Is she in dance? Why wouldn't she tell me? God damn, I thought I had made leeway with her. I've shown her in almost every way possible that she can't do much to push me away, and she's tried. Fuck me, has she tried.

His hands are on her body, the way her body is moving...this looks a lot like the way we fuck. So what *the fuck-* is she fucking him, too? I want to fucking kill him. I watch as they move in sync like they belong together. My hands are balled into fists and I'm shaking. I can't move, don't want to move, because if I do, I'm yanking her right out of this little shrimp's arms. He's muscular for a dancer but he's nowhere near as tall or as athletic as me. Definitely not as handsome. So, what the fuck is she doing?

His hand grazes over her plump ass and I lose it. *That's it.* I make my way to the table where I noticed the remote is sitting. I see his hand trace down her spine. Mine. That's the only thought that comes to my mind. The crowd is radiating energy for them, shouting, and cheering for the couple on the dance floor. Only they aren't a couple, that's MY girl. I hit the power button on the remote and silence consumes the room. Her head pops up in my direction and her eyes widen in shock. That's right, Angel, I'm here.

"What the fuck are you doing with your hands on MY girl?" I growl as I stalk toward them.

"My bad, bro. I thought she was single, we were just dancing." He looks afraid. Good.

"Kohen, what's wrong? We were just dancing." She walks away from me and grabs a towel from the shelf, wiping the sweat from her forehead.

"I don't give a fuck, it looked like you were practically fucking. Is this what you do when your phone is on *do not disturb?* You meet this little pussy bitch to dance and then what? Fuck?"

"It's not like that." She rolls her eyes and gathers her shit. I step directly in front of her, she needs to answer this. I can see her evading the situation mentally and I'm not having it.

"Hey, bro, back the fuck up. We don't fuck, I don't even know her name." Oh, pussy bitch thinks he can speak.

I walk right up to him and before he knows what to do, my fist is in his face. His hands go to his nose, and he cries out. "What the fuck, bro?!"

"Don't touch what doesn't belong to you, bro," I say sarcastically.

"Are you nuts?" she shouts.

"Yes, Angel, as a matter of fact, I am. YOU drive me fucking nuts." I grab her by the back of the neck and pull her into me. "I will not be disrespected." I crash my lips to hers. The crowd still surrounds us as I suck the soul from her body. The soul that belongs to me. I've never been possessive like this. I don't know if it's from being cheated on by my ex Erica, or if it's Alex and what she does to me, or both. She moans into my mouth, enjoying the ravaging of my tongue inside her mouth. I pull her face back by her hair so I can look at her.

"You're mine, understand?"

Her eyes are wide as she takes me in, pupils dilated and her breasts rise and fall dramatically while she catches her breath. I bring my mouth to her neck and suck and bite, salt coating my lips and tongue, but I don't care. It's delicious, *she* is delicious. I move back to look at her once more, my hand still in her hair. She hasn't answered me.

"Do you understand, Angel?"

"Yes," she says, simple, short, and sexy leaving her lips in a breathy sigh.

"Mmmm, that's right, Angel." I bring my lips to her ear and blow gently, cooling the hot skin there and whispering only for her to hear. "Good girl." I release her hair and toss the remote on the table.

Grabbing her hand and taking her bag, I lead us out of the studio. "Let's go." To my surprise, she doesn't argue or resist. She must know she fucked up. The pussy I hit is nowhere in sight and I'm glad. One hit was enough to know I wasn't playing. Now let's hope Alex learns that I won't be playing her little games when it comes to her being my girl. I already made that mistake once, I won't be making it again.

We get to my car. I don't even know if she drove herself at this point but I also don't give a fuck. I will bring her back to get her car if needed or send someone for it. She hasn't said anything yet but I'm sure I'll catch a few words once we are in the car. It can't be this easy to get her to comply.

I open the car door and she gets in and buckles up. I lean in and kiss her already-swollen lips before closing her door. I run around the back of the car to get to her. My feelings for this girl are stronger than I ever anticipated. Maybe I'm the pussy bitch, because I just want her, and I want her to trust me. I'm a hard ass, I've had to deal with my asshole of a father, but my mother kept my heart soft. She loved gently and taught me to love. She loved hard, up until she passed. She taught me to be a loving, kind gentleman. While he taught me to be a man, cocky, strong, tough, and dedicated to my future above all else. I guess I'm a mix of them both, but I'd rather be more like Mom. I want to love Alex like my mother loved.

I reach for the door handle and the little *click* sounds right before I can pull it open. She fucking locked it.

"Stop playing, Alex. Open the door." I throw my head back in frustration. This is why she was so submissive.

"No, you ruined my class." She sits, staring out the windshield, her lip pouting like the brat she is. Her arms are crossed over her chest, showcasing her tits.

"Alex, if you want me to fuck you, I will. But, baby, you have to open the door."

She side-eyes me and then rolls them. "Don't fucking flatter yourself. I'd rather go fuck...whatever his name is with a broken nose than you." This girl is going to end me.

"Oh yeah, then go," I say. "I'll drop you right in front. Open the door."

She rolls her eyes.

"Your tits look good, can you cross your arms a little tighter so I can see more of the juicy mounds pouting out of your top."

She doesn't say anything but reaches to put her jacket on.

"Oh come on, Angel, don't put your jacket on. When you open the door, it's just going to come back off anyway." She scoffs. My phone rings but I ignore it, not even looking at the screen.

"Fine, I'll go find a sexy little ballerina to dance with." I start to walk away toward the studio and the sound of her door opening makes me smile. She can't see it, though.

"No, the fuck you won't!" she yells across the parking lot. Thank god for long legs. I know her little ones can't catch up. "Kohen!" she shouts.

"Yes, Alex?"

She laughs, not liking the use of her name while we're arguing. "Where are you going?" She sounds close, so I take the opportunity to turn and jog toward her. She doesn't notice at first, which helps my plan to catch her off guard. When she finally looks up, I'm about two feet in front and she turns to run. It's no use, again, long legs for the win.

We're both laughing when I scoop her up and throw her over my shoulder.

"Kohen put me down!" she shouts, laughing and hitting my lower back.

"No," I say simply as I spank her ass hard. She yelps.

"What was that for?" she asks, confused.

"For pretending to be a good girl, after being a bad girl, and then being a bad girl again."

"That doesn't even make sense." She tries to wriggle around, making it hard for me, so I spank her again.

"Ouch! Kohen. WTF!"

"Yes, Angel?" I say, questioning her as if I don't know what she's complaining about. Finally reaching my car, I toss her in and climb in after her.

"What are you doing?"

"Oh, I'm going to fuck all this brattiness out of you."

"The fuck you are."

"Oh, I am, Angel, and you're going to fucking love it."

She licks her lips, curiosity in her eyes. She's so fucking beautiful, a pain in my ass, but absolutely beautiful. I sit here looking at her.

"What?" she asks quietly.

"Are you fucking him, or..." I pause, not sure if I want to know. "Are you with him?"

"What? No, Kohen. Omg. I'm not a whore. I've only been with you. I wouldn't hurt you like that."

"Y'all looked so...good together. I don't fucking know, but I do know he definitely wanted to fuck you."

"Well, I don't want him," she says, climbing on my lap. "I want you."

"Fuck, Angel." She grinds her pussy on my already rock-hard cock and I groan.

"Can I tell you something, though?"

I play with the ends of her hair that sit at the arch of her back. "Yeah."

"I felt this weird feeling in my stomach when he started dancing with me. Like I wanted to throw up. I didn't ask him to dance, I was dancing alone and he joined halfway through and my body just reacted."

"Reacted, how?"

"I don't know how to explain it. Like, you're right, dancing is intimate to an extent but not how you think, but I did feel guilty. As soon as I felt his hand on my stomach, you popped into my head. That's never happened to me before."

"Yeah?" I tug at her hair a little harder and she exposes her neck to me.

"Yeah, I'm sorry. I should have stopped it."

"You're right. You should have, but you're with me in my car, on my lap, and I'm about to fuck your pretty little pussy until you're begging me to make you come all over me."

"Are you mad?"

"I was. I saw red. You are mine, mine to fuck, mine to possess, and mine to love."

She gulps audibly. "Love?"

"Not yet, but yes." Her brown eyes search my hazel ones. Looking for inconsistencies, lies, or anything really. Anything to give her an out. I won't give her one. Not ever.

She pulls her jacket off and I run my hands down her arms. Goosebumps erupt everywhere our skin touches. She reaches for the hem of her shirt and pulls it over her head. No bra, bad girl. I won't give her shit for it, though. I reach down and unbutton her shorts. She lifts off me to pull them off and then I realize she has fishnets and heels on. So, she climbs off me and strips down to nothing. The way she displays herself for me is the hottest fucking thing I've ever witnessed. I reach out to pinch her nipples and she bites her lip.

I push down my sweatpants and pull my cock out. Spitting on my hand to wet it, I pump it a few times. She climbs back on my lap, taking my cock in her hand and placing me inside of her heaven. She slides down my length easily. "So wet for me."

She moans as she rides my dick. Bobbing up and down and rolling her hips at just the right time, every time. She is my greatest sin and I will gladly burn in hell for her.

I wrap my hand around her throat and she gulps. Pushing herself into my hold, I tighten my grip. She moans and her pussy clenches around me. She loves this shit. I pull her toward me and bite her neck, then I kiss it and suck gently at the place I know I brought her a little pain. Her pussy gushes down around me, soaking my sweats in response.

"That's right, Angel. You love it when I hurt you, don't you?"

"Yesss." She gasps.

"Fuckkk, Angel, lean back and show me what it looks like."

She listens like a good girl, leaning back as she pops her pussy on my cock. Watching it go in and out of her is so fucking beautiful. I see her, her wetness, her pretty pink pussy swallowing me up, taking me like a good little slut. *My slut.*

I push her back further, holding her by the throat. She wraps her hands around my wrist. My other hand at her hip, I'm controlling her thick little body now. Pulling and pushing her up and down on my dick. Her walls are clenched so tight around me with her arousal, causing my spine to tingle, tension building as I plunge into her. She starts to moan, digging her nails into my skin.

"Fuckkk, Kohen, keep going. Make me come."

"Say. Please. Like. A good. Girl."

"Please, Kohen, please!"

I grind up into her as I pull her down onto me.

"Oh fuckkk, you're so fucking deep!"

"Say my name, Angel."

"Kohennn, Ahhh!"

That's all it takes. I thrust up into her hard, grinding and thrusting. Then I feel it, her orgasm radiating through her as her whole body tenses and then relaxes.

"Thank you," she sighs weakly. Those two little words push me over the edge and I fill her up with my come. My cock pulsates inside her relentlessly as I release everything I have into her. Anger, insecurity, doubt.

She moves to rest her head on my chest and I hold her, playing with the ends of her hair. The softness comforts me. She's breathing softly as if asleep, but when I look down at her, she rests her ear over my heart. She looks up at me without moving her head and I wink at her.

"Your heart relaxes me," she admits, looking away shyly.

"Your hair relaxes me," I admit back.

She smiles against my chest. "I know."

She knows.

I don't know what's going to come from this, us.

It could be great, but it could also be catastrophic. I guess we will find out.

Chapter 31

Kohen

Alex's house has become a safe place. I think what I like the most is that X isn't here. He isn't lurking in the hallway or asking to hang out with Alex and me every waking second. I swear sometimes he's knocking before we even eat breakfast. We get to her place and shower after the hot car sex session we had earlier because we both needed it.

I had been training and she had been dancing.

"Why didn't you tell me you dance?" I ask, watching the shampoo rush down her beautiful body.

"You never asked." Typical Alex response, always avoiding any conversation that bears a part of her soul.

I scoff and she turns around, confusion spread across her gorgeous face.

"What's wrong?" Her arms wrap around my waist. This is what drives me crazy and keeps me dangling on her hook like a baited fish. She shuts me out of emotional shit and then lets me in physically. Yet here I am- pussy whipped. I can't get this girl out of my head. She has consumed every thought since I met her.

"Nothing, Angel..." I start to say, moving her hair away from her shoulder. "...I just hate when you don't talk to me."

"What do you mean? I talk to you all the time." She moves her head back to look up at me.

"Not about anything that matters."

She turns to shut off the water. "I'm not doing this, Kohen. Let's just chill, okay? Dancing is a need to know and I just don't think it's something you need to know." She storms out of the restroom and I follow her.

"Okay, cool. I got it. I won't ask anymore." I pull my jeans on and grab a t-shirt from my bag, rushing to get out of here before I say shit I don't mean.

"Good, don't," she says, sarcasm lacing her voice like venom.

I stuff all my shit into the bag and panic fills her features.

"Where are you going?"

"School. I have to meet my trainer to go over my diet plan for the upcoming meet."

"Well, are you mad?" she asks, following me down the stairs.

"Nah, I'm good." I don't even look back at her as I make my way to the car.

"Kohen, can you pause for one second." I glance at her quickly, hoping she won't notice. It's not that I want to teach her a lesson, but damn. I feel like a dog begging for scraps when I've given her a whole damn meal.

I shut the car door, not wanting to hear anything else she has to say right now. I'm too angry. I need to go work off all this aggression.

She stands on the porch watching me drive away, arms crossed over her chest and her hip propped against the door frame. I'm not giving in this time. It's her turn.

Alex

He drives away and my heart lurches. Why the fuck can't I open up? Every time my heart wants to let him in, my brain reminds me of every single reason why it's a bad idea. *He's going to hurt you.*

He hasn't yet, I remind myself.

My phone rings from upstairs and I rush up, hoping it's him. I don't want to fight, I'm just not ready to tell him my dreams of dancing. I don't want to hear more about how unreliable a career it is. The looks I get when I admit what I want to major in. Besides, right now it's just a hobby. My major is still undecided because I've never thought about doing anything other than dancing. I don't even have a general direction. I'm fucking lost and it's embarrassing.

I get to my phone too late, my sporadic thoughts slowing me. It was Xzavien. I'm not going to respond, I only want to hear from Kohen, but I also don't want to reach out first. I didn't do anything wrong and I feel like he's overreacting a bit. I'm just not ready and he should respect that.

My phone rings in my hand again and I look down at it. Xzavien's name flashes across the screen. I answer and switch to a video call, his gorgeous smile gracing my screen. Every time I see him I'm reminded of how handsome he is, but he isn't mine. Kohen is mine.

"Hey, X, what's up? Is everything okay?" I say, plastering a smile on my face so he doesn't see the sadness.

"Yeah, I just saw Kohen leaving your place like a bat out of hell. I'm just calling to see if you're okay."

I keep myself from rolling my eyes. I'm not stupid. I know that he has a crush on me, and despite my friend zoning him, he keeps pushing to be in my life. I like him, I'm just not attracted to him that way. If I were single, I'd fuck him, but he seems like he is the type who would be ready to get married tomorrow. He's just a bit too clingy for me.

"Yes, I'm fine. He just had to go meet his trainer." I put the phone down so I can find my shoes.

"His trainer? Today?"

My Spidey senses tingle. "Yes, why?" I ask, raising an eyebrow in question.

"It's not typical for the trainer to be there on a weekend, but he has no reason to lie to you, right?"

I can't tell if he is being sarcastic or not, but I decide not to take the bait this time. Kohen has zero reasons to lie. Except for the fact that he was upset and wanted to get away from me.

"Right, I may have misheard him. I was just getting out of the shower and he was putting clothes on." Pain washes over his face, but not enough for me to give an actual fuck. Kohen already told me about their little rivalry and I'm not playing into it, at least not right now anyway.

"Hey, I gotta go. I have some work to catch up on, but lunch soon, hun. We can catch up." I rush him off the phone and hang up before he can object to the call ending. I take it a step further and put his number on *do not disturb.* I dial Kohen. Nothing. The line rings and rings until it goes to his voicemail. What the fuck?

It takes everything in me to not jump in the car and show up to his training session. I call Cora to talk me off the ledge and no answer. I text Kohen's cousin and her *I'm studying ttyl* auto response pops up instantly. Fuck!

Fuck it. I grab my keys, jump in the car and head over to the gym he usually trains at on campus.

The building is huge, housing every type of sport known to man when it comes to the Olympics. The large brick building has tall windows showcasing state-of-the-art equipment inside and a huge swimming pool surrounded by a racetrack.

Butterflies attack my stomach as I walk up to this building. I have a fear of him getting mad at me for showing up here. Much like my ex would. It makes me second-guess showing up here. The trust issues from my previous relationship are raining over my current one, accompanied by a black storm cloud. I hate that he still has that power over me. I should leave, I shouldn't be here, but at the same time, Kohen left me without a goodbye and in such a bad mood.

My mind is conflicted between its usual toxicity and caring that I may have hurt him in some way. Why the fuck am I like this? This is why I wanted nothing to do with him, why I never want anything serious with anyone. I don't want to have feelings- I want to be the cold-hearted bitch I always am so I don't get hurt. Being lied to, used, and disrespected for most of my teenage life was enough hurt for one lifetime. Everyone that has ever claimed to love me has broken my heart or my trust in one way or another. Except Cora. She knows me better than everyone and is one of the only people who loves me, even though it's hard.

I wish I was easier to love but the world made me this way and there isn't much I can do about it now. I turn to walk away. This is stupid. *I* look fucking stupid standing here. If he didn't care enough about me to say bye or even finish the conversation, then why the fuck should I care if he is in there fucking someone in the locker room? I don't.

I unlock my car, climb inside, push the stupid start button, and throw it in drive. I look up to check my surroundings, making sure it's okay to go, and I see him. The cocky asshole of my dreams is leaning against his big stupid truck, *smiling.* He looks so fucking good with his wrinkly white t-shirt, grey sweatpants, and black gym bag slung across his muscular chest. His look is complete with the dimple on his cheek making a full appearance.

I melt, every single piece of mistrust, anger, and pettiness washed away by this stupid, stupid guy. He begins to walk over to my car and I put it back in park and shut it off. The butterflies are back, but this time I welcome them. I get out of the car and rush to him. He meets me halfway with arms wide open and I hate it, but his embrace feels like home.

I breathe him in, the strawberry leather scent making me dizzy.

"I'm so sorry, Angel," he says, the gravelly sound of his voice dripping with sincerity. My throat tightens and I bury my face into his chest, hiding the way my body reacts to him. "I shouldn't have left like that," he continues as he cradles the back of my head in his hand. I can't respond yet, so I stay silent, hoping he keeps talking so I don't have to.

Tears threaten to escape me and I don't know why. I don't want to cry. I didn't even realize I was sad. All I felt was anger. I shake my head and pull back, looking up at him.

An emotion I don't recognize spreads across his face and my stomach turns. Before I can decipher what it is, it's gone.

"Why are you crying, baby?" he asks, his thumbs wiping away at the wetness coating my cheeks. He leans down to kiss me and I feel confused. The emotions swirling inside me are foreign and I'm not sure how to handle them.

"I don't know why I'm crying," I admit. This man has some sort of magical powers that make me vulnerable and I don't like it. I don't like anything about this situation-ship at all. It's not what I wanted, but here I am in the thick of it.

"Why did you leave like that?" I ask him, more tears falling unwillingly. If I could force them away, I would. I feel weak. *He* makes me weak.

"I wanted to leave before I said anything I would regret. I needed to work off some of the aggression I was feeling about you never opening up to me."

I look away from his gorgeous face, ashamed that I pushed him to the point of wanting to get away from me. Self-sabotage is my bestie. "I don't know how to open up to you without feeling weak. You could break me, Kohen. You could turn what's left of my heart to dust." I take a step back from him, needing space, but he doesn't allow it. He's eating up what I put between us and pulling me to him by the waist.

"You are one of the most powerful women I have ever met. It's why I like you. From the moment I first saw you, I knew you were a force to be reckoned with." He pushes my hair behind my ear and cups my cheek. "Come on, let's get in the car. It looks like it's about to rain."

I look up at the sky and dark clouds now possess the place where the sun was shining before. Texas weather is so bipolar. We climb into my little Nissan, and as always, there is an energy between us that feels like a tangible force. Our eyes meet and a little smirk plays on his lips, but I'm not ready to be playful. He scared me, I was scared to lose him.

"Not funny," I say, breaking our connection.

His smile falters. "What's not funny?" He reaches for my thigh, and I shift away from him before he can make contact with my skin. "What's wrong?"

"I don't like how I fucking feel right now." Anger starts to rise within me, protecting my vulnerability no doubt. "I came here because you just left. You left like I was nothing."

"Angel, I said..."

I interrupt him. "You're sorry. I know, but it doesn't change the fact that you left. I know I didn't open up. I know I'm hard to love- or like, I mean- but I don't deserve to be walked out on. Like I don't matter at all." I'm crying again and he tries to touch me.

"Don't touch me, please. If you touch me, I'll melt and I don't want to melt. I want you to know how I'm feeling."

He sits quietly with his hands settled on his gym bag and waits for me to go on.

"I'm scared," I begin. "I don't like how I feel when I'm around you, mostly because I do like it."

Confusion is etched on his face and I continue before he starts to speak. I only have the courage to do this once. "I was scared to lose you tonight, scared because you make me feel safe, and I hate that because I want to feel safe by myself. I don't want a man to be my safety net because men leave."

"I'm not going anywhere, Angel," he reassures me.

"I'm not finished. Today, you walked out that door angry at me for not opening up, but I'm trying. I'm trying my best. My whole life I've had to hide how I feel so that I could be strong. With you, it's like I don't have to always be strong, but that scares me too. I'm telling you this now, scared as hell, because you can turn around and weaponize it. Like my mom did, my ex, and all the shitty people who have been in and out of my life. That is why I don't open up. I know you've been patient and I appreciate it, but I need to know you won't do this again. Because if you do, all the work you have done breaking down the walls I've built up will be for nothing." I look at him to gauge his understanding.

"I got you, Angel. I'm sorry, baby. I'm so fucking sorry. I won't ever walk away again, but you've got to give me something, at least sometimes. Like this now, it's so fucking sexy hearing you tell me how you feel. My dick is so fucking hard." He reaches for my thigh. This time I let him touch me. "Seriously, though, I promise I won't ever hurt your heart. Unfortunately, I can't make the same promise for your body," he smirks.

He leans in toward me and places a soft kiss on my lips and my core clenches. I grab his shoulders, pull him closer to me, and kiss him harder. I part my lips, licking his bottom one and he groans.

"Fuckkk, Angel. Feel what you do to me." He takes my hand from his hair and places it on his hardness. "I'm yours, Angel, and I'm not going anywhere. I'm so fucking sorry I made you feel like that, but I promise I'm going to ride out the storm that is Alex Monroe." We laugh.

"I guess I am a bit like this weather, huh?"

He looks out the window at the rain falling around us and says, "Yeah, you really are. Instead of naming a star after you, I'll name a storm."

"Ha, very fucking funny." I roll my eyes at him.

"What are you looking at up there?" I smack him for being an asshole, he always makes fun of me for rolling my eyes. "Let me drive, baby. Let's go grab some food and I'll come back for my truck later."

I climb over the middle console as he makes his way around the car and jumps into the front seat, his hair soaked from the rain.

"*We love rainy days don't we, baby?*"

"You asshole. Why would you quote that book right now!?"

"I'm sorry, kind of but not really. I'm jealous that a fictional guy can make you cry and feel all these emotions but me, I get nothing."

"I literally just poured my heart out to you, Kohen," I say, crossing my arms over my chest to show him I mean business.

"I know, and it's about damn time. If the guy from the *Ravenwood* gets your tears, I deserve them, too. 'Pick me, choose me, love me,'" he laughs out loud, his dimple pressing deep into his cheek.

"It's *Ravenhood* not *Ravenwood,* and now you're quoting *Grey's Anatomy,* too?" I ask, my laughter ringing through the car, matching his.

"What can I say? I'm a sucker for love, and you are just going to have to deal with it."

This is the second time he mentions *love* recently and the word alone is enough to make me want to vomit. There is no way we could love each other. None, but I also can't deny that there is a force between us that has pulled us together since moment one. I don't know how, why, or what it is, but I know he feels it too.

"Kohen?"

"Yeah, Angel?"

"Do you believe in love at first sight? Or like soul mates?"

He pauses to stare at me before continuing to back out of the parking spot. "Yeah, I do. Do you?"

Neither one of us is looking at each other.

"I don't know, I don't want to, though." I sneak a peek at him from the corner of my eye and he is running one hand through his gorgeous hair and using the other to handle the steering wheel.

"That's fair," he admits as he looks over to me. I can tell he wants to say something, but he doesn't. So, neither of us speaks for the rest of the ride. Kohen stares intently at the road and I close my eyes, thoughts drifting to all the what if's we could have.

Chapter 32

Kohen

I stare at the beautiful girl in my bed as I sip my coffee. I can't believe she came to find me after our argument the other day. She has really opened up and I'm hoping I have shown her that I'm not going anywhere. She is mine. I'm not giving her up for anything. The pull I have felt to her since the moment I laid eyes on her and caught the scent of her lavender shampoo as we crossed paths on those steps... I didn't know it would turn into this. Erica was the girl I thought I loved, but it's nothing in comparison to what I feel for Alex.

It's crazy as fuck to think I love her, but I do. I love this crazy fucking girl. I'm not telling her anytime soon, though. There is an invisible tether between us that binds us together, it makes as much sense as gravity holding us to Earth does. I sound like a pussy, but I'm grateful for anything in this world. It's the way my mom raised me. She taught me about true love. Her words stick with me. She always said, "Real men love deeply, and they love with their whole heart, Kohen Lee. I want you to be a man unafraid of love. Don't be like your father, he isn't capable of love, only ownership. Promise me, Lee."

"I promise, Mom."

My father cheated so often that she wanted to make sure I was a better man than he is. So, I strive to be. My first love is who I lost my virginity to. I thought we would get married. I was naive. The second girl I slept with was my first and only one-night stand. Then there was a friend I had that agreed to a platonic friend-with-benefits situation. She was two years older and we grew up around each other at our summer house in Florida, but that ended when she graduated. The last girl I slept with was my most recent ex-girlfriend, Erica. She was exotic and interesting, a model and an aspiring actress, but she was self-centered, spoiled, and righteous. She wanted to be treated like a queen but acted like a spoiled daddy's girl princess and she treated people like shit. I couldn't do it anymore, and her cheating was the icing on the fucking cake. It still broke me a little inside because I fell in love with her before I saw her ugly side, and that's why I accepted it for so long. Blinders man, they keep you stupid for a long time.

My girl stirs in the sheets of my bed and I set my coffee cup down, rejoining her. Her warmth envelops me as she moves closer to my body, wrapping her arm around my waist and placing her head on my chest. I inhale her scent, my drug, my addiction.

No one before her compares. She has intoxicated me. I hate that I have to leave her this week. I have to remain focused on my goals. This meet is important to my Olympic career. I have to go. I want to invite her but I know my father will be present and I don't want him to ruin this.

I stare down at her beautiful face, her soft golden skin, and long thick lashes. She is the most gorgeous woman I have ever laid my eyes on. I brush the stray hairs away from her face and run my thumb across her lips, down her jawline, and back up across her cheek. Her skin feels like heaven underneath my tough, calloused hands. She stirs again and I raise my arm as I stare down at her to see if she wakes up. She doesn't. I look at the clock on my bedside table and see it's five in the morning. She usually doesn't open her eyes until at least ten. I'm an early bird and I should be getting ready for today's workout but I just want to soak this in as long as I can before I have to leave. I run my fingers through her hair and my eyes drift closed from the comfort I feel from the action.

"I love you, Angel," I whisper into the silence as I fall asleep with the girl of my dreams in my arms. I hope these two weeks fly by.

Alex

I wake up to an empty bed. Kohen is gone, and as always, I look at the bedside table on my side of the bed. Just as I predicted - it's a vase of roses and a note. He does this every time he has an early morning workout. He doesn't want me to wake up and think he left like that one time. I was honest and told him how I felt. Well, not the part about being ready to text and fuck X if I had to...but that it made me sick to my stomach.

I stretch and look at the clock behind the flowers. It's ten in the morning. I grab the note and open it up. Kohen is such an old soul sometimes. Why not just text me?

Angel,

Good morning, I hope you slept well. I have training all day,

My dad will be there, he will be stalking every training until we leave for the meet tomorrow. I'm sorry. Let's go out tonight, I want to spend as much time with you before I leave tomorrow. My credit card is under your pillow, there's no limit. See you soon, gorgeous.

-KO

I feel so giddy as I fold the letter back up. He really does care about me. I've never had someone make sure I felt secure on every level as he does. I do wonder why he doesn't want me around his dad, is he ashamed or embarrassed? That's a thought I never let linger long because I don't want to meet anyone in his family anyway.

I climb out of the bed and head to the shower. I turn the water on and right when I undress, I hear a knock on the door and freeze. Who could it be this early? All the guys in this house sleep until the late afternoon.

Except Kohen and Xzavien.

I rush to the door in my towel, hoping it's Kohen surprising me, and boy am I wrong. Instead, it's a gorgeous woman, tall with short blonde hair and bright blue eyes, her skin is a golden tan color. She is absolutely gorgeous.

"Oh, hi. I'm sorry I thought you were someone else."

"Oh no, I'm sorry," she says, looking over my shoulder nonchalantly. "I must have the wrong room."

"Whose room were you looking for? Maybe I can help you. This entire floor belongs to my boyfriend."

Her eyes widen but she fixes her expression quickly. "You wouldn't know the guy I'm looking for. Sorry to disturb you, love." Before I can say another word, her long legs carry her down the stairs and out of my line of sight. That was weird, everyone knows this floor is Kohen's. Not giving it too much thought, I rush back to the bathroom to get under the steaming hot water so that I can head out on my little shopping spree. I want to be ready for my date with Kohen and I want him to eat his heart out when he sees me.

It takes me about three hours to get ready but it's fine. I know I can take my time because Kohen usually trains all day long. Usually, with my trust issues, I'd be popping my ass over to his training, but he has this way of making me feel so secure in whatever this is we have going on.

We haven't made anything official verbally, but I know Kohen, and more than that, there is something beyond words that ties us together. Call it love at first sight, fate, soulmates. I'm not sure and I kind of hate it. The magnetic pull I feel to him is unexplainable. I'm tethered to him. In his presence, I feel safe and in his arms, I feel like I'm home. I believe him when he says he will never hurt me since he has proven it time and time again. So, I'm giving my all to him.

I love him.

I feel nauseated admitting that to myself, but it's true. He makes me feel alive, worthy, beautiful, and most important, loved. With Kohen I'm not too much, or too hard. He gets me, and he doesn't hold anything against me or hold a grudge. *He's more myself than I am. Whatever our souls are made of, his and mine are the same.* I never thought I would deserve my own love story. I am

Hardin Scott, the Royal Dolce, Carter Mahoney, Heathcliff. I'm not the soft heroine who all the bad boys fall for, I'm the villain. Kohen is the king in this scenario, the hero. More often than not, I question why he wastes his time with me. Like I have a scarlet letter on my chest that I wear everywhere I go. Well, today I'm ripping it off and I'm embracing this, whatever it is, with him. I want it for as long as he'll have me.

I pull open my phone. I'm too excited for this date. I shaved everywhere and I have some sexy lingerie under this dress, thanks to Kohen and the little shopping spree he sent me on. I chose a short maroon dress. It has some ruching in the back that emphasizes my curves. The dainty little chain that crisscrosses in the back is perfect and I love the way it drapes around my neckline. Kohen is going to go nuts. I don't know where we are going, but I do know that no matter where it is, we are fucking. I'm already so fucking needy for him.

I text him impatiently.

Me: hey handsome, almost here?

Me: *sends image of my thighs*

No response. My tummy flips, he wouldn't stand me up, would he? The thought crosses my mind to text X but I would rather avoid that. He will see it as an invitation to come over. He has no boundaries and it drives Kohen crazy. My phone pings.

Kohen: damn angel, open up and let me see more. :)

Me: no Sir, you have to wait and see the rest.

Me: hurry home ;)

Kohen: mmm I love when you call me Sir.

Kohen: good girl.

Me: shut up!

Shutting the screen off, I head downstairs so I don't have to wait for him much longer. I will wait to put my heels on until I get downstairs. Kohen is on the third floor, and I don't want to fall and break my leg. I get to the bottom of the first set of stairs where Xzavien resides. I freeze when I hear loud moaning. It sounds like two grizzly bears are trying to kill each other. I giggle and run down the second set of stairs in a rush, and I run into a brick wall and fall on my ass.

"Damnnn, Angel," is all I hear, and I look up into my sexy man's eyes, embarrassed as fuck. He looks so good wearing some black skinny jeans with rips on the knees and some black-on-black vans with a band T. I don't think I have ever seen him dressed like this. I think I drool a little as my jaw hits the floor.

"You look so fucking good, baby."

I roll my eyes with a scoff and stick my hand out so he can help me up. "You don't look so bad yourself. I've never seen you dress like this. I like it."

"You do, huh?" he says, his smirk on display as he leans in for a kiss. I turn my face, causing him to catch my cheek. "That's cold, Angel." His eyebrows meet in confusion as he looks down at me.

"Well, maybe you shouldn't be a cocky asshole and should just say 'thank you, my gorgeous perfect girlfriend,' when I give you a compliment."

His eyes widen and his smile reaches his ears "Girlfriend? Where is she? I'd love to meet her because the girl I want hasn't confirmed if she's mine or not."

Sarcastic asshole. We laugh while he looks around as if trying to find said girlfriend. I push him gently and he pulls me into his chest, leaving no space between us. One hand rests at the top of my ass and the other is already tangled in the strands of my long hair. I go up on my tiptoes and kiss him on the lips gently and whisper, "I am yours, Kohen Ventura, and I don't want to be anyone else's, ever." Before I know it, his lips are on mine. He kisses me rough and unapologetic as he lifts me by my ass and grinds into me. My pussy throbs and I know I'm dripping wet for him.

He pulls back, his hazel eyes looking into my deep brown ones, searching. "You're really mine?"

"Yes," I whisper into his ear. It's simple and a matter of fact. I belong to him because I was made for him. There is no one else for me. It's him or no one. I run my fingers through his hair. "Did you get a haircut?"

"Yes, I tried something new. Like it?" I don't know how I didn't notice right away. But it looks so fucking sexy. The sides are cut short and edged up but he kept the top longer, his light brown curls on display falling halfway over his forehead. I swipe them away from his forehead and plant a soft kiss there.

"So handsome, babe"

"Thanks, sexy. Let's get going, though. We need to make it on time." He sets me down and I walk over to the main living room. The black leather sectional is empty for once. I sit down and start to put my heels on. "Let me help you." he offers.

I look up and he is already on his knees in front of me. He has a straight-shot view of my black lace thong if he sneaks a peek under my dress. I squeeze my thighs together, hoping he won't be able to see it, I want to surprise him. Images of him proposing flash through my mind like a movie, him in a black dress shirt and black slacks as we eat at a fancy restaurant with the most beautiful ring he picked just for me.

"Angel?" Kohen's voice brings me out of my hallucination. What the fuck is wrong with me? It's too soon to be thinking like that. We barely made it official. "You okay, Angel?" Concern laces his face and I stutter back a response.

"Y... Yes, okay. Are you?"

He laughs, "Yes, but I need your shoe if I'm going to put it on these sexy ass feet." I hand him my heel and lift my right foot so he can place it on me. Instead, he brings my foot to his face and kisses the arch, moving up toward my heel, peppering kisses along his trail. My breath hitches. "You sure you're okay?"

I nod, having no words and hoping we get out of this house and to our date before we fuck the entire night away. He laughs and focuses on the task before him. He gets one heel on, buckles the little strap, and taps my left ankle so I lift it for him. He gets the other heel on without all the funny business and we finally make it out the door of this god-forsaken mansion.

The drive is longer than I expected. We left the house at five and it's almost six-thirty, so we've been driving for over an hour.

"Are we going to San Antonio?" I ask as I stare out the window, looking for clues.

"Why yes, yes we are."

"Where are we going when we get there?" I'm so curious.

"It's a surprise, Angel."

I cross my arms over my chest and let out a huff of annoyance. "You know I don't like surprises." He surprised me in class for Valentine's Day with a huge bear and several dozen roses, and as if that wasn't enough, he had the acapella club sing me a song. I'm not even sure which one at this point but I was so embarrassed. I secretly love it but I won't dare admit it to him.

"You love surprises," he teases, squeezing my thigh with the hand he rests there while driving. He inches up and I smack his arm.

"Stop being a perv or we will never get anywhere or do anything."

He laughs so loud, it warms me up inside and my heart swells. I can't help but join in. I think I have laughed more with him than anyone. I love it. The light of the city comes into view and I'm filled with excitement. I feel another little squeeze on my thigh and I know it means he is watching me. He loves when I'm happy or excited. I look over at him and blow a little kiss to him. He winks back and faces the road to continue his mission as I stare out the window in awe of the nightlife surrounding us.

Chapter 33

Kohen

I look over at Alex every few minutes. I love the way she looks at everything as if it's Christmas morning. She is so tough and so strong because she's had to be, but with me, she's free. Free to be herself, to let go, and I fucking love it. Making her happy means everything to me. Sure, she has her moments, her triggers, and trauma, but I got her, and I think she is starting to see it too.

She said she's mine, all the times I have teased, pushed, and tried to please her into saying the words and she said it all on her own. I take the exit to the Tower of the Americas. She practically breaks her neck to look at me and I pretend not to notice.

"Kohen!" she shouts.

"Yes, Angel?"

"You took the exit to that restaurant in the sky."

I laugh and she smacks my arm. Her signature move. "Ouch, what the fuck was that for?"

"You." That's all she says- one word like I'm supposed to hear all the words in front and behind it.

"Me?" I question, confused.

Her angry little face looks so cute, one eyebrow raised, arms crossed, lips pouty. I want to rub my hard cock along those pouty lips, smearing my come all over them, mixing it with the gloss of her red lips. "Yes, you. You should have told me you were bringing me here."

"You're welcome," I state and she rolls her eyes. I would poke fun at her for it like I usually do, but right now I need to put out whatever fire she is trying to start. "I'm sorry, Angel. Cora said..."

She interrupts. "What did Cora say?"

"She said you always wanted to come to the restaurant in the sky." I try to hold back my smile.

"Well, she lied."

"No, she didn't." I pull into the parking lot and drop the car off with the valet. Alex refuses to get out, so the valet drives her back around when she realizes it's a far walk. She's such a brat sometimes. She walks up to the bench I'm sitting on and plops down next to me.

"I'm sorry," is all she states and places her head on my shoulder.

"It's fine, you little brat, but it would be nice to know why you were upset." I use air quotes and she bites her lip, trying not to laugh.

"I don't know. I just feel like *Pretty Woman.*"

I laugh and she pushes her bottom lip out. "Pretty woman? Why?"

"Well, because you sent me out with your black card, and now we're at this fancy place. I feel like I don't belong or like I'm the prostitute and you're the rich guy paying for my services," she whispers that last part and I laugh again. "Kohen, stop laughing at me," she giggles.

"Angel, you are a pretty woman, but you're not *Pretty Woman.* You're mine and I want you to be happy and to feel good. I want to be the one who makes all your dreams come true."

"I can make my own dreams come true, ya know. I don't need you or your money."

I grab both her hands and bring them to my lips, kissing her knuckles. "I know, Angel, but I need you, and I want to do all these things together. It's not a power play, Alex. You should know me better than that by now. We are equals, I just want you to see that you have a good man and you don't have to do it on your own because I got you."

Her shoulders relax and she leans back into me. "Okay," she states simply.

"Okay?" I ask, making sure it's all good.

"Yeah. Okay. You're right."

"Now let's go enjoy dinner." We lock hands and head to the door.

"Good, 'cause I'm hungry. This better be worth it."

I swear this girl drives me crazy, but I'd rather be crazy for her than sane all by myself. We ride the elevator to the top of the 750-foot-high building and we are both in awe the entire way up. We can see everything from up here and it's even better when you reach the top with the panoramic view.

The Chart House restaurant is highly recommended. Every table is covered in a crisp white tablecloth, and as we pass the tables filled with guests, the food smells amazing. I look at Alex and my mouth waters. Her hips sway as we walk, following the hostess to our table. I paid extra to have a more intimate experience with Alex. She squeezes my hand. My eyes meet hers and I wink. Blush rushes to her cheeks and my dick swells in my jeans. She is fucking exquisite, no woman in here compares.

We make it to our table and it's right by the window where we can see the riverwalk and the lights of the city. Her eyes are wide as she takes in the scenery. "It's so beautiful to be able to sit and really take it all in. Thank you for this, babe."

I smile so big that my cheeks hurt. "You are very welcome, Angel."

We order our food and the whole time we wait, we talk. Alex tells me about her dreams of dancing and that she can't pick a major because she really wants to pursue that career. She goes on and on about her grandparents and how they left her money that she doesn't like to use unless it's an absolute necessity. I commend her. She was raised on nothing, worked hard, and ended up blessed in the end. Karma, luck, God, I don't know but damn, she impresses me more and more every day. Most girls would be blowing that money on meaningless shit. Not her, though. She has a good head on her shoulders and is a badass woman. She just needs to see it for herself.

I listen to her talk and engage when needed, but I have a feeling besides Cora and Cecille, that no one has cared about her or her dreams. We pause to eat our food, both of us quietly eating and just being here enjoying each other's company.

The waitress returns to clear our plates and offers the dessert menu. While Alex orders what she wants, I stare at her, noticing all the little quirks that made me fall for her. The way she bites her bottom lip while she's thinking, the way she shut her eyes softly when the noise around us over stimulates her, the way she bounces her knee when she is getting anxious or angry. It's the little things that matter, and I notice every single one. She's fucking gorgeous, and no offense to the waitress, but she couldn't hold a candle to my girl.

I drop my fork and bend to get it from under the table. While I'm searching for it, I can't help but look to the heavenly place between Alex's legs. It's as if she can read my mind because she fucking spreads them for me. I get a straight view of her black lace panties, a nice surprise because she hates underwear. I'm not complaining, I actually like it. The little bit of flesh that shows through teases me. A thin barrier between me and my pussy.. On second thought, I don't like it. As soon as we leave, I'm ripping them to shreds.

It takes everything in me to not get on my hands and knees under this table and rip a hole in those panties so I can eat her pussy. Thankful for my self-control, I sit up and place the fork on the table, waiting a few seconds before looking in her direction. My dick is hard as fuck. If I look at her and her gorgeous pouty lips, I'm taking her to the restroom and fucking her senseless.

The waitress walks away and I brave a look. Just like I thought, her juicy lips are taunting me with a little smirk. My eyes slowly roam from her lips to her nose, to her apple cheeks, and finally to those beautiful chestnut eyes. They challenge me.

"Everything okay, handsome? You look like you need some air," she says, giggles escaping her.

Taking a sip of her water, she never breaks our eye contact. The waitress brings us the chocolate cake that Alex ordered. It's topped with ice cream and chocolate drizzle, perfection. Two new forks are placed in front of us and we dig in.

"Oh my god, this is delicious. It's like an orgasm in my mouth." I almost choke on the piece of cake I just shoved in my mouth at her bluntness. We both laugh and I'm dreading the moment I have to leave her.

"I'll give you an orgasm with my mouth, Angel." A drop of chocolate syrup sits in the outer corner of her lip and I lean over the table, wiping it away with my thumb. Unexpectedly, she turns her head, simultaneously sucking my thumb into her mouth. Her tongue swirls around it, removing the chocolate and making my dick rock hard all over again. It strains against the zipper, begging for relief.

"Angel."

"Yes, handsome?"

"We need to leave now," I demand.

"Why, are you okay?" Concern is etched across her beautiful face.

"Yes, baby, I just need to fuck you, like now." She gasps in response and I stand to adjust myself, her eyes falling straight to my crotch. "See what you do to me, Angel? Now be a good girl and take care of it."

Her eyes are blazing with lust. She licks her lips as she gets up to join me. I throw five hundred dollars on the table and we make our way out the door. I don't give a shit about everyone staring at how hard my dick is pushing against the fabric constraining it. I need to get to my car so I can fuck the living shit out of Alex. Her sweet pussy is the only thing I can think about. I want to bury my cock so deep inside her, filling her up with my come.

Chapter 34

Alex

We rush through the restaurant, both of us wanting the same thing. His dick in my pussy. I'm wet already. I can feel it. From the moment he dropped his fork, I knew he was going to look, so I spread my legs so he could see what was waiting for him after dessert. It worked exactly how I thought it would. With us fucking in his car. I've wanted him since the moment he came into the house.

We climb into the elevator and he doesn't even let the doors close before immediately pinning me to the wall, his grasp firm on my hip. He kisses me like a man possessed, unforgiving, a punishment. Chests heaving, he grinds against me, rubbing his rock-hard cock into my pussy. He pulls up my dress and rips the thong I'm wearing off my body.

"Don't ever wear these again," he demands.

Out of breath, I respond sarcastically, "Well, I can't because you ripped them." Redness from the fabric being forced off my body is splayed across my skin. I welcome it. He's on his knees now, this elevator ride to the bottom is long and there are no stops. He spreads my legs and dips his head, his lips making contact with my pussy. His fingertips find my entrance and he plunges two of them inside me.

"Fuck, Angel, you're so ready for me."

I moan in agreement as he continues his mission. My legs weaken at the pleasure. He pushes his fingers into me as deep as they will go, fucking me with them, claiming what's his. His tongue circles my clit and then he strokes it closer to where his fingers are.

"You taste so good, baby," he murmurs into my parted lips. He removes his fingers and picks one of my shaky legs up and over his shoulder, giving him more access to my throbbing pussy. I'm dripping for him, my wetness running down my legs. His tongue breaches my entry, and he fucks me with it, his nose rubbing my clit in the process. I don't even know if he can breathe and I really don't care. I want to come all over his face. I love the sounds of him licking all my juices up as he moans into me.

"Oh my god, Kohen, please." I know he likes it when I use my manners.

His hands come up, grabbing handfuls of my ass. He squeezes hard and I yelp at the bittersweet pain it causes, bringing me closer to my climax.

"Oh yes, please, make me come, handsome."

He moves to my clit, sucking and circling his tongue around it, his lips encasing it as he strokes his tongue back and forth. Like a waterfall, I come, squirting into his mouth and all over him. My eyes fly to his and he smiles, his perfect teeth putting my mind at ease. I don't know why I always feel like he will get upset at my mess, but he never does. He seems to like it.

"Damn, Angel, you tasted so fucking good," he pants, both of us still out of breath.

Like clockwork, the elevator comes to a stop as we reach the bottom level, and the doors fly open. The valet has the car ready and waiting for us. I notice some of them smiling wide. One of them hands Kohen the keys and makes eye contact with me. I follow the line of sight he takes when looking away, and I meet the tv they are all watching. It showcases the inside of the elevator. I nudge Kohen and he looks at the tv, eyes wide.

Releasing my hand, he rushes at them. "Were you fuckers looking at my girl?"

"No, sir, we didn't watch the whole time. We just saw some of it. It was hard to look away."

"You're welcome," I say and they all turn to face me.

"Don't fucking look at her!" he shouts, and they all turn away scared. "I better not see one of you little fuckers look our way, or I swear to god, I will fuck you up."

He follows behind me as I make my way to the car. I wait for him to open the door and slide in. Thankful for the dark tint of the Corvette, I keep my eyes trained forward as I wait for him to come in. So much for fucking in here now. He opens the door and slides in, throwing it into drive and speeding off.

"It's okay, Kohen," I say, placing my hand on his muscular thigh.

"It isn't, Alex. They saw you." I can almost see the anger radiating off him like steam. There are a few times now I've seen him get so angry that he looks like he'll explode, and every time it involves me.

"I'm sure they didn't see much. You were probably in the way."

I see his shoulders loosen up and continue to reassure him. "When I looked at the tv, it looked like the angle didn't catch much. Just a king on his knees for his queen," I tease, a little smirk on his lips.

"My queen, huh?"

"Yes, your queen." I lean over the middle console and kiss his cheek. He presses his face towards me and I pepper a few more. The intimacy we have is like no other relationship I've ever had. He is so touchy-feely all the time, I'm not used to it, but I love it so much. It makes me feel wanted. He takes my hand in his and brings it to his lips, but he doesn't kiss it, he smells it.

"I love the way you smell, Angel."

Blood rushes to my cheeks and I know they must be rosy.

"Why?" I ask, staring at him intently for a response.

"I don't know. It just comforts me in some weird fucking way."

I smile softly. "Well, sniff away."

He chuckles and brings his lips to my hand once more, kissing it gently this time. "I'm going to miss you."

That catches my attention. "Miss me? Why?"

"I have to leave for a couple weeks. I have a meet in Arkansas."

I stare at him incredulously. "Is that why you took me on this date? Because you wanted to butter me up before you left? Why didn't you tell me sooner?" I'm fuming.

"I'm sorry, Angel, my dad sprung it on me a few days ago..."

I interrupt, "Okay, you're avoiding my main question. Is that why you brought me out, left me your card, and ate me out? Because you're fucking leaving?"

"Well, yes but..."

"Unbelievable." I pull my hand away from him and turn my body toward him. I'm angry, so angry I could scream. I hate that he didn't tell me sooner, it makes all of this less special, like it was fake, or planned to appease me since he is leaving. I mean I knew the days would come when he was gone for weeks at a time, we talked about it, but what the fuck? I thought I would have some advance notice. Time I would know we were spending together before he left. I would have much rather been home with him watching movies naked under the blankets, fucking every few hours. I feel lied to.

"I don't understand why you're mad, Angel."

I scoff. "Don't call me Angel."

He sighs, "I don't want to leave on bad terms."

"Well, too bad, you should have thought about that." I continue telling him all the internal thoughts I just had. We fall into silence and a few tears fall from my eyes silently as I stare out the window into the night.

"I'm sorry. I... I didn't think about it like that."

More tears fall and I feel his warm hand on my thigh. I melt a little as he rubs his thumb back and forth across my skin. "I'm sorry if you feel like I'm overreacting, Kohen, but I just wish you would have told me. Communication is everything." I look at him, more tears spilling over.

"You aren't overreacting, you're just reacting and that's valid, but don't be mad, baby. I only did my best, too." He uses the back of his hand to wipe away the tears and I lean into it.

"Okay, let's not fight, I know now. Let's just go home and make the best of what time we have left."

"Deal." And so we do just that.

Kohen heads to the shower when we get home and I sit on the bed, phone in hand, scrolling through Instagram. I see all kinds of posts about a party tomorrow. My phone pings right as Kohen comes to grab some clothes. It's Xzavien and nerves hit me like a ton of bricks.

X: hey gorgeous, party tomorrow I hope you can make it. I know Kohen will be out of town. I can keep you company. Lmk

I don't respond. I want to go and X knows we are just friends. Kohen won't be here and there's no sense in staying home doing nothing.

Me: hey Cora

Cora: hey bestie what's up?

Me: want to go to a party tomorrow

Cora: is that a real question, duh I do

Me: okay cool, Kohen is going out of town and I don't want to be that sappy girlfriend that just sits at home all stressy and depressy while her man is gone

Cora: right.

Me: I'm serious

Cora: okay, I believe you.

Me: night, Kohens coming to bed.

Cora: night.

Kohen comes to the bed and turns on the tv, looking for a movie.

"So, while you're gone, me and Cora are going to that party tomorrow." I put my phone on the wireless charging pad built into his bedside table.

"That sounds fun, you and Cora deserve a good chill session. I feel like y'all haven't had a chance to hang."

"Yeah, our schedules have been off. I don't like it."

I roll over and wrap my arms around his body and lean my head on his chest. "Just do me a favor and avoid Xzavien while I'm gone. I still think he's pissed that you friend-zoned him, and I think he still likes you."

I keep my eyes trained on the tv as I speak to him. "I doubt. Some girl came looking for him up here earlier and when I came down to meet you I heard them fucking."

He laughs. "X? Someone came up here looking for him?"

"Yeah, she was a tall, gorgeous model-looking woman. Trust me, he isn't worried about me." Everything gets quiet, so I sneak a peek up at him and his facial expression is just flat.

"Well, either way, promise me you'll stay away from him."

"Sure, I promise," I say, fully intent on keeping a safe distance between us.

Chapter 35

Alex

It's still dark when I hear the rustle of Kohen's clothes being packed away. He was supposed to do it last night, but we ended up fucking a few times.

"Don't go," I say sleepily.

I see his silhouette moving around the room as he whispers, "I wish I didn't have to go, baby, but I have to." I groan in disagreement. The bed dips as he sits next to me, pulling the covers off of my naked body.

"Kohen, it's cold," I say, the complaint sounding a bit whiny. "Why do you always do that?" I turn to face him and can't see his face in the dark, so I reach out and touch where I think his cheek would be. Instead, I meet his lips and he kisses the pads of my fingers.

"I do it because I like it. I want to see and feel your beautiful body before I go."

"Okay, but I hate it," I lie, secretly it makes me giddy inside. I love the way he worships my body.

"No, you don't." He states as a smack lands on my thigh from his hand. It doesn't stop there as he grabs and gropes at my ass and hips. I yip at the little pressure and pinches he applies all over, followed by his lips. He kisses and sucks the soft parts of my flesh he loves.

"Kohen, stop it. You're making it harder on both of us."

"Okay, okay. I'll stop but I'm going to miss sleeping next to this sexy body for two weeks."

"Two weeks?" I sit up. "I didn't know it was going to be two weeks." I'm frowning but he can't see me.

"I'm sorry, Angel, it's not easy I know but this is my life. My dream."

Guilt washes over me. If it was me following my dreams, I would want support and understanding so I shift gears and do just that. "I know, handsome. I don't want you to feel bad. I completely understand and support you, I'll be a good... Olympic girlfriend?" He laughs. "I'm serious, like basketball wives but better!"

He kisses my hair. "You're fucking perfect, Alex Monroe."

"Stoppp," I say, pulling the covers to my chin.

"What?" he asks. "You only like it when I say you're my perfect little slut?"

My mouth waters and my pussy throbs. I know we can't have sex right now because he has to leave but, damn it, does he turn me on. "Yes, I love it."

"Oh, I know you do, Angel, and I bet your pussy is getting all juicy for me right now. I'm sorry I can't take care of it." The blanket shifts and his warm fingers find my naked pussy, spreading my lips apart so he can feel the wetness he knew was there. "Mmmm, just like I thought, filthy. Little. Slut."

I moan as he begins to kiss me. "Stop, Kohen." I hate to say it, but he has to leave. I don't want to be the reason he's late.

He removes his fingers and I hear the sound of him tasting me on them. "So fucking delicious, baby."

I'm blushing and suddenly so thankful he can't see me. I get out of bed and pick up one of his shirts off the dresser. He's so tall that it reaches mid-thigh. I inhale the scent surrounding me as I put it on, knowing I won't have him for two weeks.

"I got to go, Angel. Walk me out?" I grab my purse and keys. I don't want to be here without him. "You're leaving? You can stay here, just walk me to the door."

"No, I don't want to be here without you. X is downstairs and it's mostly guys here. I don't feel comfortable."

The light from the moon hits him as he stands near the door now. "You're right, good idea. I thought if you were here it would be better because I would know you're safe but with X here, I don't want him to pressure you into hanging out or anything."

"I agree. See? Same page! Look at us doing this boyfriend-girlfriend thing." I move towards him and slip on my sandals so we can get downstairs. He shuts the door behind us and we make our way down the stairs. The buzz of his door locks behind us. His damn smart house freaks me out. It's like it knows we are leaving. We get to the front door and lights are shining through the glass panels of the front of the house. "Shit, my dad's here."

I stare up at him, a small smile plays on his lips apologetically. "I'm a big girl, I'll be fine." I tiptoe to kiss him and he places a soft kiss on my forehead. What the hell? Why wouldn't he kiss me?

He opens the door, leading me outside. His dad opens the door to his Mercedes Benz and starts to walk over. "Is that you Kohen Lee?" His voice is a deep baritone that shakes my nerves.

"Yeah, Dad I'll be right there." The nervous tone of his voice shocks me. He always sounds so confident when he speaks. Is his dad that much of an asshole?

"Who are you with, son?" his dad asks, taking a few more steps in our direction.

Kohen rushes me to the car and kisses me gently on the lips. "I'll see you in two weeks, Angel, be good." He shuts the door before I can say or do anything else. I'm left confused. Is he fucking embarrassed of me? That was weird Right? I turn on my car and watch as he joins his dad leading him back to their vehicle. His dad takes one last look in my direction before getting in the car and taking off. What the hell just happened? I pull my phone out of my purse and text him. There's no way I can just let that shit go.

Me: that was fucking weird

Kohen: I know, I'm sorry. My dad's a dick. I don't want you to meet him and think differently of me

Me: I would never do that

Kohen: I'm sorry, but while we're together I'll be MIA.

Kohen: just know I miss you, Angel, even when I don't respond, every time you think of me know I'm thinking of you too.

Kohen: and that tight pussy, and the way it fits perfectly around my cock. Winky face emoji.

Me: K

Kohen: don't be like that

Me: like what? I'm tired AF, going home to sleep. Night.

Kohen: okay, night.

I don't respond. I put my car in drive and head home. I have to get some sleep before the party tonight. Any ounce of guilt I felt about accepting Xzavien's invite just got washed away with Kohen's red-flag behavior.

Chapter 36

Kohen

I wake up as we approach the airport and my dad is on the phone, unleashing his wrath on the person at the other end of it. Glad it isn't me. I pull my phone from my backpack and check for any messages from Alex. Nothing. I get on Instagram and see all the posts about a party happening later tonight. I wonder if she's going. I check the time and it's four pm, so I decide to text her.

Me: Hey angel, pulling into the airport, it will probably be a while before I can text you again.

I wait a minute and then notice it says her phone is on *do not disturb.* What the fuck? I check the GPS I had installed on her car and she's at the mall. Not unusual since she and Cora love to shop. I shove my phone in my pocket, she probably has her phone on *do not disturb* to focus on her time with Cora. I love the loyalty they have in their friendship. That's one of my favorite things about Alex, too. She's selfless. If Cora needs her, she drops everything to be there. X and I used to be like that, and then something, somewhere along the way it all changed. I can't trust him like I used to be able to. I've caught him in a few lies and honesty is everything to me. We've always been competitive but in the last couple of years, he has taken it too far, crossing boundaries and being disrespectful. It sucks but it is what it is.

My attention turns to my dad as he hangs up the phone. "Well, all the flights have been grounded due to weather." Anger radiates from his body.

"It's sunny, though. Can't we take the jet?" I feign annoyance but really, I am kind of glad. I want to get home to my girl.

"No son, we can't. There is a lot of wind and they see some possible tornado action."

"That fucking sucks." I try to sound disappointed but really, I'm not. I can't wait to surprise Alex.

"We can grab a hotel, and just enjoy a couple of days away. You okay with that, son?"

"Actually, if it's okay with you, I'd like to head back home and get some more training in for the next meet." He seems pleased with that and relief floods my system. I never know how he will react, his emotions are unpredictable. That must be where I get it from.

"That's an incredible idea, Kohen. Let me get you a rental car. I'm going to go ahead and stay here."

Thank fuck. I don't want to ride in the car back with him. I love my father because I have to, but I know the monster he is. Judgmental, angry, stubborn, cold.

"Thanks, Dad. Camille won't want you home?" Camille is his current girlfriend. She seems nice but I stopped getting to know his flavor of the week a long time ago. Granted she's been around a lot longer than most. I mostly got tired of them trying to fuck me while he was away. That's why I bought my house- I allow whoever I want there, no surprises.

"No, she is in Italy right now visiting her parents." His phone rings, interrupting our conversation. "Your car is here, son." The way he calls me *son* always makes me cringe. It isn't out of pride or love but something calculated and factual. I *am* his son.

I look out the window and see a black Dodge Charger. It's a black-on-black hellcat and I'm obsessed. "Consider it a gift," he says, clearing his throat.

"A gift? For what?" I ask, confused.

"You have kept up your end of the bargain and you have been focused, just make sure it stays that way."

I turn to look at him as I exit the car. "Well, of course. Why wouldn't it?" I feel like I know where he is heading with this. I knew once he saw Alex, he was going to make some type of demands.

"Let's not play games, son, I saw the girl. Get rid of her."

Fuck.

"Dad, she won't make me lose..."

He interrupts, "This isn't a request, Kohen. Do as I say or I will take you off the will, that includes your mother's ashes." Fucking, piece of shit. "Your house, your car, all the money you use to pay for your little sluts clothes, and the dates you take her on, did you think I wouldn't find out?" He checks his teeth in the rearview mirror and straightens his hair before repeating the words I have no intention of listening to. "Get rid of her, she's nothing but a hole to stick your dick in, and I need you focused. You have a future, and a girl like that will ruin it." He slams on the gas, causing the door to shut as he speeds off. I fucking hate him.

I climb into the hellcat and it's fucking gorgeous, but it's not worth losing Alex over. Nothing is worth that. Except for my mom's ashes. There has to be a way for me to have both. I'll find a way. I hate how he holds that over me. I turn the car on and the power vibrating beneath me causes adrenaline to pump through my veins. I rev the gas and the car shakes with power. God damn, this is badass. I can't wait to get home and fuck Alex in here.

Alex

Cora and I spend the entire afternoon shopping for this party. X has been texting me all day but I've been keeping it casual. I don't want him to get the wrong idea just because I'm going to this party with him. Well, technically not with him. I'm going with Cora and we are just meeting him there. He has asked about Kohen a few times but I'm not fucking stupid. He knows where he is just as much as I do.

X: hey gorgeous, want to meet for dinner before the party?

Me: can't sorry, our Uber driver just pulled up to Olive Garden and we have our name in line.

X: I can join yall, which one?

Me: oh, no sorry OG is our girl time, I just want to spend some time with Cora alone.

X: ahh okay no worries I'll see you tonight

Me: K.

I put my phone in *do not disturb* mode, guilt inching its way back into my gut. I'm still upset at Kohen, it seemed like he wanted to keep me a secret or was ashamed.

The waitress calls our name and the hostess leads us to our table. We place our regular order. I get chicken Alfredo and she gets lasagna. One of us always gets the soup and the other a salad so we can share. The waiters always give us shit and say we aren't supposed to, but sweet little Cora talks us out of it every time. We also order our usual pitcher of green apple Moscato. That's the real reason we come here. It is infused with fruit and one pitcher has us feeling good.

As soon as the pitcher hits the table, we pour ourselves a cup, downing breadsticks to keep us a little sober. It's only four pm so we have time to go home and nap before meeting.

It feels so good to be spending time with my best friend. We sip and chat about all the things we have missed.

"How are your theater classes going?" I stuff my mouth with some Alfredo while she answers, when we drink, she tends to be long-winded.

"It's great, my professor says I'm incredibly talented and I got the lead in the next production."

I swallow before responding. "Oh my god, that's amazing, C. Way to go. I knew you were going to be a star." She giggles, sipping some more Moscato. "I'm serious, ever since we were kids, I knew you would do something huge."

Tears fill her eyes. "Thank you, Alex, that means everything. You are going to do big things as well." I scoff in response, finishing up what's on my plate before washing it down with wine. "Stop, you're so talented..."

I interrupt her before she can finish, "Stop, Cora, you know I'm undecided. Dance isn't a real career." My lip quivers, the alcohol rushing through me making me more emotional than usual.

"It is a real career if you make it one. I have never seen anyone dance like you. It's captivating. Follow your dreams, it's what Cecille would want." She grabs my hands across the table, holding them to comfort me. "Oh, and fuck anything your mom put in your head." We burst out laughing.

"Cora! That mouth!" I joke, feigning shock.

"Well, I mean it. Forget her, she doesn't have a voice here."

I stay silent, grateful for the encouragement of my bestie. We spend the next hour laughing and joking, making the best of our time together. The sun starts to set, and we schedule a pick-up so we can get home, grab a power nap, and get ready for the night. Kohen pops into my head, but I don't want to go there right now.

"You, okay?" She reads me like a book.

"It's Kohen, I feel like he is embarrassed of me."

She giggles. "Alex, he is obsessed with you, and he ate you out on an elevator," she whispers that last part as if saying it any louder will get her in trouble.

"I know, but anytime his dad is going to be somewhere he doesn't want me there. Like this morning- he basically shoved me in my car and said bye when we won't see each other for two whole weeks."

"Oh, that is weird." She puts her finger to her chin as if she is contemplating the situation. Our Uber shows up and we climb in drunkenly. "Maybe it's his dad he's embarrassed of and it has nothing to do with you."

I didn't think about that. Maybe she's right and I'm overreacting. I just don't see why he would be embarrassed of his dad. They spend so much time together. "Yeah, maybe."

It only takes fifteen minutes for us to get home. We lay on the couch and take a nap snuggled up together. I'm the big spoon as always, even though she's way taller.

My phone blares on the coffee table alerting us it's 7 pm and we need to get dressed. The Uber driver must have brought the bags in because I certainly don't remember bringing them in. I pop up, stretch and stand to grab my bags before heading to the shower. I throw a pillow at Cora's head as I head up the stairs and she groans. "Get up!" I shout.

"No!" she shouts back. "Wake me up when you get out of the shower since you take forever shaving all your beastly parts." That witch.

"That's rude."

"It's also true." Fair, but damn she didn't have to call me out like that.

I throw my hair in a bun and turn the water on, waiting for it to heat up. The water here doesn't heat up in seconds like it does at Kohen's house. I miss him, but not enough to text him. I'm still mad and I'm holding a grudge. Okay, it may also be that I don't want to admit I'm going to hang out with X, he doesn't need to know that. He isn't my dad or my boss. I can hang out with whoever I want, especially because we are just friends. The steam fills up the bathroom and I step in, allowing the water to engulf me. It eases the tension in my neck and shoulders, I relish in it. I grab my lavender soap and wash the day away. Tonight is going to be fun, the outfit I got is fucking fire, and I'm going to be the baddest bitch there.

Chapter 37

Alex

The room is spinning as I dance on this table. Alcohol pulses through me as if it is the blood in my veins. I feel hands all over my body but I don't bother to look at who's touching me, all I know is it feels fucking good. Kohen is probably having the time of his life balls deep in some tight little gymnast's pussy. He can have them, as a matter of fact, he can have them all.

Camera flashes go off all around me and I feel like a movie star. "Show us your tits!" someone shouts, and I do. I want to be numb. Everyone shouts as I bring my top back down to cover my bare tits. The music flows and my body follows its rhythm, grinding into Xzavien. I look back at him over my shoulder as I pop my ass up and down on his dick. He has pants on, but I don't think it would matter to Kohen otherwise. I wish he could see this, but fuck him. It's not just what he did this morning. It's everything that transpired after. X filled me in on him and his ex and showed me a picture of them in the same clothes he was wearing this morning. I'll say it again- fuck him.

I feel Xzavien's hands on my hips gripping me like handlebars as he grinds his pelvis into me. I wonder where Cora is. I straighten up and look around for her. Something in my brain reminds me of some faint idea of where she is. I can't quite remember. I'm so drunk. X has been grabbing me shots and mixed drinks since we got here. I only ate lunch so it's hitting pretty hard. I feel around my pocket for my phone and don't have it.

"Looking for this?" X questions, waving my phone around. I reach for it and he pulls back. "Nah ah ah," he teases. "We don't need you drunk dialing Kohen, looking desperate."

"X, give it to me now." He laughs. He fucking laughs at me. I smack him, but there's no strength behind it given how wasted I am.

"Be a good girl, Angel," he mocks Kohen's nickname for me. My stomach turns. I plop down on my ass and attempt to climb down off the bar. "Where are you going, Angel?"

"Do not call me that!" My body feels hot as anger takes over every rational thought.

"Why not? You like it when Kohen does."

I try to slap him but he catches my wrist. "You're not Kohen," I say, anger lacing my tone as I snatch my wrist away. I jump down, grab my heels and rush to the restroom. I need to pull myself together.

Thank God the restroom is free. I wobble in, swaying as I slam the door shut. I lean over the counter, looking at myself in the mirror. My lips are still painted a crimson red, my smokey eyeshadow my mask for the night. Hiding how hurt I am. The eyeliner and mascara smeared a little underneath my eyes. I wipe it away and fix my hair. It's curled down my back but the sweat has it looking a little frizzy.

"How the fuck did I get so drunk?" I ask myself quietly. I turn on the water and drink some from the faucet. I need to sober up, I need my phone. I don't like to feel this drunk, it makes me feel out of control, and weak. But I also don't want to be sober. Fuck. Where the hell is Cora? She would never leave me alone like this.

I stare at myself one more time as I adjust my top. What the fuck are you doing, Alex?

A loud knock on the door startles me, causing me to jump.

"Hurry the fuck up," someone says as they pound on the only thing keeping them safe from me. I open it quickly and the mousy little bitch that was knocking falls into the restroom on her hands and knees. "What the fuck?" she says, staring up at me from the floor.

"Want to act like a little bitch, I'll put you on your knees like one," I tell her as I exit the restroom.

"Fuck you!" she shouts at my back.

"You wish, pup." Somehow in my drunken state that felt like more of an insult than the word *bitch.* The music thrums throughout the house and I can feel the surge of energy flowing back through me. I walk the crowded halls, heels in hand, to find another drink. I want to keep the buzz. I don't need the sadness of my relationship to ruin this night. It ended before it even really began. I feel like it was some big joke to Kohen, he got into my panties and that's all he wanted. To prove he could get me. He did it, he got me. Joke's on me.

It doesn't take long to find the kitchen, and the bar surrounded with buckets of ice, beer, and liquor bottles. *Pick your poison,* a familiar voice says. I turn to look and it's Edward. "Where is Cora?" I ask immediately.

He chuckles. "She's upstairs putting her panties back on, I just ate her pussy out." I want to slap the smirk off of his cocky face. This feels full circle. The first time we met, we were at a party, where he was a complete dick to me. The party, his best friend's party. The one that tied me to Kohen for the last few months.

"You're a dick," I spit at him.

"And you're a nasty bitch." I slap him across the face before I even know what I'm doing, and he charges at me, his nose touching mine. "Don't you ever fucking slap me with your dirty fucking hands, you are nothing here you little bitch. I will end you."

I square back up to him, not scared for a fucking second, years of abuse with Walker prepared me for this. "I dare you to fucking try, you little prick. You think Cora will stay with you once I tell her what the fuck you just said?"

He scoffs, "She's so caught up on how my dick feels in her mouth, that she wouldn't believe you. What do you think she'll say if I tell her you tried to touch my dick?" He grabs my hands and forces it to the bulge in his pants and I fight with all my strength to remove it. "I'll fuck you so good, Alex, and then I'll go make your best friend suck your juices off me before I take her virginity."

I'm shocked, not at his behavior, but at the fact that he thinks Cora is a virgin. What the fuck? I know she lost her virginity the night we went to the hospital.

If not with Edward, then who? I step back, eyes wide, and confusion spreads across his face. I turn and rush down the hallway and I don't even know what I should be doing. Do I confront her? Ask her who it was she lost her virginity to? No, I can't. I don't want to cause a scene, she is all I have right now, and she will tell me when she's ready. I just wish she told me the truth.

"Woah, woah, where you headed, gorgeous? You okay?" My eyes meet X's and comfort floods my drunken system. A familiar face, a safe face. I hug him, even though I almost smacked him, too. "You okay, love?"

I look up at his handsome face, swirly memories of when we first met flashing through my mind. He was the one I wanted, we clicked, and we had chemistry. Why did I throw it all away? His interest in me has never faltered.

"Here, I got you another drink, cheers."

I take the cup and chug its contents down, needing to be more drunk. I don't want to sober up now. I want to be so drunk I don't remember a fucking thing. If X and I hook up, so be it.

Kohen

I stomp my way up the front steps of this fucking party. I can't believe Alex actually came to this. I tried texting her several times with no response. It wasn't until I checked her location again that I saw she was here. I call her phone and it goes straight to voicemail. I walk past the threshold of the front door, my body is radiating with anger. I know X is here, it's his party. He had it at his teammate's house so he was free to have Alex over. Everything he does is strategic, I'll give him that. Why the fuck does he always want what's mine? *Alex* is mine.

I stalk down the hallway, ignoring the people trying to fist-bump or shake my hand. I'm here for one thing and one thing only- my girl.

I see Cora and Edward, and head straight for them. "Hey, bro." We fist bump, and he looks nervous seeing me but I don't have time to decipher why. He's a little bitch and Cora deserves better than him. "Have y'all seen Alex?"

I see fear in Cora's eyes as I make eye contact with her, and she stutters before responding. "She's with Xzavien." I turn to go find them. "I'm sorry, Kohen, but you had to know how she would react after you were just with your ex."

That stops me in my tracks. I turn around slowly, trying to keep my composure. It all clicked into place. Erica was waiting for me in my room when I went home to see if Alex was there. She played her usual games. Talking shit about Alex and how she saw her leave with X. I made sure she knew I also saw her on camera, heading into Xzavien's room and I even heard them fucking when Alex came downstairs to meet me for our date. That shut her the fuck up. It also gave me another reason to come here and drag Alex's ass home.

"What are you talking about, Cora?"

Edward steps in front of her protectively and she places a small hand on his shoulder as if to tell him it's okay. He should know better. He knows me prior to anger management. I will destroy him. "She, well... She saw the picture of you two together and you were wearing the same clothes you left her in this morning. She's also pretty pissed that you are embarrassed for your dad to know about her."

I slap a palm to my forehead. "She has it all wrong. I wasn't with Erica- she showed up at my house. I don't want anything to do with her, as a matter of fact, she and Xzavien have been fucking for a while, I'm sure."

She gasps, her hand covering her mouth now. "Oh my gosh, Kohen. I'm so sorry."

I nod, letting her know it's okay. "As for my dad, he is a toxic, narcissist. I didn't want him to ruin what we have. I didn't want him to treat her badly." Tears well in her eyes as I explain why I'm here, how the plane was grounded, and what my dad said.

"Well, go find her. She's drunk, she's hurt, and we both know that she isn't herself when she's drunk."

I look around in defeat. "She will never believe me, and I'm sure X had a huge part in setting this up since he's wanted her from day one."

She steps in front of me and places a hand on my bicep. "So, go and show him who she belongs to." Her smile is huge as she and Edward head out the front door together.

I decide to follow the music since wherever music is, is where Alex will be. Drunk or not. It doesn't take long to find the main living room, this house is much smaller than mine and way more basic. Plain white walls with ranch-style furniture. Typical Texan decor. I step into the dance area and I see her.

She is exquisite, just like the first time I saw her. She is dancing and it takes a minute before I can see Xzavien's hands on her waist following the flow of her curvy body as she sways to the sound of the music. It's sexy as fuck to see her in her element. Dancing like nobody's watching. I'm sure dancing is to her what the bars are to me. The world around fades away and nothing matters.

She bends forward and grinds her juicy ass on him, her hips moving in a circle on him. I feel the blood rushing to my cock as I imagine her riding me reverse cowgirl, bobbing that juicy pussy up and down on my cock as I finger her asshole. Rage boils inside me. I don't want him to picture her like that. Every part of her belongs to me. I have marked her and filled up every hole with my tongue, dick, or fingers. I will never let her go, she's it for me. I know she's pissed, mad at what doesn't make sense, and hurt. Hurt more than anything, but she's hurting me now too, jumping to conclusions when I have proved time and time again that I'm not going anywhere, and I'm not going to hurt her.

As I'm watching her, our eyes meet and hers widen in surprise. I turn away from her and head down the dark hallway that leads to the basement. I know she will follow me, maybe not for the reasons other girls would follow, but because she is Alex Monroe. She wants to give me a piece of her mind about what she thinks I've done.

She reaches the place where I stand. It's too dark and she's too drunk to notice my presence, so I grab her and slam her into the wall. She gasps, her chest heaving and her scent fills my nostrils, driving me wild.

"Why do you insist on being such a bad girl, Angel?"

Her breath hitches and she tries to speak but I don't want to fucking hear it. I kiss her, punishing her for her sins. My hand moves down her body and makes its way between her legs. She's fucking naked underneath this skirt! What the fuck? A growl works its way up my throat and I plunge two fingers into her pussy. She's already wet.

"This pussy is mine, Angel. You are mine. I better not see his fucking hands on you again, understand?" I push my fingers deeper into her as I wait for a response.

"I understand. It's yours."

"Good fucking girl."

She melts into my palm as I glide my fingers in and out of her knuckle deep, the other hand around her throat as she swallows. The sounds of her wet pussy gushing around my fingers, the scent of her, and the way she's looking at me set me off. I pull my fingers from her pussy and unbutton my jeans. She reaches down and pulls my boxers down for me and my dick springs free. She drops to her knees and tries to take me in her mouth, but I deny her.

"I hate you," she seethes.

"Tsk tsk, no you don't, Angel. You fucking love this dick but you have been a very bad girl and I need to punish you."

I pull her back up to her feet and lift her top, exposing her tits the same way I saw her do in that Instagram video. Then I grab her up by her ass and thrust myself inside her tight little pussy. She moans loudly as I push myself deep into her. I slam her back against the wall again and her hands wrap around my neck, she grinds her pussy into me, meeting each thrust, taking the forceful pleasure like a good little slut.

"You like being punished don't you, Angel?" A tear falls down her cheek as I wrap my long fingers around her delicate throat again. She leans her head back against the wall as I fuck her like a rag doll. "Tell me, you like being punished, Angel." I buck into her hard, my cock fully seated inside her.

"I like it," she moans.

"That's right, you love it, you're such a pretty little slut." I run my thumb across her bottom lip, smearing her red lipstick. "Mmmm I would love to smear this lipstick with my cock, but you ruined that didn't you?" I stick my thumb in her mouth and she sucks it without question. "Didn't you?" I ask again.

She groans around my thumb. I thrust into her, each stroke harder and deeper than the last. The aggressive way I'm pounding into her causes the décor on the wall to fall. She is moaning so loud for me, and I love it.

"Fuck, Kohen, oh my god, don't stop."

And I don't. I see a shadow move from the corner of my eye and turn to catch Xzavien watching us fuck. Good. He will never have my girl. We are tied together by something greater than he can ever understand. He walks away in defeat as he should. I'll deal with him later.

I bite Alex's ear gently before whispering, "Now come for me, Angel." Her moans and groans as I fill her up with my come are so fucking sexy. Her pussy pulses around my cock, milking every drop of come I just released into her. I feel the moisture leaking down my dick as she relaxes in my hold.

"I'm sorry, Kohen." The words tear through the anger I have for her.

"Don't be sorry, you couldn't have known."

"I'm still mad," she admits, tears falling down her face.

"That's okay, baby, I'm still mad too. Just not really at you. X played you, he knew."

"What?" she gasps, hurt, lacing her tone.

"Get dressed, baby. I'll tell you everything and then I'm going to fuck him up."

Chapter 38

Alex

My mind is spinning and I feel confused as we make our way to find Xzavien. "What do you mean he knew, Kohen?" I feel the tremble in my tone.

"I mean he set this up, he knew I would be gone. He sent Erica to meet me at home when I texted him. I was headed back. You weren't answering. I saw your location here, and I let him know my plane was grounded due to weather and I was headed back to you."

I try to keep up with his pace, but his long legs make it difficult. "Can you stop for a second and talk to me?"

He pauses, pulling me to the side. "What, Alex?"

"Why are you being rude?"

"Because all I can picture is his hands on your body, my body, and I want to erase it."

"I'm sorry, but it wasn't easy seeing a picture of you with your ex either."

He scoffs. "That's exactly what they wanted. She was already there and they've been fucking. I caught her on camera knocking on our door the day of our date, and then when you closed the door she went to Xzavien's room."

I feel like I've been punched in the gut. "That's who he was fucking?"

"Yes, Alex. My best friend was fucking my ex-girlfriend."

Does he care?

As if reading my mind, he responds, "And no, I don't care, but what I do care about is they set it up to look like I was home with her, and you were here with him and that's fucked."

I nod in agreement, still shocked at the revelations. "Why though, why do all this?"

He begins moving again, his body radiating with anger that I can feel. "Because he's fucking jealous and he wants you."

I shake my head, disagreeing. "No, we are just friends and he knows that."

Now he's shaking his head. "Don't be so fucking naive, Alex, you're smarter than that." I try to touch his arm to calm him down and he jerks it away from me. Hurt and embarrassment flood my mind and I turn to walk the other way. He follows. "Alex, wait. I'm just...angry."

I don't say anything. Instead, I keep walking until I'm outside, and it's as if it's a divine intervention. Xzavien is outside with Erica. Before I can react, Kohen charges X, tackling him to the ground. Kohen doesn't even give X a chance as he slams his body into the ground by the collar. X looks like a rag doll in comparison to Kohen.

"Kohen, stop!" I shout. I don't want him to get injured, his Olympic career would suffer.

"What the fuck, bro?" X yells, trying to get some type of footing to get off the ground. Bones crunch as Kohen punches him in the nose. Xzavien's hands go to his nose as he yells, "Motherfucker, what the fuck is wrong with you, Kohen?"

Some of the guys they hang with pull a thrashing Kohen off of X. Panic floods my system, and although I know X didn't get a chance to defend himself, I rush to Kohen. He isn't hurt but his chest is heaving, and his eyes look wild as he continues to fight them off to get back to X.

"You're what's fucking wrong with me, you little bitch." It takes four grown men to hold him back and not one person is holding X. Even though I know it's wrong, the sight of Kohen raging turns me the fuck on. The veins in his muscles are bulging and the utter strength it's taking to contain him is fucking sexy.

"What did I do, bro?" X questions as he steps closer to Kohen with his hands raised in question.

"X, stay the fuck away from him!" I shout.

"Don't you fucking speak to him," Kohen spits out at me. His pupils are dilated, and he looks savage- like he could rip me to shreds with his look alone. Fear floods my system and even though his anger isn't pointed at me, I feel it down to my toes. It radiates through me like an orgasm does.

"You see, gorgeous, you deserve better. This is the true Kohen- a fucking monster."

"I hope you have a good fucking reason for trying to steal my girl, bro, because once I get my hands on you, you're fucking done." The guys release him, staying close by just in case.

"Y'all settle this shit like men- you're brothers," one of the guys tries to remind them.

Kohen scoffs as he walks up to X like a predator. A lion, while X is a lamb. "I don't know what you don't understand. Alex is mine."

I look over at Erica and she's just watching. It's taking everything in me not to go over there and smack the smirk off her face. I shout, "You like this, don't you, coming in between them?"

She rolls her eyes. "It's you between them, little whore, not me."

I bring my attention back to Kohen and he is face to face with X, their noses practically touching. He chest bumps X, and X pushes him back with all his strength, but it just doesn't compare.

"Look, Ko, I don't have a good excuse, man. I just feel like you swooped her from me, I met her first, you weren't even there."

Are they really talking about me like I'm not even here? "I'm sorry but fuck you both. I choose who I belong to and I'm sorry X, but I told you we are just friends."

He takes a few steps away from Kohen, his hands running through his hair. "That's bullshit Alex and you know it. All the little jokes about wanting to fuck me when we met, the dancing, the dates. You fucking wanted me, until him." His eyes shoot to Kohen. "Give me a chance, Alex, you deserve better than him. He will never get over Erica, and even if he did, she will never let him go."

Kohen lunges for him again. "Stop putting negative thoughts in her fucking head. I don't want Erica, she is a gold-digging bitch. I will never want her again."

I rush to stand between them, not wanting Kohen to hurt himself. "Xzavien, I will never want you. Say I never met Kohen- it still wouldn't happen between us. I am not a relationship girl. We would have fucked and maybe even more than once, but it wouldn't have turned into anything."

He starts to speak but doesn't get the chance to finish as Kohen shoves me to the side. He swings, uppercutting X in the jaw. He falls to the floor in slow motion like Apollo getting knocked out in *Rocky IV.* Xzavien hits the ground hard. Erica rushes to check on him and he gets up onto his elbows, looking straight at me.

"This is all your fault." X stands and begins the walk to his car, opening the door before getting in and confusion stirs inside me. He looks...hurt? I just can't seem to find the energy to fully care. Look at everything he's done. How is any of this my fault? I was upfront from the beginning, I don't know how much clearer I could have been.

I grab Kohen by the arm when he charges at X again like a bull, relentlessly attacking the guy. His knuckles are bloody and there are gashes from where Xzavien's teeth punctured the skin. I take his hand in mine anyway, kissing them. I cup his cheek and pull him to face me, hoping I can calm him down.

"Handsome, look at me. I'm yours, let's go home. You handled your business, now let's go. He isn't worth it."

Erica laughs, she fucking laughs and I ignore her. "You aren't worth it, honey. You don't deserve either of these men and why they are risking their lifelong friendship for a little whore like you is beyond me."

Xzavien walks back our way and I feel Kohen tense. "I'm curious..." X begins, "...was it Alex or Erica that you're actually upset about? Or maybe it's both." He laughs as he continues, "Because the way I recall the night we met Alex, you were upstairs fucking Erica, were you not? Erica correct me if I'm wrong."

"Don't antagonize him!" I yell. "It's you, you're the problem. You and that stupid bitch." I step in his direction. "Stop trying to get in my fucking head, if he wanted to be with her, he would." He feigns confusion. "Don't play dumb, X, you're not innocent here. You were fucking her. Your best friend's ex."

"She doesn't mean anything, Alex, and I don't mean anything to her. We just both want you and Kohen to be over. And what- do you expect me to wait on the sidelines like a lost puppy?"

I scoff.

"Don't you already, begging at my feet every fucking minute, texting, calling, trying to get me to hang out behind Kohen's back?" He throws his hands up, gesturing toward me.

"Yet here you are with me, you came here to meet me, you didn't think Kohen would be here, what does that say about you two? Is it the money? Is that why you chose him?"

I rush up to him and slap him across the face. Red marks splay across his skin. "Fuck you," I say, tears streaming down my cheeks. Xzavien looks like I just stabbed him in the heart, the painful look on his face is heartbreaking to see, but he brought this on himself. I feel bad for him in a way, I hate him for doing this.

"Well, you just lost me as a friend, Alex, congratulations. Don't call me when he breaks your pathetic ass heart." He wipes the blood from his lip, turns, and stalks off to his car, taking off like a bat out of hell.

I see Erica walking to Kohen, and I rush to intercede, stepping in front of him. "Don't even think about it, you stupid cunt. You're disgusting, accept that he chose me."

She *tsks.* "Better be careful or you'll lose him too. I was his fiancé, what are you a little rebound?" My heart stops in my chest. "Oh, he didn't tell you, did he?"

I look up at him over my shoulder as he grips my elbow. "There's nothing for him to tell me, I don't see a ring on your finger today, do you?" I hate feeling blindsided with this, it hurts but I'm not going to show her any sign of weakness.

"You're a fool, just a tight little hole for him to fill until he realizes I'm it for him. Our families have decided we will be married. Now, it's just a matter of when. We are made for each other. You are nothing. His father will never let him be with you."

It clicks. That's why he doesn't want me to meet his father.

"Y'all are delusional. You both want people who don't want you. So, who is more pathetic here?"

She smirks. "You," is all she says before turning away and getting in her BMW.

My heart aches, my stomach turns, and a tear falls down my cheek without permission. "That's why you didn't want me to meet your dad," I whisper where only he can hear me.

"I'm sorry, Angel," he whispers back, squeezing my elbow.

"You're pathetic!" she shouts from her window and zooms out of the driveway sending pebbles flying behind her tires. I fucking hate her, and I have a gut feeling this won't be the last time we hear from her.

Chapter 39

Kohen

Alex is in the shower. She insisted we come to her house in case X was home. I'm not scared to get into it again, but she's right. One wrong move and an injured hand could set me out for a while. Tonight was a shit show. Part of me is fucking angry at her still, she shouldn't have been there. How could she fall into this trap? I hear the water shut off and it pulls me from my spiraling thoughts.

The beautiful girl I'm in love with comes walking out stark-ass naked. Puffy pink-rimmed eyes tell me she was crying in there, but why? Does she honestly care about him that much, how close were they? I have never had feelings of jealousy even when Erica cheated, I was like good riddance, but I am jealous of any part of Alex that cares for him. If she cares for him, there's that much less of her to care for me. I can't fucking help it, she makes me crazy. I stand up, pulling her soft body to mine, wrapping her up in my arms, and squeezing her tight to my chest. She smells amazing, that intoxicating lavender and pear combination I can't get enough of.

"Kohen, I'm so sorry."

Is she honestly apologizing to me? Guilt consumes me. "No, Angel, don't be sorry, it wasn't your fault." What am I saying, some of this is her responsibility, I just can't hold her to that when she looks so broken right now.

"Yes, it was. I should have waited for your explanation, I shouldn't have jumped to conclusions when he showed me the picture of you and your ex. I shouldn't have agreed to meet him at the party when you asked me not to go. I felt like you were ashamed of me when your dad showed up and I reacted."

I rest my hands on the arch of her back and kiss her softly, comforting her the best way I know how. The way she loves me to. "It's okay. I mean I wish you would have talked to me, but I get it."

She looks up at me, wrapping her hands around my neck and locking them there. She kisses me now, pushing her chest into me, nipples hard, she needs this. Me.

We are both a work in progress and there are tons of unanswered questions, but right now we just need each other. I'm bonded to her, in more ways than one and nothing can separate us. I hope she sees how hard I'm falling for her, how hard I can fall for only her. Her body rocks into mine, my cock hardens between us, and she moans into my mouth. No one ever mattered before her. I sit on the edge of her bed, breaking our kiss to stare at her beautiful lush body. She stands in between my legs, still naked. I run my hand down her body from her shoulder to the valley that sits in between her breasts, and continue slowly down her stomach, relishing the softness there. Finding the mound of her pussy, I cup it, sliding my finger in between her lips. She's dripping wet, and I let out a groan. She's always so ready for me.

"That's my good girl," I praise her. She places a hand on each of my shoulders and throws her head back as I fuck her pussy with my fingers.

"Fuck me, handsome." Her pupils are shot as the need for me grows. "Please."

God damn she's fucking sexy, she said please all on her own like a good fucking girl. Her hands drop to the waistband of my sweats, and I lift so she can get them off. I stand to remove them from my ankles and switch positions placing her on the bed. She lays back and I crawl on top of her, using my knee to spread her legs apart. She opens up for me like a butterfly, showcasing her pussy to me like a gift. Mine. Her pussy glistens with arousal and I run the head of my cock through her slit, teasing and she writhes under me.

I slip inside her and her hands grip the bed sheets, I pump inside her slowly at first appreciating the feeling of her pussy gripping my cock. "Fuckkk, Angel."

She bites her bottom lip as she stares at me while I quicken my pace, grinding into her. I use one hand to hold me up and the other to grip her love handles. She is curvy in all the right places, my perfect girl. "You feel so fucking good, Alex." I grab the headboard to stabilize myself and pound my cock into her fast and hard, her sleek pussy gushing as I enter her over and over. Her back arches off the mattress causing me to hit a new spot inside her and I nearly come. I feel her pussy convulsing around me, her breath quickening as she scratches her nails down my back.

"Oh my god, Kohen," she moans.

"Come for me, Angel."

"I love you Kohen, fuckkk I love you. I'm yours." The words leaving her mouth do something to me, causing me to see red in the best way. I pump in and out of her and she meets me thrust for thrust.

"I love you too, Angel."

She reaches up to kiss me, sucking my bottom lip into her mouth, biting it softly and my cock twitches inside her. Her face is flushed, her hair a mess and yet she looks like a goddess. I lift her by her ass and plunge my cock into her, bouncing her up and down on it, she clenches around me so tight when she reaches her orgasm. I come instantly. "Your pussy feels so fucking good." I pull myself out of her and let her fall back on the mattress, her hair a tattered mess around her. She spreads her legs open for me, knowing I like to see my come in her pretty pussy. She's fucking mine.

I take two fingers and smear my come all over her pussy, shoving what's leaking out back inside. She squeezes my fingers with her pussy, and I raise my eyebrows at her, and she winks. I fucking love this girl, I am in love with her. I pull my fingers from her grip and put them in her mouth. My good girl sucks our mess off my fingers and swallows.

"Angel?"

"Yeah?"

"Can you promise me something?" I ask, sleep taking over, eyelids heavy.

"Yes?" a question is her response.

"Next time can you please just talk to me before you jump off the damn cliff?"

She laughs and I don't know if I'm making any sense half asleep, but she responds as she runs her little hands through my hair. "Yes, handsome. I can ask before I jump off the cliff, now go to sleep."

"Goodnight"

"Night," she responds.

I swear I hear her say something else, but I'm too far pulled into sleep to make it out or respond.

Alex

Kohen is sleeping peacefully in my bed. I kiss him softly on the cheek and slide off the bed carefully so I don't wake him. He stirs but grabs a pillow and seems to get comfortable. I grab an oversized t-shirt from the top of my dresser and pull it over my head. I grab my phone and climb up onto the bench near my window. Guilt pulls at my heartstrings, and I let the tears fall. I love Kohen but that love doesn't excuse the lies I found out about him. I can't believe I told him I loved him, and he told me it back. Does love overrule everything that happened tonight? I found out Erica wasn't just his ex- she was his fiancé. I found out their families have basically arranged their marriage like some fucked up Shakespearean play. How do I even compete?

I can't believe Kohen punched X in the face, the way he was acting was like nothing I've ever seen before. The rage and anger that consumed the sweet guy I have come to know and love. Is he a monster like X said? X was a good friend, maybe I did lead him on, maybe it is all my fault. I pull a blanket from the foot of the bench up over me, hugging it tight to my chest. This is all so fucked up. The one thing I know I'm sorry for is going to meet X, knowing it would upset Kohen. Old habits die hard. I really should grow the fuck up and stop trying to get even before I know the truth. Toxic trait number 1065. I keep telling myself that I'm trying my best, that's all anyone can do, right?

I would be lying if I said a huge part of me doesn't want to hear Xzavien's side. I just don't understand why he would try and sabotage my relationship with his best friend. I look over at Kohen who is still fast asleep, so I unlock my phone and text the one person I know I really shouldn't be texting,

Me: Hey I don't know if you're mad…

Me: but I really want to talk, I have to know why you did this. you ruined our friendship. I mean were we ever really friends?

I really can't believe X was the one to set all that up.

It shows he read it immediately, and yet no response. My gut feeling tells me I shouldn't have sent anything, but the damage is done. He didn't respond and I delete the thread. I climb off the bench as I put my phone on *do not disturb* and crawl into bed next to Kohen. I place my arm around his waist, and he rolls over, pulling me in close. A moan slips from his lips as he brings his nose to my hair and inhales. It's insane how fast we have fallen for each other, but I couldn't imagine it any other way.

It's a huge relief hearing he feels the same way. I choose Kohen. I will always choose Kohen. I've let my walls down for him, and that's something I can say I have never done for anyone. I need to update Cora on all of this. Oh fuck, I forgot about Edward! I don't even know where to begin with all that shit. Maybe I'll just chalk it up to us all being wasted. He must have been confused, Cora lost her virginity to him, I know she did. My eyes feel heavy, and I place my ear to Kohen's heart, the steady thrum comforting me, pulling me into a deep sleep with him. My man, my safety, my soulmate.

Chapter 40

Alex

A week goes by of us staying at my house so we can avoid X. He never responded to my text. Things between Kohen and I have been great so I'm not too worried about it. We haven't broached the subject of her being his ex-fiancé or his dad wanting them to get married. I would love to talk about it but any time we spend together we try to make the best of it. He is busy training for the next meet and that really limits the time we have. We both have a break this weekend so tonight we plan to hang out at home and watch movies. Kohen says he will cheat on his diet for me, which means tons of junk food. I changed his name in my phone to Handsome, it's a weird nickname but I call him that more than anything else. It makes me feel giddy when I see a text or call from him.

Handsome: I can't wait to see you tonight, Angel. Love you

Me: same. Counting down the minutes for this class to be over so I can rush home and shower. Love you more

The 'I miss you's, and 'I love you's come easy now. We did talk about that. The watch Kohen got me vibrates, alerting me that class is over. Come on summer break! I plan to get tons of beach time.

Cora: We need to get some new swimsuits.

Me: I know, tomorrow? Kohen and I have the evening all planned out.

Cora: gotcha winky face

Me: see you later, love you best friend

Cora: who do you love more me or Kohen

Me: YOU. Always you.

I shove my phone in my pocket before feeling it vibrate. Instead of pulling it back out, I check my watch.

Handsome: I can't wait to fuck that dirty little mouth

It vibrates again,

Handsome: and that pretty pussy

Hypnotized by his dirty words, I bump into someone and apologize as I make sure nothing fell. Looking up, I meet a familiar pair of green eyes. Xzavien's.

"Oh, sorry," I stutter.

"It's fine, gorgeous." He flashes his pearly whites at me. "I miss you, though."

My stomach flips and not in a good way. I don't know if I should mention the text or not. I can't even bring myself to make eye contact with him.

"I'm sorry," is all I can manage to get out. I don't want to be seen making more conversation with him than necessary. He is trouble and even though I love the thrill of being a brat, this is not a line I'm willing to cross again. I texted him, and I gave him the opportunity to reconcile this friendship and he didn't. It's probably for the best anyway.

"What's there to be sorry for, gorgeous?" The mischievous smirk gracing his lips makes me nervous and I don't like it. I'm not doing anything wrong but the way he is talking to me and looking at me makes me feel like we are doing something wrong.

"I don't know, X. I'm sorry that you're such an asshole." I shove past him and he grabs my arm.

"Does Kohen know you texted me that night?"

I gulp. Of course, he's been waiting to bring it up. Suddenly my surroundings catch up to me, and X shouldn't be in this building. It's the fine arts building. He is a sports medicine major. "Why are you even in this building, X?"

"I thought so," he says, letting me go and walking away.

"Of course, he knows!" I shout. He doesn't say another word as he shoves the door open and walks out of the building.

I'm nervous as I shower, thoughts racing as my anxious body shakes. I finally have something worth losing and I'm terrified. Scared to death that X called him and told him that I texted him. I should have just told him myself the next morning but every time I gain the courage to, I chicken out like a little bitch.

A knock sounds at the door and I jump. "Alex, are you naked?" Cora shouts through the door.

I release the breath I was holding and my body relaxes, knowing it's Cora. "Yes, I'm in here and yes I'm naked!" I shout back. I turn the water off and the door flies open, Cora not batting an eye at my naked body. "What ya doing?"

"Having a party."

I roll my eyes sarcastically. "Ew, rude much?" I wrap my towel around my body and face her.

"I'm sorry, I'm just anxious," she sighs in response.

"It's fine, but just so you know, your man is downstairs." She stares at her manicure like it's no big deal.

"Fuck," I whisper and she looks up at me as she sits on the lip of the tub.

"I knew you were acting weird because of him, what's wrong?"

I sigh in defeat."I did something stupid," I admit, eyes welling with tears already.

"Oh god, Alex, what did you do?" She stands, wiping the tear that fell from my cheek.

"I can't tell you, I think it's best if I tell Kohen first."

"Okay, no worries. I'm leaving anyway. Edward and I have a date." The reflection of my best friend in the mirror makes my heart swell. She is beautiful and worthy of all the love. This brings up thoughts of the conversation I also have to have with her.

Fuck, I'm just screwing everything up with the only two people I love in the world. "You deserve better than him," I spit out.

She looks at me incredulously. "Alex, stop. You don't know what I deserve." What the fuck is that supposed to mean? Her phone rings and she looks at it a second before ignoring the call. "Okay, I'm leaving but I love you and whatever happened, don't worry. Kohen is freaking obsessed with you. Have you seen the way that man looks at you? He would hang the moon for you." She kisses me on the cheek and rushes out the door, leaving me in a whirlwind of emotions behind her.

I smell popcorn and smile, he's making snacks. The stairs creak and butterflies erupt. I'm just going to tell him the truth. I should have just asked Cora for advice about it. He taps his knuckles on the door, even though it's open.

"You decent in here, Angel?"

I don't respond, my mouth is dry, and my throat feels like it's closing up. What the hell is wrong with me?

Damn, he looks good, he looks like a damn GQ model in the simplest shit. He walks straight over and kisses me on the forehead, the tip of my nose, and then he plants a soft kiss on my lips. "Hey, beautiful," he whispers. The intimate gesture pushes me into a panic. Guilt overwhelms me and the words fly out of my mouth like word vomit.

"I texted Xzavien the night of the fight after you fell asleep."

He stays frozen, hunched over the bed with his lips still inches from my lips. He scoots back, the room going quiet. My stomach is in knots waiting for him to say something. He bites his bottom lip and I move to get up, but he holds a hand out to stop me, shaking his head in disappointment.

"Why?" The words leave his lips so quietly, I almost didn't hear him. He stands silent one more time, his eyes trained on me, filled with questions. The look on his face isn't one I've seen before, it is not angry but hurt. Heartbroken?

"I don't know, handsome. I just... I guess I wanted to see why he did all of that. I thought he was my friend. I..."

He interrupts me and now I see the emotions in his face that I expected. Anger. "Bullshit!" he yells, and I flinch at the unexpected volume. "I call absolute fucking bullshit, you fucking like him don't you?"

I start to say no but he doesn't let me get a word in.

"You know what, Alex? Don't even answer that. I don't want to hear the fucking excuses that are sure to come out of your mouth. I fought my best fucking friend for causing issues between me and you by not only crossing lines, but he also knew how I felt about you over and over, but he also fucked my ex and tried to set us up."

"You mean your ex-fiancé," I scoff, my anger rising as armor surrounds me with its protection.

"Do not change the subject. We aren't flipping this on me, you fucking texted him while I was asleep, making me look stupid."

"I'm sorry, baby. I was confused and I wanted to know why. This is all new to me, Kohen."

He scoffs, pacing the room like a madman, his hands running through his hair as I continue.

"I haven't ever been with someone who treats me like you do and sometimes I don't know how to handle it. I'm doing my fucking best here. I'm coming from one extreme to the other. I told you I didn't want this, but you kept on and kept on, and I mean...you tell me, Kohen. What are the rules here? I know I need to learn to deal with shit more healthily but I'm doing my best."

His phone rings and he ignores it. "I don't know, Alex, but what I do know is if the shoe was on the other foot, and I texted a girl after they started shit between us, you would have my balls for it." He isn't wrong but before I can respond, his phone rings again. He is about to ignore it when I grab for it. Erica flashes on the screen. Perfect timing. I answer.

"Hello?"

"Hello? Kohen?"

The fucking nerve.

I don't know who the fuck this Erica bitch thinks she is, but I am not a person she should be messing with. She might run shit in her world, but I run shit in mine. Kohen is *mine.*

"Umm no, this is Alex. Do you need something? I don't know why you're calling him when he already made it clear he doesn't want you." It's like she and Xzavien have psychic abilities and knew today would be the day to try and ruin us one more time. She laughs and I can't help but be petty. "Anyway, he is getting dressed right now, would you like me to give him a message?"

"Sure, honey." Her condescending voice irks me. "Tell him the love of his life called and it doesn't matter who he buries himself into these days, I love him, and I'm endgame."

It's my turn to laugh. "You're old news, bitch, hanging on the sidelines desperate for some dick. Keep begging for it, go ahead, embarrass yourself." I hang up and turn my rage over to Kohen. Now he isn't the only one who is pissed off.

"What?" he asks, anger and venom lacing his tone, triggering something deep inside me.

"What the fuck do you mean, *what?* Don't fucking talk to me like that. That was your fucking ex-fiancé calling, claiming to be your endgame. Looks like I'm not the only one keeping secrets."

He raises his voice again and my entire body is shaking in anger. I clench my jaw to keep my teeth from chattering. "Wow, well you're right about one thing Alex, she is my ex, and I never gave her false hope or led her on unlike you."

"What the hell is that supposed to mean?" I stand toe to toe with him, making sure he knows I'm not afraid. I will never give another man the satisfaction of my fear again. I feel my chest tightening and the fight or flight in my brain is pushing me to respond accordingly. Lights are flashing behind my eyes and sirens are going off inside my head, telling me I'm not safe and that I need to protect myself.

"It means yes- she is my ex, but you... You are currently in some fucked up little love triangle with me and X. I'll tell you right now that I want no part of it."

I gasp at his accusation. "I don't want him. I chose you, I want you, I love you. I was clear from day one it's not my fault your friend can't get a damn clue."

A chuckle escapes him, and a tear escapes me. "Sure, Alex. Look, I'm out. You want him, have him. I'm not doing this shit. I. Don't. Give. A shit."

My body reacts faster than my brain and I just need to stop him from leaving. Desperation floods my senses and I shove him. "I want you, is that not clear? Nothing is going on with me and Xzavien."

"Yeah right. I'm sure you probably fucked him downstairs before I fucked you upstairs." Before I even know what's happening, I feel heat on my left hand from slapping him across the face. I *slapped* him. Realization hits as the tears fall down my face. I slapped him, I slapped the only man who has ever treated me with an ounce of respect. His eyes are empty as he stares at me, a black void replacing the look of love that resided there less than an hour ago.

What the fuck did I do?

His voice is calm, like the steadiness of a heartbeat. "You just crossed a line. I cannot believe you just slapped me, I need to leave right now, I... I have to go."

I'm frozen as he moves around the room calmly gathering the things he has laying around and stuffing them into his gym bag. I watch him go and my heart is screaming at me to follow him and apologize. Pushing me to be vulnerable, own up, and not let the best thing that has ever happened to me walk away. Though, my brain says, *Protect yourself, Alex, you don't love him. You aren't really falling for him, and he definitely doesn't care about you. Don't make yourself look pathetic. A desperate little girl, begging for love and attention. If you chase him, he has the power.*

I feel torn. I have never felt this way before. The choice was always easy, it was always me, until Kohen.

I hear his shoes tap the wood as his feet rush down step after step. I throw caution to the wind and ignore every red flag in my brain telling me not to chase him. My brain keeps shouting at me to let him go, to stay in the safety of my room so I don't get hurt, my mind doesn't want me to care. Only I do care, I care way too much. It scares the shit out of me, but I want this, I want him. I've never wanted anything in my life more than I want what we have.

I run down the stairs in my towel. Not caring that I'm not dressed, nothing else matters right now. I have to make this right, I cannot lose him. I hit the bottom step with a thud and lunge toward the front door, yanking it open. My heart sinks at the sight of him, his shoulders slouched in defeat, his head hanging in disappointment. "Kohen!" I shout. He pauses, looking over his right shoulder in my direction but then continues his walk. "Kohen, just listen for one second, please."

The words sound all too familiar when they leave my lips. A flashback of my ex chasing me down and asking me the same thing after the first time he hit me.

"Look, I know I crossed a line, baby. I'm sorry. Just talk to me, please," I beg, not caring how weak I look. He turns slowly to face me. His eyes are red and heartbreak is written all over his face. "I don't do this, Kohen. I have never chased anyone for anything. I push people away but I don't want to do that anymore..."

"Alex," he interrupts, surrender in his tone.

"Wait, please. Don't say anything. I know I shouldn't have slapped you, but I was triggered, and I panicked. I know it's not an excuse, but I promise it won't happen again."

He runs his hands through his gorgeous hair.

"Please, handsome, don't walk away. I don't want you to run and I refuse to let you go."

A small smile graces his lips, but it doesn't reach his eyes and something in me breaks. *I* did this. I caused this beautiful man to look so broken. The words that leave his mouth rip my heart out of my chest.

"I wish this never happened, Alex, but it has, and I don't know if I have enough strength to withstand your storm anymore. I have worked so hard to become the man I am today so I need to leave, and you need to let me, because I love you and I would do anything for you."

"Kohen," I whisper, wiping tears from my cheeks angrily.

Kohen

I wrap my arms around her gently as she sobs into my chest, pulling her into me so that there isn't any space between our bodies. I shouldn't still be here, but I can't help it. I love this crazy girl with every fucking bone in my body. She is my other half, the missing puzzle piece that makes me feel complete. Before her, something was always missing in my life. Sure, I'm on the fast track to compete at the Olympics, I have it easy because I come from money. But those things don't make life better, not like she does.

Her mere existence in this world matters, and before me, no one showed her that was true. I breathe her in again, filling my lungs. Her lavender shampoo overloads my senses, making me dizzy. The energy between us is so palpable that I want to kiss her. I would die for her, and that's why I have to walk away. She has to learn to love herself and let go of all the pain and trauma to allow herself to be loved. The choices she makes every time something seems off to her is proof she needs help.

As if sensing that I want a kiss, she looks up at me through her lashes, black mascara running down her cheeks. My heart breaks for her. I told her I would never walk away, never leave like everyone else that left her. The difference between me and them is that I'm not leaving because she's too much, or because I don't want her.

I'm leaving because I love her too fucking much.

I have tried to show her in every possible way that it doesn't matter how broken she thinks she is. I want her but the shards of glass from her broken heart pierce mine. Through every obstacle, we have overcome and every moment we spent tangled up in each other, she cuts me. Some pieces are small and insignificant, they can be removed and bandaged up. The other pieces, though...the big sharp ones that she throws at me like daggers cut deep. Those are the ones that hurt me, and when I pull them from my flesh to repair the man staring back at me, he's a little emptier in the eyes each time.

I would gladly let her have every ounce of my soul if I thought it was healing her and bringing her out of the dark corners of her mind, but I can't fix her. She has to want to fix herself. I kiss her gently and pulling her away from my body feels like I'm tearing half of my soul apart.

I back up and she advances towards me again, knowing her touch will pull me back in, but I hold up a hand to stop her and pinch the bridge of my nose. I take one last look at her, the toxic girl I fell in love with as I turn to walk away.

Chapter 41

Alex

The silence is loud. Not having Kohen here is killing me. Not having the safety of his arms around me. Holding me. I promised myself I would never let a man make me feel empty and alone again. It isn't his fault, though, is it? It's mine. I play these fucking games and I never win. Does anyone actually ever win? I pull my phone out of my pocket and open up the text thread. I start to type but I can't bring myself to hit send.

Me: I miss you

I began to delete the words when I see the three little bubbles pop up on the bottom left corner. He's typing!

My heart races and my stomach turns. I begin to shake. The bubbles stop. So I muster up all the courage I have and hit send. The bubbles begin again. My heart leaps at the words.

Kohen: I miss you too, Angel. So much.

I immediately type out the words '*come over*' and as if he knew what I was going to send, he texts.

Kohen: please don't say come over, because if you do I will. I don't have much willpower to stay away Alex.

He called me Alex. My eyes fill with tears.

Kohen: We still very much need this break. I love you, that's clear, but I need you to learn to love yourself.

I began to type and again he read my mind.

Kohen: you don't love yourself enough to let me love you. I miss you Alex but just wanted to check in and make sure you were okay.

I stare at the screen as tears roll down my cheeks. I lean forward and hug my abdomen, feeling sick to my stomach, empty, and unworthy. The phone pings again.

Kohen: remember, beautiful girls don't cry, Angel. I love you.

It's too late. I'm already crying. I hate this fucking feeling. It's indescribable. It's an ache inside that feels like it radiates to the deepest parts of my soul. I'm too broken to love. How do I come back from here?

Me: I'm sorry I'm not the girl of your dreams. I'm sorry I'm fucking broken. What do you want from me? Huh? Tell me because I have no fucking idea what I'm doing!

No response. Guess I'm just not worth it. I double over, clutching my abdomen. The heartache is just too much.

Epilogue

Alex

He is the sun and I am the earth and one can't exist without the other.

-Alex

The waves hit me over and over, the pain crashing into me like bricks. The black cloud is heavy and I feel so numb inside. I never felt love before this. I thought I had but I was wrong. I swore I would never let myself get involved with anyone like this after Walker. My first heartbreak.

This is deeper, though. The cuts run so fucking deep. I don't see how they could heal because it seems impossible. The scars from this love will be ugly, and the torn flesh in my heart will never repair fully.

I take another drink of wine from my cup. I don't know how many bottles I have finished at this point. Cora went out of town with Edward, I had to make her think I was fine. She was worried since Kohen sent me roses. I stare at the place where the vase sits on the table. There is a note sitting next to it I haven't had the courage to read. I pretended it didn't affect me. I smiled and hugged her and acted it out perfectly so she would go on her trip. It worked, and now I get to wallow in self-pity.

The truth is I'm empty. It's dark in this hollow shell. Love was never meant to touch me and when it did, I warped it into toxicity. Of course, he doesn't want me.

"*Learn to love yourself,*" he said.

What the fuck does that even mean?

I'm pissed. Hurt. Hopeless.

He fucking left, he left when he said he never would. Fuck him. I hate him, he's nothing to me.

That's a lie, the little angel on my shoulder whispers. *He is everything.*

But he doesn't love me anymore, I whisper back

The worst part is when he left, he took every ounce of light with him. Reducing me to nothing.

More waves. They roll and roll over my body and I welcome them. Deserve them.

Pain, crash.

Heartache, crash.

Damaged, crash.

My mom was right. No man would love me if my own father couldn't. No one would stay if he didn't. The man wired to love me left me before I could even learn his name. My phone goes off and I see Crystal's name.

I ignore it. She can't make me smile. Only one person can make me smile. I sob into my blanket. The empty ache of loss punches me in the gut.

I thought I wanted love, but that was a mistake. It's a blessing and a curse. It destroys. I wouldn't wish it on anyone.

The highs, the lows. It's good when it's good but when it's bad, it's disgusting.

I can hear the words he told me to comfort me.

"*Beautiful girls don't cry, Angel.*"

"*You are the most gorgeous woman I have ever seen.*"

"*You aren't so broken that you can't be made into something new with every fragment perfectly placed. We can fit our pieces together because you aren't so far gone that you don't deserve love.*"

"*You can close your eyes, Angel. You can rest. I'll always be right here.*"

Lies. All of it.

He didn't mean a fucking word he said. I know I'm hard to love. An all-consuming black hole of trauma, but damn if I didn't love him back the best way I could. The best way I knew how. No one showed me how to love. I'm fire and he was my gasoline- he lit me up in the best ways but it became too much, incinerating our love. It's all my fault.

I pick up my phone, drunk dialing his number without thinking, and instantly regret it because he answers immediately. Only it's not him.

"Hello," a sweet voice greets my ears.

The joy in her voice pierces me.

"Kohen, your phone was ringing."

My broken heart slumps to the bottom of my dark soul.

"It did? Did you answer it? Who was it?"

I stay quiet, listening.

Music, the buzz of people conversing. He is at a party. As he should be, living his best life, without me. Just like Walker. He gets the happy ending and I get nothing.

"It says My Angel on the screen. Here."

I hang up, block his number and stand up urgently. I'm dizzy from all the wine. The room spins, and shades of maroon, black, and gray surround me. I grab the sofa to ground myself and make my way up the stairs. I turn on the water and stare at my reflection as I undress.

"You are broken."

Saying it out loud feels good.

"Worthless. And everyone would be happier without you."

Stepping backward until my feet hit the tub, I step in and turn the shower head on.

Rinsing away the sadness, and disgust, I feel pathetic. I'm here crying for him and he is just partying.

No, this doesn't work for me. I'm going to shower, sober up, and get dressed to go out all by my damn self. All I need is me. I will fuck the first hot guy I see, even if it's in the goddamn restroom because I want to rid my body of any traces of Kohen Lee Ventura.

Acknowledgements

I want to thank my family for supporting me, especially my husband Mr. Issa and our kids. They believe in my dreams and I appreciate it more than they can ever know.

Mom, thank you for stepping up, washing clothes, running errands, cleaning, and making dinner so that I could write, do lives, and grow my business. You are the real MVP.

Megan, my beautiful sister-in-law- thank you for being here with me from my Wattpad days, reading and re-reading every version. I love you.

My brothers- Jesus, Javier, Jacob, and my sister-in-law Rachel, thank you for listening to me rant, loving me, and believing in me.

Annabel and Amanda, I love you.

Ruben, this was my dream and you were the only one who said, *"do it."* You saw it was a passion and you fueled the fire. Constantly checking on me, my Wattpad, ranks, asking about chapters until 2 am. I wish you were here to get the call when I wrote the end. I love you and I know you are here with me. One day we will meet again brother, I love you.

To my bookish girls, hot damn ladies, I wouldn't be here without every single one of you. I truly love and appreciate every member of my team. Y'all are the absolute best ever.

To Sam thank you for staying up late on live with me to write all the words! I appreciate you more than you know.

Britt, Kayla, April, and Stef- you all make this beast I created work and without you four, it wouldn't be possible at all. Thank you so much, I love each of you like sisters. Accept the love twin, you know you want to! Lol

To my author friends that inspired, encouraged, and believed in me- H. L.Swan, Delaney Foster,. Danda K, A.L. Maruga, Rachel Leigh, Selena, Sam Mariano, Brit Benson, Rosie Alice, LJ Shen, Nicole Fiorina, Mika Rayne and more thank you! And to Christina Santos for believing in me and helping me pimp myself out at parties, you're the best.

Autumn, brother, you have been my day one. Supported all my dreams of writing, reviewing, and everything. We started this whole shebang together and I couldn't have asked for a better best friend than you. Thank you. I more than love you and never too.

To anyone in my life who has ever tried to snuff my light, kill my vibe, and or tried to sabotage things for me- thank you too. Without you, I wouldn't be who I am today. Strong, empowered, and unbothered. I was born to fight wars, I am the storm. I'm sorry that something in you is hurting and I wish you true light, love, and healing.

Thank you, God, to you all the glory.

Also By

Want more? Check out what I have on Amazon!

Pre-Order *His Daggered Heart* now, the conclusion of Alex and Kohen's story.

My Battle with The Enemy, a poetry book that contains my real life journey to healing. Use it as an introduction to me, Issa Marie, and why I write what I do.

Claiming What's His, A New Year's novella that introduces you to the other side of Texas State and that is a prequel to my upcoming dark romance.

Pre-Order *Fool Me Twice,* a dark secret society romance with twin brothers who love to share.